"GOOD NIGHT, SWEET AND TASTY PRINCE"

Sam smiled up at her host, giving thanks that she hadn't been booted out on her butt or brought within an inch of her life—or twelve inches of her dignity. Even though she was a hard-boiled preternatural pest controller, a nemesis to nasties everywhere and nobody's pushover or sure thing, she found Prince V. to be temptation on the fang. But she had a company to save, and save it she would. Petroff Varinksi would be glad he had hired her in the end—if not in the beginning.

Waving good night, she started for the stairs. Petroff watched her walk off.

"Where are you going?" he asked.

"To bed. Solo," she answered resolutely.

Other *Love Spell* books by Minda Webber:

JUST ONE SIP (Anthology)
THE RELUCTANT MISS VAN HELSING
THE REMARKABLE MISS FRANKENSTEIN

BUSTIN'

Minda Webber

LOVE SPELL   NEW YORK CITY

LOVE SPELL®

January 2007

Published by

Dorchester Publishing Co., Inc.
200 Madison Avenue
New York, NY 10016

ISBN 0-505-52705-7

Visit us on the web at www.dorchesterpub.com.

To my sister Marilyn, beloved friend,
the best of aunts to my son Jake and a wonderful
creative writing partner. Without her I wouldn't have
gotten to do Saturday morning cartoons. I thank
you for your advice and making me laugh. Also,
for putting up with my eerie habit of hexing
all mechanical or technological machines.
Thanks for fixing them for me.

ACKNOWLEDGMENTS

I want to thank Chuck Baltzell and Brian McDaniel for computer help; Beverly F., Christine D. and Mary Alice C. for reading this book when it was a mere second draft; Mary Jane M. for bringing the teddy bear babies to visit; my son for letting me drag him to every sci-fi movie since he was knee-high to a very tall grasshopper; Jeff G. and Steve C. for waltzing across Texas in my younger years (in reality, the Texas Panhandle); my cousin, Willie, for loving one of the best scary, funny movies, and running around saying, "Who you gonna call?" for six months after viewing the film; and last but not least in memory of my grandma Vick, for knowing how to tell a scary story better than anybody, like her potato story. Generally a potato story shouldn't be scary, but when my grandma told it—watch out!

Gargoyles, Wings of Darkness and Spitting like Camels

Vermont, 2007

Bustin' wasn't an easy business to be in. Courage, agility and expertise were required by those involved. Paranormalbusters, as those in the industry were called, had to be quick and skilled in all methods of capturing, communicating with, and moving all manner of supernatural creatures. One of the best Busters in the business was Samantha Hammett, known as Sam to friends and enemies alike. She was a hard-working, hard-fighting and soft-playing-the-piano kind of gal.

Tonight, Sam had been hired by the Lady in Red to clear out the old warehouse on the outskirts of town. It was due to be renovated in a couple of weeks, made into apartments, but first a nest of gargoyles had to be removed.

The routine clean-up job should have been just like any other, but something this time felt different. Trouble was brewing; Sam could feel it in her bones. But then, trouble was nothing new to her—not after working as she did for the family business. The Paranormalbustin' Pest Pursuers—Triple-P—had been founded in 1925 by Sam's great-grandfather. Those were the Roaring Twenties, the decade so named for the werewolves, vampires and werelions who first burst onto the mortal scene, howling, roaring and snarling. It was an era of bathtub gin and tubby goblins, flappers and flapping gargoyles. Jazzy blues played and blue ogres danced in speakeasies across the country, while speaking spectrals began haunting people everywhere. Triple-P should have been an instant success—and it was.

Originally the company dealt only with ghosts, but later grew by leaps and bounds to handle werewolves, wererabbits, vampires, and a whole new catalogue of fiends, monsters and otherworldly creatures. The werewolves or vampires they dealt with were usually rogue, exiled from their principalities if they were vampires or packs if they were werewolves. Otherwise, those two species tried to fit in. Usually, they did a good job.

In the supernatural world, vampires were tops. They had their own feudal system, and a king ruled over each continent. Princes and princesses helped maintain discipline and paid tribute. Werewolves had their own hierarchy, each with six or seven packs forming something they called a clanship. In each clanship, the king's rule was absolute. The location of each pack and the large number of pack members, however, meant that those packs each needed a chancellor. Each chancellor ruled over one or two packs with the help of blood kin, who were usually also some form of royalty. Packs even had knights, which were called *gellogs*, who helped keep the wolves in line and hunted down and destroyed any rogues. Sam had run afoul of a *gellog* a time or two in her career, but fortunately the encounters had only left her with a few scars. Those blended in nicely with the other scars she'd received from the rest of the otherworldly creatures she had helped capture and relocate.

Just as Sam's family business had evolved, so had the term Paranormalbustin'—Bustin'—which had become a generalization for anyone extracting and removing paranormal pests.

Yes, these days the company dealt with everything; some nights, fire-breathing demons or runaway dragons. Other nights, Triple-P might be chasing a gruff weredog who wanted to put the bite into crime, or a rogue vampire looking to devour Mr. Whistler's grandmother. And at holidays, Sam could always count on the grinches. They were a hard-drinking, rowdy bunch; indulging in too much spiked eggnog, they would put on their red Santa caps and start stealing Christmas presents. They were in the Hoo's Who of paranormal pests.

Occasionally Sam ran into some really nasty poltergeists, like the Amityville Horror. Other times she captured grouchy gremlins—all cute and fuzzy when they had full stomachs. When hungry they'd go after your body parts. Then there were card-carrying witches and warlocks who might turn a person into a frog as soon as look at them.

A few times she'd run into nice, normal ghosts, like the Captain and Mrs. Muir—a lovely older couple who loved to sail around the world in once sunken ghost ships. Or Casper; he was always a friendly face.

But tonight there would be no friendly faces. As she now listened to the gargoyles crunching away inside the dilapidated old warehouse, she tossed her younger brother his safety helmet, complete with its large nightlight attached to the front. She turned her own light on. "Here's looking at you, kid," she said, quoting the movie *Casablanca*.

"You're starting to sound cliché," her brother teased.

"You're one to talk," Sam replied. Both of them had been bottle-fed on film noir; from the time they were born they'd lived in a home where dogma, dress and dialogue from 1940s movies was commonplace.

"Now rig up tight, Bogie," she reminded him. "You know these guys would just love to snatch you bald."

Gargoyles were notorious for plucking hair and using it to feather their nests back at the buildings to which they were so often attached. It was a particularly vile tactic in Sam's opinion, as she had always secretly longed to be a hairdresser. But then her family business would have gone down the drain.

Glancing over at Bogart, she shook her head in regret. "Jeez, they wouldn't have far to go." Her brother had cut his long brown hair last summer, tired of her poking and prodding him with scissors and curling irons. Now he wore a military style, a buzz cut. At least he still let her highlight his hair, but there wasn't much challenge in highlighting hair that was less than an inch long.

Even with the military cut, her little brother was a good-looking man, one who had girls on the brain and other strategic places. These pesky females called him at all hours of the night and day. Some even pretended to have ghosts in their homes so that Bogie would come by and scope out the situation . . . and them. More often they had bats in the belfry.

The last lust-driven girl had donned a white sheet. After she'd jumped out shouting "Boo," Bogie had told Sam, he'd whipped off the sheet to discover the lady naked as the day she'd been born. How Bogie handled that particular paranormal pest was anybody's guess.

Every once in a while, Sam wished she were half as attractive to the opposite sex as her brother. Instead she was perky cute in a girl-next-door sort of way—if the girl next door happened to bust ghosts and other things that went bump and howl in the night. No, she would never be able to compete, and that was driven home to her every day with the drop-dead gorgeous female vampires she sometimes ran into while working, or with the sexy femme fatales of the werewolf and werecat world. It might have bothered Sam more, but her philosophy was that when life gave you lemons, you learned to like things sour.

"You ready? We need to make this quick. I got a date with a long-legged redhead," Bogie bragged, glancing down at his sister. His five-foot-eleven frame towered over Sam's diminutive stature.

"So what else is new?"

"Do I feel lucky?" he joked, doing his Eastwood imitation.

"Talk about clichés."

Laughing, he got down to business. "You ready to rock and roll a few gargoyles?"

"Yeah. But be careful. I smell trouble in there. So keep your mind on the business at hand and not the pleasure to come. I mean, your date."

He gave her a dirty look. "I'm not a kid anymore. I can take care of myself—and you, too!"

"Just humor me."

Sometimes Sam felt thirty going on fifty, while Bogie was twenty-three going on sixteen. He truly loved getting decked out in weird work outfits and being attacked by all kinds of bizarre creatures; he saw it as a neverending adventure. To Sam, this was business pure and simple. It was pride in a job well done. Although, to be honest, she would probably miss the action if she ever worked at anything else.

"Don't fire until you see the yellow of their eyes," she warned. "Stay with me. No winging it, and no flying solo. We play by the rules or we don't play at all." Her baby brother sometimes forgot procedure in his desire for adventure.

Bogie rolled his eyes, muttering under his breath as he checked his steel-mesh coveralls for extra dart cartridges. They wouldn't want to run out. In the dangerous task of hunting supernatural prey, preparation and precaution were the watch words of any day or night.

"On the count of three, we bust in and shoot them with the dart guns," Sam said. "Remember to look to the rafters. Our visual scans from last night showed ten of the ugly little critters up there."

"Gotcha," her brother replied. He clearly didn't like being told what to do.

They both tensed, adrenaline running high, ready to do combat with the four-foot creatures and their extremely sharp teeth and claws. Gargoyles were also dynamic aerial artists; with their three-foot wingspans, they had the ability to dive bomb victims with startling accuracy.

"One, two . . ." she began, but was interrupted by her brother's gleeful, "Three!" Then they were off at a fast run, Sam trying hard to keep up with the long-legged gait of her brother.

Cursing his brief head start under her breath, she ran harder, her tranquilizer rifle heavy as her feet pounded into the dirt. She hated it when Bogie took point, since she was the elder sibling and it should have been her who first courted danger. After all, Bogie and her Uncle Myles were all the family she had left after that unfortunate Godzilla incident had killed her parents eleven years ago.

Bogie hit the old slat doors hard, slamming them open. From inside Sam could hear the gargoyles' cries of rage and shock. The crunching noises stopped abruptly, and the sound of flapping wings filled the air.

Inside, Sam got a good look at the gargoyles taking to flight. She immediately raised her rifle and began firing. On her right, Bogie did the same. Her first two shots were aimed true, and two gargoyles plummeted to earth. Her brother wasn't as lucky: his first shot went wide.

"Hey, you hit my gargoyle," he called out in frustration.

"You snooze, you lose," she replied. She had to keep him on his toes.

Her baby brother responded by hitting a gargoyle

dead-on. His third shot was high, but it clipped a fiercely hissing gargoyle in the wing, doing enough damage so that the creature was forced to land, barely able to flap. It quickly passed out, and the score was tied; between the siblings' shots, four heavily clawed gargoyles were now lying on the cement floor.

Bogie shouted with glee and Sam grinned, when a sudden loud noise caused Sam to duck.

"Nuts!" The gargoyles were regrouping to pluck some hair, which meant soon they would begin the thing she disliked most about this kind of assignment: the spitting. Gargoyles spat like camels but were less attractive. Sam gritted her teeth.

Yep, she realized as she felt a large wad of spittle hit her chest. She'd been right. And the mustard yellow goo with bits of wings and thin legs sticking out reminded her of her car window on a warm spring day when she was out driving in the country.

Sparing a quick glance at her brother, she noted he too was covered in regurgitated bugs. Really it wasn't surprising, considering a gargoyle's main diet was insects. But, oh, how she hated these glob-spitting pests. Getting bug guts out of her work clothes was harder than getting them off her windshield.

Firing rapidly, Sam managed to hit two more of the dive-bombing little buggers. Bogie also hit another two, which left them with two. That pair, suddenly realizing their fallen comrades still had not risen, fled into the rafters.

"Rats! I hate it went they hide there," Sam griped.

Ignoring her ill humor, Bogie pointed after the largest of the gargoyles, one which had just finished hacking a huge glob of yellow at them.

"Wow! Did you see that? I bet that fellow spat his wad at least nine feet. That's pretty impressive. I'll have to measure it for the record books."

Sam gave him a disbelieving look. "Here we are, covered in crud, and you're impressed with these spitting suckers?" Boys would be boys, she decided cynically, even in her line of work. "You guys and your pissing contests."

Grinning, her brother gave her a high five.

She ignored him and said: "Get off your duff and let's see if we can sew up these last fly-by-nights."

Fifteen minutes later, the final gargoyle fell to earth. Checking her watch nervously, Sam noted that the first of them had fallen over twenty minutes ago. That left less than ten minutes before the knockout serum would wear off, less than ten minutes for them to bake these gargoyles with their sunlamp.

Since gargoyles reverted to stone once the first rays of the sun hit them, it was fortunate for Paranormalbusters everywhere that a high-powered lamp could get the same effect. Sam sighed wistfully. It would be so easy to just buy a huge sunlamp and turn it on full blast when entering a gargoyle-infested building, morphing all the creatures to stone; the problem with that scenario was, as soon as the bright light hit them, the gargoyles would go rock hard. If they were in flight they would then crash to the earth, cracking to pieces and literally biting the dust.

No, while she might not like the nasty bug-spitting bastards, since they played hell with her laundry bills, she didn't want to cause their deaths. The Hammetts had always gone to great lengths to see that whatever supernatural pests or monsters they captured were removed and sent to some other location, preferably one that wanted them. Also, gargoyles were on the endangered supernatural species list, and the fine for killing them was hefty.

Yes, Sam was conscientious about her family vow to do right by Busted creatures. She had moved ghosts to castles in Scotland, enjoying how fine they looked in kilts, and had turned attention-grabbing apparitions who could project into skeletal form over to universities where medical students could study them to their hearts' content. She had delivered gremlins to Spielberg in Los Angeles, and had herded bath-loving, fire-breathing dragons to Arkansas to fuel that state's numerous hot springs. Sam had also laid a few ghosts to rest, but only at their request to receive their heavenly reward.

Tonight's captives were going to be sent to South America, where a scientific expedition was underway in the Amazon jungle. There the gargoyles would be used for pest control: the scientists would work in bug-free comfort, while the gargoyles would have the feast of their lifetimes.

"You got the sunlamp ready?" she asked her brother as she watched a few of the creatures twitching. The sedative was clearly starting to fade.

"Right here," Bogie answered. He turned to switch the big lamp on.

"Cool. Let's shake and bake." Sam liked this part best, because it reminded her of cooking a big batch of chocolate chip cookies—with the exception that these cookies had sharp teeth and deadly claws that could rip a heart out.

10

BUSTIN'

As the sunlamp came on, Sam's sigh changed into a gasp. The lamp's usual bright white glow had been replaced. "What the hell? Not again!" Her eyes flew wide with disgust and horror as deep purple fluorescent light flooded the warehouse. The bright color might be pretty, but it was essentially useless in gargoyle capture.

Two dazed gargoyles stumbled upright and took off in flight, with a third not far behind. Sam and her brother stood stunned and helpless, out of ammo. The three gargoyles fled, their wings flapping loudly as they raced out into the wide black yonder.

"No more Miss Nice Guy," Sam growled, gritting her teeth while her blue eyes flared with rage. "I'll beat those dirty rats at their own game!" Enough was enough!

Bogie looked confused. "Rats? We don't have anything scheduled after this, sis. Certainly no wererats."

Sam rolled her eyes, raised her clenched fist to the night sky and shook it fiercely.

The Gilded Age of Ghostbusting

"Sabotaged again! Somebody's really giving us the shakedown. Boy, do they have a death wish or what!" Sam cried out in anger. "Somebody is going to pay and pay big!"

Tonight's fiasco made three times in the past month that her family business had been undermined by some devious, dastardly deed. The first time had occurred with that mockery at Venckman Manor. The second had happened two weeks later, when a shipment of goblins on their way to Texas had been rerouted to Spielberg and tagged as gremlins. To say that the director was not amused was an understatement; there were more than enough goblins already in Hollywood.

"Quick, grab the cable netting," Sam urged, her voice taut with anger. Cable netting was difficult to wield and hard to throw over the gargoyles, and despite it being made of metal, many of the gargoyles could still slice through. Still, it was the best they had.

Over the next half hour they managed to contain four of the original ten gargoyles, the rest flying off into the night sky. She knew that the wily creatures wouldn't come back to the warehouse now that their sanctuary had been invaded. They were lost to capture for a time, until they settled in some other poor unsuspecting slob's building.

Bogie shook his head regretfully. "I sure hope they don't breed."

"Nuts!" was Sam's angry retort. Gargoyles bred like superenergized werebunnies.

She was in a foul mood by the time they finished, her blue eyes bright with anger. Paranormalbustin' Pest Pursuers Inc., had failed tonight because of one fiendish greed-ridden man: Mr. Nicolas Strakhov. She just knew he was to blame. He was the ominous owner of Monsters-R-Us, a Russian-based company that had relocated recently to the United States. This company of comrades was a brother, brother and brother act.

"Who does he think he is, some Russian Rockefeller? This isn't the Gilded Age. That remorseless rat needs to learn some American history!" She swore, her rage running rampant. "We always win."

Bogie shrugged. "Monsters-R-Us doesn't seem to have problems competing against us," he said.

She ignored him. "How can such a cold-blooded creep of a man own a Bustin' company with such a cutesy name?" she asked in sheer frustration. It had been three months since the Strakhovs had moved into her hometown of Dodge, Vermont. Slowly but surely Monsters-R-Us had been stealing her family's business, even though she and her brother were once known to be as dependable as the Maytag Man.

But obviously that didn't count for anything with the American public—not with Mr. Serial-Saboteur Strakhov around. Oh, no. And Mr. Slimebag had to mess with her projects as well as steal her clients. Three lousy months of underhanded tricks, and disloyal customers were switching to the other monster removal company in droves. It was just plain unfair, Sam thought heatedly, kicking at the tire on their truck. "Ouch," she yelped. "That hurt."

"Hey! Don't take your bad temper out on the tires," Bogie said. Sam ignored him.

"He thinks he can take us down playing dirty pool and politics? Well, not on my watch!" Her life's blood was in this company . . . literally. Too many times to count. And no rotten-dealing Russian was going to usurp her territory. A showdown was coming, and she intended to be the winner.

Cursing softly under her breath, Sam climbed into their specialized removal truck. Her brother did, too. "Doesn't Strakhov know that cheaters never win and winners never cheat? I'll teach him a lesson he won't forget. Those dirty Russian rats will regret the day they were born." Sam put the truck in gear and started driving toward their warehouse.

"What?" Her brother leaned wearily back against the seat, his shoulder aching from a particularly vicious whack he had taken. Gargoyle capture was always a tough business, but tonight's sabotage had made it much worse. He called and canceled his date.

Sam continued ranting. "Mr. Damn-Him-to-Hell Nicolas Strakhov—although even hell will probably slam its gates to him. How dare he throw a monkey wrench into our works? Who the heck does he think he is?" Then, ignoring her brother, she quickly answered her own question.

"He thinks he's some caviar-snuffling Mafia don of the supernatural world—I'd bet my bottom dollar. But just because he's from some former communist country doesn't mean he can ignore the American way! Doesn't he realize that capitalism is just that?"

Bogie looked at her, a confused expression covering his face. He loved his big hairdress-hankering sis, but when she went off on a tirade like this, which was rare, there was no turning back. His sibling was hard-driven and sometimes hard-bitten, tough as nails, full of sass. Of course, she was also sweet as molasses, with a heart of gold. A person or monster had to really back her into a corner before she came out swinging. But once she did . . . DUCK!

Slapping the steering wheel, Sam winced. Her hands and arms were already a little stiff and sore from their gargoyle misadventure. Focusing back on her anger, she added scathingly, "You stand up for what you believe in. This is America, for God's sake! You give the other fellow a square deal, don't knock him on his ass when he's on his knees! There's enough room for more than one Bustin' company in the northeastern U.S.! That's what makes America great—all these companies working against each other. What would we do without competition?" Sam peeked at Bogie, taking her eyes off the road long enough to give him a knowing glance.

He smiled and shrugged, knowing to remain quiet when his older sister was on one of her tirades.

She liked old-time America better, preferably with fast-talking guys and glamorous dolls.

She went on: "Why, we'd all be wearing the same style jeans and going to one fast food restaurant. Can you imagine? No, of course you can't. That fast food restaurant might not be Mexican food or pizza. That stupid, smug Strakhov is ruining our country's capitalistic tendencies with strongarm commie tactics. And communism is so yesterday's news. If Mr. Strakhov is an example of Russian fair play, then no wonder people called it the Red *Scare*."

Bogie grimaced. Fast food was a staple at their house, which they shared with their uncle. Even though Bogie was quite a cook, he still idolized the drive-thru. And when his sister was right, she was right. Without capitalism, you might have communism and only one fast food restaurant. Forget that! He wouldn't live in a country with only Big Macs.

"Doesn't that scavenging shark Strakhov realize that this is a free country?" Sam rattled on, gaining speed. "Well, maybe not free," she corrected, thinking of the rent on their warehouse where their new offices were located, and of the price of asparagus and popcorn at the movies. Still, she had a point to make, even if only to herself. She noticed Bogie's eyes seemed glazed over like freshly made donuts.

"Are you listening, Bogart? I'm not talking just to hear myself talk."

The glazed look vanished and her brother tuned back in.

"Just think how proud the Founding Fathers would be of us. I mean, they were into trade and all. And Jefferson! Why, we would probably get a congressional medal of honor if he were alive. Too bad none of them came back as ghosts. I always wanted to ask Adams about the Alien and Sedition Acts."

"How do you figure that, about medals?" Bogie asked, glad he was paying attention now. He'd always wanted a medal.

"Why, our great-grandfather made a business out of zip, nothing, *nada*. He saw an unexplored market in the supernatural world and tapped into it. That's what America is about: seeing a need, filling it and getting paid damn well for it!"

"We do get paid the big bucks," Bogie agreed. Bustin' work was dangerous and ofttimes deadly. Poorly trained Paranormalbustin' companies had very high mortality rates.

"Besides, we Americans are a driven bunch. All of us are going for the American dream—a four-car garage and six-television household. Now some rat-faced Russian decides he can come stomp all over our hopes with his chiseling comrade boots?" Sam finished grandly, proud of her thesis on American capitalism.

Bogie shrugged again, wondering what chiseling comrade boots were.

"We'll dump these cages with the gargoyles at the warehouse and then go home. Uncle Myles should still be up. I have a job for him," Sam decided.

Bogie glanced askance at her, wondering what devious plan his scheming sister had in mind that would involve their nutty relative. "Uncle *Myles?*" he asked.

"Uncle Myles." she said, smiling evilly. "I've got a scheme for that sleezebag Strakhov! I'll teach him to mess with me, that vodka-loving, sabotaging stooge of a Slav! I bet he doesn't even know the Star-Spangled Banner or who Willie Nelson is! I bet he hates maple syrup. And in Vermont, that's hard to swallow!"

Bogie shuddered. He knew that evil smile of his sister's and, Mafia don of the supernatural world or not, it didn't bode well for one Mr. Nicolas Strakhov.

Against the World—or the Strakhov Brothers, Anyway

As soon as Sam walked through the door of the Hammett household she felt like she had stepped onto the set of a 1940s film—one starring Humphrey Bogart and complete with a baby grand piano. It really wasn't surprising; this was how she always felt. Her family had always been nuts about Bogart movies.

Her parents had named her Samantha—Sam, for the Samuel Spade character adapted from the movie *The Maltese Falcon*, the Dashiell Hammett novel. It had made it more inevitable since their last name was also Hammett, though no relation to the author.

Her middle name was Sabrina, chosen from the movie with Bogart and Hepburn. Her brother, of course, was named after the late and great film star himself. Both brother and sister privately thought that her parents, children of the sixties, had been bogarting each other's joints when they'd come up with the names.

Her uncle was the same. He relished the fact that his name was Myles; Myles Archer was Sam Spade's partner in the detective agency from *The Maltese Falcon*. However, his moniker had more to do with the fact that his grandfather had been named Myles than any movie nostalgia.

Walking into the vast den, Sam took a quick scan of the room filled with bookshelves. Some of the books were just good reading, while others were references and research materials in various dealings with ghosts, gargoyles and other things that flew or bit by night. Titles ranged from *Raising Dead Children*, by Dr. Spook; *The Road to Hell*, by Goode N. Tentions; *Dancing with the Devil*, by Ginger Astaire; *Stoned Until Dusk: a Gargoyle Study*, by T. O'Leary; to, of course, the ever popular *Thirteen Ghosts*, misleadingly compiled by Two Ghosts and a Banshee.

She spied her uncle in his favorite chair by the fireplace. He wasn't a handsome man; his nose was too big and his features too large for his thin face, but he was a good man who loved both her and her brother. He had once again fallen asleep reading.

Uncle Myles was in his late fifties, and tonight he was dressed in a dark pinstripe double-breasted suit. His typical fedora lay on the coffee table beside him. When it was on his head, he wore it slightly cocked to the right side of his face. Everything he did, he tried to emulate his idol, Humphrey.

Sam smiled. Her uncle had been looking for the Maltese Falcon for the past eighteen years, but other than that odd quirk he was fairly normal— considering the guy acted, talked and dressed like a reject from a Humphrey Bogart film festival. He even called women "dames" and "dolls." Fortunately,

Sam wasn't into feminist sensibility issues. However, when all was said and done, there was nobody better at scouting out information. The years of practice her uncle accrued while looking for the black bird had sharpened his reconnaissance skills even more than Sam's own tracking skills of shadowing black vampire bats, black gargoyles and any other preternatural flying hazards that came her way.

Sam gently tapped her uncle's shoulder. "Time to wake up."

Opening his eyes, Myles reached for a toothpick in his suit pocket. "Hello, sweetheart, what's stirring?" He stuck the toothpick between his teeth and looked her over from head to toe, noticing the large mustard yellow bug stains on her coveralls. "Rough night?"

"You could say that again."

"Rough night?" her uncle repeated, his silver hair shining in the golden glow of the lamp.

She nodded wearily. Well, maybe he had another odd quirk. Sometimes he took everything literally. "He's at it again."

"The Fat Man?" Myles asked curiously, his eyes suddenly bright and alert.

"More like the Fat Russian," Sam corrected, wondering if Nicolas Strakhov was overweight. She knew he was in business with his two younger brothers, and that Monsters-R-Us was a family business, just like her own, but she didn't know what he looked like. Nor did she much care. Probably he was some macho, squatty foreigner with hairy eyebrows and fish breath from all that caviar. But was he overweight? Probably not. It was too hard to chase sharp-toothed little gremlins and leaping goblins if you were carrying around a bunch of excess baggage.

She addressed her uncle: "Strakhov's certainly not a straight shooter. The dirty rat hit us again—sabotaged us by switching our sunlamp for a fluorescent one. We had to use the iron netting and lost six of the gargoyles. No, the job tonight didn't go down easy—as you can see," she added grimly as she glanced at the rips in her steel-mesh coveralls. Not only could the gargoyles' slashing claws have hurt her and her brother, but also they both were now going to have to replace their coveralls. It was an expensive but necessary prospect, as a Paranormalbuster didn't capture creatures without the right equipment; there was too much room for error, and too much chance of ending up disfigured, put out of commission or killed.

"Tough break. You all right, precious? And Bogie?"

"We're fine," she replied. "Baby brother is cleaning out the truck."

Myles pulled an old Colt .45 out of his inner jacket pocket. "That dirty-rat Russian better watch out, or he'll be picking iron out of his liver."

Sam would have been concerned about her uncle waving around the Colt, but she knew he never loaded it. "Forget the threats. I'm on to Nicolas Strakhov's tricks now, and I've got a plan."

"Yeah, doll?" Myles put the gun back in his jacket pocket. "What's that?"

"I want you to find out when and where Strakhov's next two extraction locations are. I've heard a rumor and if one of his locations is where I think it is, he's gonna be up a creek without a paddle. Nicolas Strakhov isn't the only one that can play dirty pool."

"Does this wise guy cheat at pool?" Myles asked. "I could always challenge him to a game. Loser leaves town."

As tired as she was, Sam laughed. Her overly literal family was her family in spite of being fruitcakes. She loved them dearly—warts, blackbirds, fedora hats and all.

"No, the rotten louse doesn't play pool, Uncle Myles," she told him. "Just get the scoop on their doings as quick as you can. We'll give these brothers grim a surprise or two. You know, the bigger they are, the harder they fall." Her uncle had quoted these words as long as she could remember, and so far they had held true. The last giant she had taken down had knocked over a house.

"Got it, doll. You know, for a real looker, you also got brains. Must run in the family."

She kissed him on the cheek. "Yeah, it does." And with those words she wearily climbed the stairs to her bedroom.

Another day, another dollar. What a way to make a living. She should have been a hairdresser. Or she could have played piano in a bar. Well, if her husky voice didn't scare little children and goblins alike.

Actually, she sometimes played on an old honky-tonk piano to an audience at the Casablanca, the club owned by her Uncle Myles and his longtime friend Rick Bergman. And after a rough night of busting up monsters, when the bar closed at one o'clock, Sam would go over and play and sing to her heart's content.

Yes, her life was at times a lonely one.

Although she had quite a few friends, she did not have too many close ones. It seemed at times that her life was to have and have not, and if at times she found herself in a real lonely place in the desperate hours after midnight, so be it. No, she didn't have much time for herself or a social life, but she would take it on the chin and come back swinging. There was no reason for her to feel like a woman marked by fate, by her family and by her job. This was the nature of the beast, of this Bustin' business. And she loved the thrill. The work had gotten in her blood, infecting her with adrenaline lust just like many other Bustin' junkies around the country.

Her fate had been ordained at nineteen, when her world had come crashing down around her; her parents died and suddenly she was in charge. She had taken on the family business and learned to run it like a pro, juggling work, college and raising her twelve-year-old brother all at one time—always on a deadline. It had left her little time for hairdressing, undressing with a member of the opposite sex or even just letting her hair down, but that was how life went. Her life, at any rate.

Oh well, she thought as she pushed down her lacerated coveralls, her internal conflict was just that—hers alone. If at times her life might seem a Pyrrhic victory, leaving her like a frozen tree in the Petrified Forest with no love on the horizon, that was okay; she was what she was.

Washing her face, Sam glanced in the mirror. Maybe sometimes her life did seem like a dead end, but fortunately she had a good head on her shoulders and knew what was important. She could thank her lucky stars that she had a roof over her head, a family who loved her, a job that never left her bored, two pianos, a cuddly pet goblin and a big, soft bed.

Smiling, Sam climbed in between the soft green flowered print covers and closed her eyes. Tonight, Lauren Bacall or Humphrey Bogart had nothing on her; she was more than ready for the comforting embrace of a big sleep.

Trolls—Cheaper by the Dozen

Nobody ever walked across the Madison County Bridge unscathed, not with the bunch of trolls who lived underneath. Trolls were the biggest scavengers of paranormal pests, and they had very distinctive body odor, like the smell of a pigsty in Fourth of July heat.

Sam might have felt sorry for her unsuspecting quarry, the Strakhov brothers, who were about to take it on the chin and everywhere else, but she didn't. Life was a series of tough choices. She'd learned that in the school of hard knocks—learned mostly from demons, shapeshifters and grinches, the latter who could pack a mean punch when denied their Hoo pudding. She wouldn't take losing her business to Monsters-R-Us lying down, nor would she pretend that them stealing her clients was just water under the bridge. No, what was under the bridge wasn't water.

Discovering that the Strakhovs had somehow gotten tonight's troll-removal job from the three Billys—grandfather, son and grandson—Sam had put her plan in motion. Now she was waiting patiently for the payoff.

The three Billys, though gruff in manner at times, had thrown Sam and her brother a lot of business over the years, so she didn't know how Nicolas Strakhov had talked them into switching sides. She figured it wasn't on the up and up.

The grandfather, Billy Senior, whom Sam had never particularly liked, was retired. He was a randy old goat who was always pinching her rear. The grandson, Billy Double, was generally a whiner and fairly lazy. But the randy old man's son, Billy Junior, was okay by her. Junior was the mayor of Dodge, and he ran a construction company that dealt with all the county's roadwork; bridges, too. Their defection to the competition hurt.

Well, if the competition wanted to play dirty, Sam would oblige them. She would butt heads with Nicolas Strakhov any day of the week; she swore valiantly as she climbed to a bump in the middle of a hillside above the bridge. Bogie trailed a few paces behind, his eyes carefully scanning the darkness.

Kneeling, binoculars in hand, Sam scouted out the entire location, the world progressing in shadowy motion. Tonight the dark was like an old friend; it was good company, and needed. Soft patches of misty fog rose like cold fingers and stretched into the night.

Methodically Sam scouted the old bridge with her infrared binoculars. She and her brother Bogie were about a mile off, hidden in some brush among the gently rolling hills. "Hmm, it appears all is quiet on the Eastern front."

"Nothing good ever happens after midnight," her brother replied, raising his own binoculars to quickly check out the dirt road that trailed down to the bridge. He frowned as the smell of trolls floated up on the breezy night winds. "Phew, they stink!"

"How I love the smell of trolls in the evening," Sam muttered sarcastically, grimacing as the rank odor wafted past them.

Below, she could see the dark outlines of the bridge with her infrared scope and the red forms huddled in slumber underneath.

Trolls. Unlike some supernatural creatures, they slept at night and wrought their havoc during the day. People had to pay a toll if they wanted to cross an infested bridge. Though they truly would have preferred goat meat, bridge trolls were also partial to donuts. Therefore, informed people would buy two dozen donuts and then throw them over the metal handrails of the bridge. After said tribute was paid, the trolls would then move whatever blockade they had set up and a car would be allowed to pass over. Heaven forbid the car's occupants didn't have any donuts or goat meat; those unlucky few that didn't pay the troll's toll were in for one big stinking surprise. No food meant disaster, for their car and personage would be pelted with large chunks of troll dung. And while trolls were unsightly, short and chunky creatures, they had pitcherlike precision when throwing their waste. They rarely missed. Sam had always thought it a shame that major league baseball discriminated against them.

Personally, Sam thought some of the trolls were kind of cute, what with their big four-toed feet and long, shining rainbow-colored hair. Sam knew she would give her eyeteeth for a chance to style and cut troll hair, but it was a fool's wish; trolls were feisty, mean-tempered little creatures that died in captivity and disliked human touch. Whenever she and Bogie made a troll haul, they literally moved the beasties in the same night from a well-used bridge to some other place.

Her brother hunched down beside her and shifted uncomfortably. "Anything stirring? I wish those lousy Strakhovs would hurry up and get here. I have a hot date tonight."

Sam rolled her eyes. "Swell. Just when don't you?"

"Well, you have to admit that sitting down to a bite of dessert with Mary Alice Lorz beats the crap outta sitting here in the dark, a bite for mosquitoes, waiting for Nicolas Strakhov to get his just desserts—a crap-filled beating."

"That remains to be seen. Nicolas Strakhov and his brothers are at the top of my shit list. What could be better than seeing them get pelted with troll turds?" Tonight's revenge would be a feast for the senses, like sipping champagne and eating strawberries or trying out a new hair color—though on the grosser end of the spectrum. "I can't wait to see the trolls' welcome wagon for those rotten Russians. Every time I think about them, I see red," she added heatedly. "I can't *believe* those sneaky Slavs are giving discounts on creature capture." Earlier, her crafty uncle had handed her a flyer snatched from the Strakhov warehouse. Monsters-R-Us was now giving a discount on captures of supernatural creatures in groups of a dozen or more. In big print, their sleazy advertisement read: TROLLS, GREMLINS, GARGOYLES AND GHOSTS—ALL CHEAPER BY THE DOZEN! The price-cutting creeps.

Frustrated, she mumbled, "What this country needs is a good ten-cent cigar, another Roosevelt in the White House and Nicolas Strakhov expelled. I bet he doesn't even know who Kermit the Frog is. And I bet he hates apple pie."

"What do apple pie and Kermit have to do with anything?"

"Oh come on, Bogie. What's more American than apple pie or Kermit the Frog?"

Her baby brother thought a moment. "I think you're wrong. Not about the pie, but about Kermit. Frogs are French. Baseball. Baseball is the big American thing. And football. And don't forget Star Wars and Lord of the Rings." Losing interest in the conversation, he began to scope out the trail below again. "Maybe they're going to be a no-show. It's been dark for over two hours, and they still aren't here."

Sam shook her head. Her brother could be a lot of fun sometimes, but patience wasn't one of his virtues. "You really should learn to be more patient."

"Ha! This from the woman who throws a temper tantrum if I'm ten minutes late to go on a job."

"Time is dough."

Bogie shrugged, then stiffened as he glanced back down the hill. "Sam, look!"

She nodded. "They're here at last. Dumb, dumber and dumberest." Her whole attention was captured by what was going on down the hill and under the bridge. Her night vision binoculars allowed her to see three men slowly and cautiously heading forward—toward the big fat booby trap she and Bogie had engineered.

All three men were tall, well over six feet. They moved with catlike grace and assurance, despite wearing heavy coveralls designed with steel mesh to protect them from troll bites. Those bites could make a human go crazy for a couple of days, since troll saliva had compounds that resembled really bad LSD.

With a thumbs-up at her brother, Sam pushed down on a remote control switch connected to a set of speakers and a CD recording of Beethoven's "Ode to Joy," which was located close to the bridge in some underbrush. She grinned, her white teeth shining in the dark. She knew only too well that there were three things trolls hated absolutely.

Captivity.

People ignoring their tolls.

And classical music.

"Ode to Joy" was an inspired choice, Sam felt.

"Tonight's the night. This time the Strakhov brothers won't come out smelling like a rose," Sam remarked slyly as the sounds of Beethoven saturated the night, clashing cymbals and pounding piano.

Between chuckles, Sam saw that the three men were frozen in their tracks. As the music burst forth, within seconds the trolls had woken from their sleep, shrieked and loped over to gather up their bodily wastes from the spot beneath the bridge where they stockpiled it in case of emergencies. And with remarkable aplomb they began lobbing their missiles at the interlopers, who busily began trying to cast their troll netting.

It was a scene straight from a farce. Sam covered her mouth to dampen her laughter. She could feel her brother beside her shaking with mirth. "To Russia with love, courtesy of the Hammetts," she muttered.

Bogart nudged her. "They don't look like happy campers, these Krapov brothers. Or maybe we should call them the Krap-on brothers."

"What can I say? Shit happens."

Her words cracked both of them up.

Still chuckling, her brother said, "You know, Sam, sometimes you are just plain evil."

Wiping tears of mirth from her eyes, she sighed. "Time to go. I would give a week's pay to see them up close, but I think discretion is the better part of valor tonight. They may suspect that we did this. This way, they won't know for sure."

Bogie nodded, and they crept away in the opposite direction.

Before they completely crested the hill, Sam took a quick glance back. Her infrared binoculars showed two of the men holding up their arms as they were being hit by flying objects, while another was being pelted from behind. Oh yes, the shit had surely hit the fan. Or in this case, the fam. The Strakhov family.

Without a Paddle

Angry took on a whole new meaning as Nicolas Strakhov yanked off his protective headgear. He was covered in troll dung from head to toe. Running a hand through his ebony black hair, he stared at his brothers. His smoke gray eyes held a ruthless gleam.

"Somebody sabotaged us!" His voice was coarse and raspy.

Nicolas, known as Nic to most, was a product of both the old and the new Russia. He was a supremely confident man, a natural-born leader. He took what he wanted because no one was usually foolish enough to stand in his way. He was in essence a man who could move mountains. He was also fiercely loyal to his friends and family, although he saw himself as essentially alone, a persuasive, pervasive and perplexing personality.

"*Merde!* This diabolical dung-throwing means war. We will show no mercy to our enemies!" Nic spat as he began unzipping his protective outerwear.

His two brothers, Gregor and Alexander, nodded in agreement. They too had pulled off their helmets, their pale gray eyes glittering in the twilight, their features taut with anger.

Alex, who was the youngest of the three, remarked slyly, "I bet I know who sabotaged us, Nic."

"I think, so do I. Paranormalbustin' Pest Pursuers, Inc. Who else would care if we rounded up these trolls and sent them off to Russia but our competition?" Nic growled.

Gregor, the middle child, more studious and even tempered, was less resolute. "We don't know for certain. We have no proof. Just because they are unworthy Americans doesn't mean they are behind this morass."

Nic gave his brother a glacial stare. He had made it his business to learn something about his competition, which was this brother and sister team. The sister probably looked like a sumo wrestler and cussed like a sailor. Why else, Nic reasoned, would any reasonable female be in the business of monster removal? Certainly no one dainty or attractive would want to wrestle ghosts and get their pretty white hands dirty—like his own were at this moment. Ugh, troll dung.

Of course, Nic had also gathered that the Hammetts, including their strange old bird of an uncle, were enamored with that Humphrey Bogart fellow and his movies. And after renting some of those classic forties films, he had unwillingly admitted that, though he didn't trust or care too much for his business competition, he did appreciate their taste in entertainment.

"Who else would ruin this troll run? Who else would dare?" Alex argued. "Our surveillance showed twelve trolls living and breathing under the bridge. Because of this sabotage, we only captured seven. *Seven!* We Strakhovs never fail! But tonight we did, *and all because of them.*" He spat the last words out with great distaste.

Nic's eyes were smoldering, their gray smoke almost afire. He added, "And the five we didn't capture will now head for the hills. We'll have to try and track them to their new lair. Only, now they'll be leery and hard to track. Someone will pay for this fiasco! No one makes a fool out of a Strakhov, or causes him to rescind on his word!"

Nic's ruggedly handsome features were hard, making him appear a bit older than his reputed thirty-nine years of age. Yet, that hardness did not diminish from his natural, rugged good looks. He had prominent cheekbones and a full, firm mouth. He was a man who women looked at not once or twice, but for whom they would wrench their necks trying to get a third or fourth glimpse.

Still, as the years marched on Nic had stayed alone for the simple reason that he never met a woman he wanted to spend time with on a day-to-day basis for the rest of his life. His shortest relationship had lasted one night, and there were more than a few of those. His longest relationship had lasted six months.

His brothers, who were peeling out of their filth-covered uniforms, were also handsome men. Not as attractive as Nic, but close enough. They were both well over six-feet tall, with hair so black it shone with blue highlights in the daylight.

Alex was cunning, sometimes unprincipled, and

loved playing pranks. Gregor was thoughtful and more reserved. Nic was the aggressive one, unafraid to show his feelings and ruthless when crossed. And none of the brothers had any trouble with women. In fact, they could beat them off with a stick if they were so inclined. But they weren't. They loved women, were worshipped by women, were spoiled by women and rarely had a serious thought for any particular woman. They were playboys at their best and worst. Likely it was because they were raised from birth with wealth, privilege and the punishing need to win at all costs. Like tonight's treachery—that would not go unforgiven or unpunished.

"Alex, make sure you find out who did this by tomorrow night," Nic ordered. "Then I will take appropriate action. We're going to crush those Hammetts! They'll rue the day they were born."

Alex grinned. He loved it when his brother got that feral glint in his eyes. Nic was a man others revered or feared, and it looked like the Hammetts were going to get a chance at the latter. "What will you do to punish them? Shall we hang them by their thumbs with corkscrews, or should it be the rack?"

Gregor choked. Nic laughed harshly, then grudgingly said, "Ah, for the old days."

Gathering up his equipment, he opened the door of their specialized van. He reminded Alex, "I need the answers soon, before I leave for my trip to help out our cousin. Once I know for absolutely certain who did this, *then* I will decide which method of punishment fits the crime. I'll think on it while I'm gone."

"But you'll be gone a good week," Alex argued. "What was done tonight deserves swift retribution.

Triple-P Inc. needs to be ground into dirt beneath our feet. We need to strike at their hearts, their pride!"

Only half listening to Alex, Nic was letting his mind revolve; it was spinning quickly as he came up with scenarios. Glancing at his youngest brother, he nodded. "Yes, you always hated competition. But remember the Russian saying, 'Revenge is a dish best served cold.' And I intend to serve these Americans cold cuts."

Getting into the van and sitting next to him, listening to his brother's harsh warning, Gregor shuddered. Nic was formidable even before the added stimulation of being angered. Angry, Nic was a force to be reckoned with.

His eyes on the road, Nic added in a voice filled with grim determination, "*Merde!* Nobody but nobody—and certainly not some insignificant little American nobody—crosses Nicolas Strakhov and gets away with it!"

Driving off toward their warehouse, Nic turned to his brothers, eyeing them with heat. "What is that saying . . . ?" Snapping his fingers, he suddenly nodded. "Ah, yes. Samantha and Bogart Hammett will soon be up *that* creek without a paddle."

Public Nuisances
Nos. One, Two and Three

Sam and Bogie had gotten home a little over ten minutes earlier. Her baby brother had gone to shower and get dressed for his date while Sam headed for the den. As she passed, she noted the furnishings here had a distinct look of wear and tear, but it was the sort of look a house gets that has been well lived in.

As Sam stared at the flickers of flame in the den fireplace, her Uncle Myles wandered in. A cigarette was pinched between his fingers, smoke wisping into the air.

"So how'd it go, kid?" he asked.

"You know how those Russian brothers all think they're Ivan the Terrible? Well, our scam ran like clockwork. The music played, the trolls danced, and the Strakhovs got pelted. They got their noses a little dirty tonight, I'd guess. And everything else."

"I get the picture."

"I would have given a fiver to see their faces underneath those helmets" Sam remarked, laughing. "That'll teach them to play chicken with us."

"You said it, doll." Myles chortled and ground out his cigarette in an ashtray. "You didn't happen to see the black bird, did you?"

Sam shook her head. Over the years she had gotten various artists to design replicate Maltese falcons, but her uncle had never been fooled. Now the decorated birds sat on the mantle and bookshelves, while her uncle was still patiently looking for the original.

He sighed. "I didn't find the bird tonight, either, but let me tell you how it went down. Casing the Strakhov joint was tough. They put in more security. Even so, I beat their system. I got the info you wanted," Myles explained, his light blue eyes alive with excitement.

Sam's grin widened.

"The Strakhovs are in contact with Prince Petroff Varinski, the vampire prince."

Her grin faded a bit. Prince Varinski was the bigtime. He was rich beyond all get-out, and was literally a royal vampire of the Tolstoy-Vlad lineage, the very top of the old royal line. At one time he had ruled a large part of Russia, but had abdicated to come and live in America. If blood was blue, his was a shrieking cerulean, the color of deep-frozen icebergs.

"You see, sweetheart, they're talking to that prince fellow about doing a Bustin' job, and it ain't gonna be a pretty one."

When her uncle called her sweetheart, things were going to move. And move fast, like a runaway locomotive. Anyone on the tracks better get out of the way double quick.

"Varinski, it seems, has got a real doozie of a problem with that castle of his he bought in upstate New York. He's got not one ghost, or two ghosts, but *three* of the little buggers, a real paranormal pest parade. And all of them are causing mayhem in that fine new place."

Sam took in her uncle's words. The competition had been contacted and she hadn't even been called in for a consult? This harsh reality not only made her angry, it made her stark-raving mad. Gritting her teeth, she thought about the client, wondering if all of Russia was intending to move to Vermont. First Prince Varinski and his entourage, then the Strakhov brothers themselves. She supposed it wasn't surprising they were sticking together. Russian bears of a feather, as it were . . .

Myles continued: "They've got a ghost called Andy whose been painting scenes all over the house."

"An artist ghost, huh? I've handled a few of those before." They were usually highly emotional and often messy, leaving turpentine and oil paints all about a place. Noticing her uncle's grimace she asked, "What? He's a *bad* artist?"

"Don't know about his talent, but I did hear that Andy only paints one scene, over and over."

Sam raised an eyebrow, encouraging her uncle to go on. Myles lit a cigarette, rolling it beneath his fingers.

"Well, sweetheart, that's the problem. Andy only paints cans of soup."

Sam laughed. "This wealthy aristocratic vampire prince has a castle full of soup can paintings?" Since the royal vampire's move to Dodge about eight months ago, she had been curious about him. Unfortunately he was rarely in town, and when he was in Dodge, the Prince ran in a different circle. Her circle was more square. Prince V. was an extremely attractive vampire with raven-dark hair, and he was considered to be a top-notch heartbreaker, painting the town red with his arm candy when in residence. Sam might be cute and even sexy at times—when she went all out—but she wasn't anybody's arm candy. She wasn't even a main course—especially not for a bloodsucker. Her IQ was too high, being in the triple digits, and she didn't have the kind of legs that stretched from here to eternity.

Rumors were that the Prince was descended from Peter the Great. His vampire heritage was less clear, although it had been suggested that Prince Petroff Varinski was descended from Vlad the Impaler. Prince V. was said to be over six hundred years old—old enough now to stand the early morning hours of daylight as well as the last few hours before twilight.

She chuckled. "Just think. Instead of Rubens or Toulouse-Lautrec's can-can dancers, this very royal Prince is stuck staring at Campbell's commercials. How fitting for his very expensive American castle."

Myles shrugged. "I hear he's a straight Joe." That lingo meant the Prince wasn't a people person—at least not one with a *taste* for people. He might snack a little on a human, but he wouldn't drain them dry.

"So, he's into synthetic blood then?" Sam remarked

thoughtfully. "Good. Much safer that way." She could trust this playboy prince with her neck, just not her virtue. Though that particular problem probably wouldn't come up. "Okay, so Andy's ghost has got to go. Who's next in this lineup of silly squatters?"

Myles chuckled. "I thought you'd never ask, doll. We got ourselves a galloping gourmet. A ghostly one. His name's Jules, and he's a regular wine guzzler. He's fighting with Varinski's human chef, who's fit to be tied by her apron strings. Which by the way Jules has done to her, along with throwing crepes and Russian caviar all over the place and sucking down their oldest, boldest wines with a vengeance."

Sam pursed her lips, thinking. She bobbed her head as a realization lit her up like a bulb. "Of course! The famous Chef Jules. He died, what—ten years ago? He cooked for royalty and was a renowned winer."

"And apparently he still is. Hence, he's at the Prince's castle, and is creating a real stir. And no matter how many cans of it are painted, you know the saying: Too many cooks spoil the broth."

"Even if one of them is dead," Sam agreed. "Or maybe more so when one of them is dead." She shook her head, since everyone with any sophistication whatsoever knew that chefs' temperaments were more notorious than those of artists. "The Prince really does have a ghost of a problem. So give me the rest of the story. Who's behind door number three?"

Myles crushed out his cigarette, narrowing his eyes. "You ain't gonna like this one, angel. Rasputin."

She gasped. "The Mad Monk? The monk connected to Czar Nicholas and his wife Alexandria? That monk?"

"Yeah, doll. That's the one. The worst apple in Varinski's barrel."

Pursing her lips tightly, Sam shook her head. "Rasputin. That's not good. Not good at all." The Mad Monk had been almost impossible to kill when he was alive: poisoned, drowned, stabbed and strangled—all in one night. Which was amazing, since the mad, bad monk hadn't been a shapeshifter or a vampire. Now that Rasputin was dead, it would be even harder to get rid of him. But she didn't really have a choice; her family's business was on the line. If Prince Varinski had hired Monsters-R-Us to do this ghost removal, then he would continue to hire them for any other properties he had. And he had plenty. Sam could not afford to lose this kind of business or publicity. Not now. She couldn't wait for her ship to come in.

"I'll just hijack the damn boat." she muttered.

"Is the castle on a boat?"

"No, just thinking out loud. When will the Strakhovs do the removal?"

"They're tied up for a few weeks. They have a couple of scheduled jobs around here, and of course they have to track those trolls they missed tonight."

"Serves the supernatural-business-stealing bullies right," Sam declared emphatically. "Now, what about the Prince? When will he go to the castle?"

"He's out of town for a few weeks more. Traveling on business across the country."

Sam smiled like the cat that ate the cream. "Well, if those Strakhov brothers think I'm going to let them claim royal clients from right under our noses, they've got mush for brains."

Myles stared at her. "What do you have planned in that pretty little head of yours?"

"Capitalism at its finest." Her self-satisfied smile grew bigger. "*Real* competition. I intend to go up to the Prince's castle and clear out those ghosts before Prince Varinski comes back—and before the Strakhov brothers know what's hit them. Bogie will just have to work the rest of our jobs alone for the next week or two."

Myles raised an eyebrow. "For a bird, you're getting foxy. Still, I'm not so sure about this. You always think you know what you're doing, that you're too slick to get into trouble. But a lot of things could go wrong on this deal, Sam. Russians can be a crafty lot. They're smart apples, all in all. A determined people, able to endure a licking and keep on ticking."

Sam agreed—and disagreed to a degree. "I'm not worried. We beat them at the atomic race and the space race, no? I think some Yankee ingenuity can beat them at the race to see who gets whose ghost. Besides, I'm like the Canadian Mounties—I always get my ghost. Especially if it will get Nicolas Strakhov's goat. Er, and never mind that the Canadian Mounties are Canadian."

And again, she really didn't have much of a choice. Right now, necessity was the mother of both invention and outlandish strategies. "I'll clear out the ghosts. Once that's done, I'll explain to Prince Varinski that my ghost extraction and relocation were a courtesy service provided to show him how efficient we Triple-P'ers are. When I prove how good we are, he'll forget all about the Strakhov brothers, comrades from the Mother Country or not."

"You can't just show up on the doorstep, doll!"

"I can if I'm the prince's latest squeeze."

Her uncle looked shocked. "No way, Sam. I am putting my foot down. You ain't ever gonna be some Russian vampire goon's floozy!"

Patting him on the shoulder, she replied humorously, "Of course not. The Prince *isn't in residence.* I'll just say he told me to go ahead of him until he can meet me. That way I have free rein of the castle. I'll clean the suckers out before the bloodsucker arrives. Then, when he does show up, I can give him a clean bill of health. See? All's well that ends well."

Myles shook his head. "I still don't like it. You got a dark passage and a deadline. If you miss, there is gonna be one dead reckoning—and I hope you ain't the one dead. You gotta remember, sweetheart, that these aren't angels with dirty faces, these are vampires with bloody fangs. And crazy ghosts! Don't let 'em tuck you in for the Big Sleep."

"I won't." She hugged Myles, loving him for being his usual goofy but caring self. He had been a fixture in her life for as long as she could remember, and in spite of his living out every 1940s Bogart movie, she wouldn't have it any other way. Family was family. And if they didn't love her, who would?

No Use Crying over Spilt Milk—Unless it's the Last Carton

Sam had gotten an early start on her trip to Prince Varinski's castle, dubbed Mandelay. After a three-hour drive, she found herself headed up the winding gravel path to the castle. Staring out her window she took in the beauty of the place: dark green lawns with huge flowering rhododendrons, large shaggy bushes sculpting themselves against the gray-black rocks of the coastal cliff, and gnarled trees twisted by the sea's high-saline winds lined the background.

Ahead of her the massive castle, four stories tall, was isolated on a tall cliff overlooking the ocean. The gray stone was covered with ivy that wrapped its tenacious tentacles onto the stone like a lover's embrace. Built back in the 1880s, this was a standing monument to the wealth of the Gilded Age.

"Nice homey little place. If home happens to have twenty kids and twenty sets of grandparents," she muttered to herself. Still, Sam had to admit that she was a little surprised, as she had been expecting something more along the lines of Frankenstein's castle.

Minda Webber

When the butler opened the door, her impression of the place was again one of vastness and wealth. The floor was white marble with deep blue veins. The walls were also stone, with magnificent tapestries in place and an odd can of chicken soup splashed here and there. She didn't have to be a genius to know that Evil Andy the Spook had been hard at work.

The butler was a retiring man in his sixties. He had a spare frame and was dressed to the nines in a dark suit with a white shirt and a very starched collar. He looked very nifty, Sam observed.

"I'm Mr. Belvedere," he informed her.

After a lot of lying and false smiles, the butler seemed to accept her explanation that she was the Prince's latest squeeze. In fact, the butler seemed delighted to finally meet someone connected so intimately with the Prince. It seemed he had yet to meet his new employer.

Sam was shown to a spacious bedroom on the second floor of the castle with a lovely ocean view of rocky coastline and foamy white waves. Taking in the view, she allowed a big grin to cover her face as she congratulated herself on her deception. Just until Nicolas "client-stealer" Strakhov found out that she had scooped him on this phantom pest parade! She'd bet the sneaky Slav would be green with envy, and she couldn't help but wish to be a fly on the wall or an invisible woman when he discovered her deceit.

Leaving her room, Sam discovered more signs of the brush-wielding bogey. It seemed Andy had been a busy little ghost. Not that it took much detecting skill. Huge cans of soup were painted haphazardly all around the castle. Sam shook her head. Andy wasn't much of an artist.

Familiarizing herself with the grand old residence, she finally found herself in the castle kitchen, where the cook Mrs. McCutcheon was busy creating a masterpiece of a cake with chocolate cream frosting. Sam smiled. Anything with chocolate was a masterpiece to her way of thinking.

Within minutes she and the cook—"Rebecca"— were good friends, and Sam sat down to tea. She also got a piece of that marvelous cake. After savoring the first few bites, Sam got down to business: "I hear you've been having a few problems with an apparition named Jules."

Rebecca McCutcheon groaned. "That ghost is a monster! He's also a cocky, crabby chauvinist chef," the cook added bitterly. "He believes that a man's place is in the kitchen and a woman's place is to peel his potatoes. He's also jealous of my pastry-making."

Sam had to agree. This lady had a way with desserts. "So, give me the scoop. What does Jules do and when does he show up?" She could tell that this was just more than a cook and wine steward's sour grapes and cooking envy.

"He throws food, curses in French, guzzles the wine, makes the pots and pans fly," Rebecca explained angrily. "He is an evil ghost. An evil ghost, banging his pots and pans and making my sauces boil over, while he flies around the room swigging sauvignons. And I make a much better quiche," she added smugly.

"Horrible. The fiend." Sam didn't really see a major tragedy, but if the cook wanted to bellyache, Sam would let her. After all, everything was relative in life. What was one cook's demon could be another's devil food cake.

"That fraudulent foreign chef makes the milk go sour in the cream for my pastries. It's tragic. *Tragic,*" the woman complained tersely, her pretty round face red with indignation.

Sam nodded politely. She had seen other ghosts do much worse things than throwing temper fits with food and pans or getting soused on good wine, but then again this wasn't her kitchen and Sam hated it herself when milk went sour. There was always that first bitter, surprised gulp, followed quickly by a curse and milk spewing everywhere. Still, there was no use crying over the stuff.

"That idiot thinks he's so special, since he studied in France. Like a Frenchman's taste buds are better than my own hardy Irish stock. He's always *bon appétit*-ing me. As if I'm too stupid to know what that snooty spectral is doing when he ruins my food or what he's saying in the meanwhile."

Suddenly, the cook began speaking in French. Sam watched in fascinated amusement as the woman got her Irish up, but she couldn't tell what the cook was spouting since she didn't speak any foreign language except goblin. She also didn't know if the cook was repeating the ghostly chauvinist chef's curses or simply showing off her knowledge of a foreign language.

"English, please," she suggested.

"Sorry. Sometimes I forget myself. But I am *so* angry. That madman of a spook won't leave my utensils alone. Sometimes I see him with a bottle of wine and a ladling spoon. Sometimes I see him with his faux chef's cap. Sometimes I find pastry cooling on the cabinet shelves—pastry I didn't prepare. The ghost is a fiend. Imagine, leaving *his* pastry to cool on *my* shelves? His favorite is chocolate-covered éclairs, but he uses too much cinnamon," the cook confided.

Sam's mouth had begun watering. Perhaps she could entice Chef Jules to spend a few months at the old Hammett home. Her brother was a decent cook, but he still didn't do desserts.

Helping herself to another small slice of cake, she quickly took another bite, closing her eyes in ecstasy as she tasted the sensual softness of the creamy frosting. Eating chocolate was her favorite activity, even more than making love or riding dragons.

"I don't know what I'll do when the Prince arrives. What will he think when the kitchen is covered in potatoes au gratin and cream puffs with green slime? That temperamental menace even throws grapes!"

"Ah, the grapes of wraiths. Unfortunately I've seen that before." The image wasn't a pretty one, not Sam's ideal decorations. "Perhaps I might talk with Jules. I have some experience in ghostly manifestations," she bragged slightly.

"You do?" Rebecca McCutcheon's voice was full of admiration and awe. Her assistant, Beverly, a girl in her early twenties, with a lush figure, quickly joined the adoration society.

Sam explained briefly a few of the things she could do to handle the temperamental chef. When she was done, she checked up on the other situations. She left with an earful from the cook's assistant about Rasputin. Of all the ghosts he was the worst, which wasn't a big surprise to Sam. In life Rasputin had been evil; she doubted death had sweetened his disposition.

So, Andy was an artist with awful taste and bad technique, but he just wanted to be universally loved for his originality. The galloping ghostly gourmet, Jules, was a spoiled, chauvinist chef who had a tendency to drink too much wine, even in ghostly form, and who had a really nasty temper. But Rasputin was the ghost of a different color. In fact, he was downright dangerous. It appeared that the afterlife had had no good effects on the malicious, promiscuous poltergeist whatsoever. He was still into drinking himself stupid and arranging orgies in all shapes and sizes, and his favorite place to play and disrupt lives was the library, where he was known to appear at all times of the day and night.

Hoping to learn a little more about the galling ghost, Sam sat down in the library for a couple of hours, waiting for a sudden flash of white or signs that the vodka on the sideboard was beginning to diminish. But she waited in vain.

As she rose to leave, sighing, a little kitchen etiquette reminded her that a watched pot never boils, and a mad, bad Russian monk who had been a ghost for almost a century would probably appear when she least expected it. He'd want to get the drop on her so to speak.

"Ha!" A ghost would have to get up pretty early in the day to get the drop on her. She was a good egg but a hard-boiled ghost detective, and she hadn't lived with her uncle so long without some of his detecting skills rubbing off on her. "Mr. Rasputin, you don't stand a ghost of a chance with me," she warned the empty room—just in case the malevolent monk was playing hide-and-seek. "I'll be back, and then you can just make my night."

Five People You Meet at an Orgy

Shaking her head, Sam glanced again around the castle's large library, which was filled with the Prince's servants. Everywhere people were in states of undress, with the loud strains of "The Stripper" blaring from a CD player. The room was now filled with candles of all scents and sizes, and was oozing lust like a leaky sieve. The mood, Sam reasoned was supposed to be one of romance, with buckets of champagne littered here and there, but it would be a cold day in hell before she would consider this group romantic.

Sam was too stunned to be totally repulsed, and a faint curiosity was wending its way through her brain. She watched in morbid fascination as if watching a train wreck in slow motion.

"Well, well. This is certainly a hot time in the old castle tonight. And it isn't even a demon convention, just a devilish ghost with lust on the brain," Sam muttered, her fingers pattering a beat on her jeans. Yup, Rasputin was at it again, and it appeared that his old black magic, that same old feeling he had engendered while alive, was alive and well even though he was dead.

The beyond-plump housekeeper, Mrs. Winters, who was not a day under sixty, was dancing a tango in her slip for the head gardener. Mrs. Winters, a woman who had greeted and treated Sam with a frosty civility, had evidently begun to thaw considering the way she was gyrating her hips. To make matters more bizarre was that the good-looking gardener wasn't resisting; he seemed more than willing to plant some seed in such an abundantly fertile and willing field, even though Mrs. Winters was December to his May-ish twenty-four. But then, in orgies, anything went. At least, that was what Sam thought. She really wasn't up on her orgy etiquette.

Glancing to her right, Sam spied the aging butler, Mr. Belvedere. Usually the epitome of everything proper and regimented, he now had his coat off along with his tie. He was licentiously taking a garter off the cook's assistant's shapely leg, and Beverly was giggling and blowing kisses at him or a bust of Napoleon; Sam wasn't sure which.

Tomorrow, Sam thought wryly, Mr. Belvedere was going to regret finding out that the butler *had* done it—and in front of a roomful of people. But tonight his libido was apparently on fire, and he stood leering at the sexy cook-in-training.

Sam had heard of orgies. Roman, mainly. But she had never before had a front row seat. Pinching herself with one hand helped to remind her of her duty to save the day and to stop normally circumspect people from faux fornication due to one mad monk's infamous inclinations. "Rasputin always loved to corrupt the innocent—or hell, even the wicked for that matter."

Subconsciously Sam fingered the amulet around her neck, Bustin' ghost-protection amulet given to her by her mother when she was five. The amulet protected her from all kinds of nasty poltergeist spells and was a required trinket for all serious Paranormalbusters.

As Sam played with the amulet she continued to survey the massive room, trying hard to catch a glimpse of the shadowy spook of the moment; Rasputin had to be around somewhere, most likely conducting the orgy like an orchestra maestro, complete with his big stick. Narrowing her eyes, she caught a glimpse of a luminescent shape off to her right.

"Gotcha," she muttered. The rotten phantasm was fading in and out, blinking on and off like a neon sign, and catching her first glimpse of him, she couldn't help but stare.

The Russian ghost was dark-haired and dark-bearded and very tall. He had bright scarlet eyes, was dressed in monk's robes and sat on the steps of the library's oak ladder, high amidst a stack of books, his big baton in hand. His smile was so cold that Sam shivered.

Once again touching her amulet for good luck, she started forward, willing herself not to fall under his spell. She was still worried, even though her amulet was top of the line. Like condoms, amulets weren't foolproof. An extremely powerful spell could affect the wearer, and since Rasputin was a prime phantom Sam had a right to worry. Luckily her amulet worked and she appeared immune to the spell, with only the faintest twinge of desire tugging at her hormones.

"Now, how to stop a full-scale orgy," she muttered. They hadn't covered this in her college class, Ghostly Enchantment 102. "Things are heating up and quickly. It's every female for herself." If she didn't want to end up down on the floor or the top of a desk with her feet in the air like a dead bug and doing the horizontal mambo, she needed to figure out a solution and quick. "Double-time quick," she mused as she saw Mr. Belvedere go for his pants.

She made a moue of distaste. She loved and respected older people, since they had seen and done things that she hadn't. "But I don't want to see old people naked. No way!"

Frowning, Sam concentrated hard on her dilemma. She could ring the fire alarm, but the way these people were moaning and carrying on, she didn't think they would even pay attention. Perhaps she would just turn on the fire sprinklers she spotted on the ceiling. Thank goodness the renovation of the castle had included safety issues!

"Yes, extinguishers might work. Rain on their parade, so to speak." It worked with dogs in heat, so maybe the same principle would apply with Rasputin's lust-driven stooges. Now, if she could just get Rasputin off that ladder, she could climb up and hold a candle under the sprinklers.

Sam made her move, her attention focused on the ghost, but she ran smack-dab into a hard chest. Her nose and breasts smashed against a muscular build. Startled, she stepped back and glanced up into the face of one of the most handsome men she had ever seen, the stuff that dreams were made of. He was tall, dark and devastatingly masculine, with thick wavy hair the color of deep midnight. He wore it several inches below his shirt collar. It was hair that made the hairdresser in her itch to run her fingers through it. The man had a physical strength as well. His expression was arrogant, in command, but he wore it well, along with an armor of cynicism.

The breath exploded from her lips in a rush. This man she had just tangled with was all male sexuality, a sexuality that curled her toes. And that was just the highlights. He was clearly a heartbreaker, able to section a girl's heart before breakfast and serve it like a grapefruit. No doubt, this was Prince Petroff Varinski in the flesh.

He was the night—nothing more and nothing less, she thought as the air around her began to hum with some strange current. Suddenly she felt like she had her own personal electrical storm stationed right above her head. Taking a deep breath, she scented him. He smelled all male, the odor of frost and damp woodsy earth, and some scent uniquely his own that tingled her senses.

"What in the hell is going on here? Perhaps a failed palace coup?" He had an excellent command of the English language, with only a faint hint of an accent.

"A . . . a . . ." Sam cursed silently. This was a first. She was at a loss for words, due to the sneaky vampire springing a surprise visit to his castle. What nerve! Fortunately he had caught her with her pants up. Unfortunately her mind seemed stalled and in the gutter. And her hair was a disaster, pulled back in a loose ponytail.

"It's difficult to explain." *Brilliant,* she sneered at herself. But she so wanted to run her fingers through his hair. She loved thick hair. And she wanted to strip off his shirt, his boots and then his . . . "Oh!" What if her protection amulet had lost its power and she was in the grip of a mad, bad lust?

"Oh? Difficult to explain?" The Prince asked in his cold clipped voice, clearly determined to get to the root of the problems surrounding him. The luscious female standing here didn't look like one of his servants; she held herself too proudly and she also wasn't in some varying stage of undress. Who was she? he wondered even as he glared at her.

Studying her from the bottom of her tennis-shoed feet to the top of her lovely blond hair, he conceded that she was a pretty woman, although in his long life he had seen far lovelier. But there was something about this female that was different, and that frustrated him. He couldn't even seem to tear his eyes away to watch the orgiastic shenanigans around him.

Something in this woman's chemistry called to him in a wild primordial way, urged him to move closer. Following his body's command, he stepped closer and breathed in the scent of wild jasmine and a honeyed essence that was totally hers. His nostrils flared.

"What's going on here?" he asked with an arrogant lift of his eyebrow.

Ruthlessly stomping on her growing lust, Sam answered. "What does it look like? An orgy, or rather the beginnings of an orgy are what's going down. And not your run-of-the-mill orgy either."

"I deduced that myself. What I want to know is, why?"

"Rasputin the ghost has put a spell on them," she explained warily, licking her lips and gazing at his tall, hard body. "I was trying to find a way to break it up when I ran into you."

He cocked a brow. "Really? How?" The Prince studied her carefully. Who was she? She had a wonderful body, and those worn jeans showcased her muscular, curvy legs, and her tight sweater encased full, firm breasts. She also had the loveliest hair the color of ripe wheat. And bedroom blue eyes. And he now intended his to be the bed in the equation.

Sam pointed to the ceiling. "Water sprinklers."

He shook his head. "I don't think so." Turning to the room, he almost took a pair of panties to the face.

"Enough!" he commanded the library's libidinous occupants, his voice loud, harsh and utterly quelling. Such a commanding presence might have looked ridiculous dodging flying underwear and scowling at half-naked servants, but somehow Prince Varinski managed to pull it off.

Pointing a finger at the salacious specter, he commanded, "Leave at once, Rasputin. I'll attend to you later!" Then he spoke some words in Russian, and the malevolent monk dissolved with various vile curses.

Once Rasputin left, the orgy participants seemed suddenly subdued. Their faces and various other body parts flushed red, and a mad scramble for clothes hastily ensued. Sam couldn't help grinning at the half-naked servants' antics.

The Prince turned back to face her. His command was impressive, and she wondered if he would teach her the words he had called out in Russian, perhaps bespelling the horrid, horny monk, and definitely causing him to leave the library posthaste.

"Who are you?" he asked, his stern eyes alight with curiosity. Life had long since grown boring. He had become jaded over the many long years of always getting what he wanted, often before he even asked, and so this blond female stirred something primal in him—an acute appetite to taste and savor her. This was sexual chemistry at its height.

Believing in fate as the Prince did, this sudden business trip to the castle to deal with his ghostly intruders had suddenly taken on a brand new light. He would make love to the stranger. He knew he wasn't being conceited, since women tumbled right and left for him, along with various other gymnastic tricks to capture and hold his attention. But being from the Old School he would first learn her name.

Before Sam could answer, Mr. Belevedere began to speak. He hastily tugged on his black butler jacket, looking askance at his employer. "Why, she's your girlfriend, Samantha Hammett, my prince. Is the room too dark for you to see?"

Within seconds the butler had lit the library's large crystal chandelier. Bowing from the waist, he added solemnly, "And my name is Belvedere. I'm your butler. And I must apologize for this appalling lack of decorum. It's that infernal ghost, that monk, who is making us behave in this less than civilized fashion. I must beg your humble forgiveness. For all of us. Your Highness, we truly do not normally behave in this fashion. . . ."

Seeing the fierceness in the Prince's eyes, Sam wondered if he was going to put his foot downright smack-dab in the middle of the butler's back. Instead, the haughty vampire waved the explanation off, halting the butler abruptly as he turned back to Sam.

Ignoring the embarrassed servant, the Prince stared at his uninvited but very much wanted guest. His blood began singing in his veins, and his heart began beating faster. "Ah yes, my *lover*."

Watching the vampire prince, Sam's heart began beating so fast and furious she wondered if the whole room could hear it. Would the vampire kick her out without a chance to explain? Would he denounce her in front of all his help? Would he carry her off on his shoulder and have his wicked way with her? She stood taller, her chin thrust out.

"Your girlfriend!" she said.

The Prince knew what this female was thinking. A grim smile lit his features as he recognized whom and what she was—an uninvited Paranormalbuster. So *this* was Samantha Hammett. He had heard that she had a backbone of steel and balls to match, that she was a tough-talking, hard-driven businesswoman, who was hell on ghosts, goblins and demons alike. From the gossip he'd heard, he'd formed a completely different (and unflattering) image of a deceitful and devious female. Yet tonight she stood before him filled with sweet vulnerability in both her voice and stance. An interesting conundrum.

Smiling deviously, he formed a plan to deal with

her. "My lover, Sam," he stated, his expression wicked.

"Your girlfriend," she protested again.

Talk about going from the frying pan into the fire, Sam thought. It appeared he was going to play along with her lie, but at what price? And would she mind so terribly paying?

Perhaps she should buy a new amulet, because she didn't normally behave or feel this way about men. Well, she did occasionally lust after Mel Gibson and Robson Greene, or men she saw in the movies, but she certainly hadn't ever encountered a lust that threatened to knock her over before.

She had fallen in love once, when she was twenty-one. The relationship hadn't worked out. Her boyfriend at the time couldn't stand the thought of her risking life and limb in corralling supernatural creatures. His fear had gotten in the way of their relationship.

Her resentment at his constant complaints had added to the problem. When she had busted him in bed with another girl, well, that had been the end of everything. Since her fiancé-bustin' days, she had been man-free and mostly sex-free, with an occasional splurge. But the last splurge hadn't been for many years, many, many years.

She managed a faint smile as she stated again, "Girlfriend. You're my boyfriend, and I'm your girlfriend."

He seemed affronted. "Princes are never boyfriends. But don't worry, my dear. I haven't forgotten you. How could I? Not when we've shared so many happy times." He grabbed her arm and held it, though not painfully. "I'll escort you upstairs, myself. After all, we have lost time to make up for."

Although she didn't like the sound of his words or the underlying threat, Sam kept her mouth shut.

Glancing grimly back at Belvedere, the Prince stated in a voice dripping with derision, "Make sure I don't interrupt another scene like this, not ever again." He held up his free hand to stop the complaints and excuses he saw coming from the butler. "I will deal with Rasputin. Now, no more orgies behind library doors—or any doors for that matter. I don't approve of this mischief."

"Mischief?" Sam muttered under her breath—but obviously not as quietly as she'd intended, since the Prince sent her a gravity-defying look. If he considered naked servants, an insane malicious ghost and library orgies mischief, she wondered what he'd call bigger problems.

Turning her attention back to the servants, she watched in disbelief. They all bowed and scraped so low, she was sure some of them were going to have backaches come morning and be in desperate need of some heavy duty painkillers.

The Prince's X-rated Diaries

While the Prince guided Sam away from the library and his meek disorderly servants, she found herself wound up tighter than a watch. She waited for the other shoe to drop, waited for him to order her out of his home into the cold, cruel night—or else into his hot, soft bed. Even though she ached to have his lips on hers, she wasn't easy, and she didn't intend to go to bed with this fiendish Don Juan of the Undead; not within fifteen minutes of meeting him.

Whether her sexual ache was the lingering effects of his lust-filled library, his bloodsucker charm or the man within the vampire, she didn't know, but she did know one thing, one very solid thing: She never mixed business and pleasure. No matter how sexy a vampire prince might be, she couldn't move this fast. Going to bed with Varinski might be one small step for him, but it was one giant leap for Samkind.

With those thoughts clacking around in her head, Sam pulled at the Prince's hand. "Thanks, but I don't need an escort," she said.

"But I insist. After all, I'm a gentleman, Samantha. You don't mind me calling you that, do you?"

"It's Sam. But you know who I am, don't you?" she continued without equivocation. "What I do for a living?"

"I suppose it's too much to hope that you're a high-priced call girl."

"Please," she said. "I saw the recognition in your face when Belvedere introduced us. You know I'm a Paranormalbuster." Who did he think he was, letting her pretend to be his girlfriend when he knew damn good and well that she wasn't? This crafty Nosferatu was up to something, but whether it was getting into her pants or somewhere more nefarious, she didn't yet know. But she would know, or her name wasn't Samantha Sabrina Hammett.

"Perhaps. And you can call me Petroff," he remarked, an odd quality to his voice.

"Aren't you curious why I'm here? And what are *you* doing here? I thought *you* were out of state. Don't you read calendars?" What kind of bad luck was this? If she didn't watch it, she was going to end up losing Prince Varinski's business before she even had it.

"Daily and I decided matters here at the castle needed attending to immediately. Isn't that fortunate for us?"

"There is no us."

"But there could be," he said, grinning wickedly.

Sam Hammett had a beauty that was definitely classic, the Prince decided. Such a shame she was who she was; not to mention that she was a liar and a sneak. Those were two traits he hated in females he

intended to bed. But he would overlook them somehow.

"I'm here to help you," she remarked; then seeing
his grin widen into a knowing leer, she added
quickly, "with your phantom pest problems." Now, if
he would only let go of her arm so she could scam-
per off into the darkness and get away from his
touch.

"Perhaps you're the pest," he suggested wryly. He
wanted to make her sweat for her subterfuge, and
for making him want her. For being Sam Hammett,
scourge of the ghost world and havoc-wreaker on
the Strakhov Brothers.

"Thanks a lot. I know this looks bad, me barging
in and all, but I have a plan to help you out," Sam
replied. "Yes, I admit this looks bad. But it really
isn't."

He smirked, feigning ignorance. "The orgy?"

Sam scowled. "I meant me being here, pretending
to be something I'm not." The vampire was too
good-looking for his own good. It must be true: a liquid diet was good for the system.

"But you could be," he interrupted seductively, his
voice caressing her, "my mistress." The Prince added
with a wicked grin, "I seem to be momentarily without one, and you're here. I'm a firm believer in answering the door when opportunity knocks. Or on
knocking, myself."

It shouldn't have surprised her, his willingness to
knock her up; vampires were notorious for seizing
the night. Fast on their feet, they had to provide
their own opportunities, pounding on doors and entering people's homes with only the slightest invite.

"Well, don't hold your breath," she advised him coolly. This vampire prince might be wily and domineering, but he would have to rise out of his coffin pretty early in the morning to put the bite on her.

The Prince grinned at her; he did so love a challenge, and Samantha Hammett was proving the ultimate.

Noting his cat-that-ate-the-canary grin, Sam narrowed her eyes. She wasn't in the mood to be lunch. His proposal had been lacking in charm, and was highly insulting if slightly erotic. She wouldn't be anybody's plaything, although she might fantasize a bit sometimes. "Look, Prince V., you've got worse problems than not having a mistress at the moment. Let me make this short. You've got three ghosts in your castle that are devious, deranged and downright dangerous."

"So you decided to come here and hunt them, since you're from a family of renowned ghost removal experts. You install yourself at my castle, pretending to be my lover—"

"Girlfriend," she interrupted.

"Why quibble over words? You came here to do some Bustin'."

"Yes. I came here to get rid of your ghosts," she agreed.

"Without me hiring you. What if I have decided on another firm? Is this justice and fair play? Is this how business is done in America?" he taunted her.

Sam hawed and hemmed, then finally answered: "Haven't you ever heard of Yankee ingenuity?" With her dying breath she would fight to the bitter finish, and not under any condition, not under any circumstance, would she let Monsters-R-Us keep the Prince as a client. Especially not after the illuminating episode of skullduggery the dirty rotten scoundrels had perpetrated against her.

The Prince scowled, shifting his legs as he stood, hands on hips, waiting and watching her like a big spider. And she had walked willingly into his web. "Perhaps I like to choose my Bustin' companies without any help."

She shrugged. "Then I guess I owe you an apology. I meant well, really. And I wasn't expecting any payoff for capturing and removing your ghosts. I just wanted to show you what Paranormal bustin' Pest Pursuers Inc. can do. What *I* can do."

He was dying for her to do just that. But in the bedroom. All night long. Forget the ghosts.

"Hmm," he began thoughtfully, examining her like a succulent piece of meat. "How did you learn about my little problem?"

"I make it my business to know these things. And your problem's not a little one. Not with Rasputin."

"No, the problem isn't a little one," the Prince admitted. "And you seem to be one of the only Busters available to help." She was making him aroused just with her delicious scent. Rubbing his thigh muscle, dangerously close to his growing erection, he noticed that her eyes had focused on what his hand was doing. She blushed.

Sam froze, mortified to see that he had caught her staring at his crotch. She never blushed; and at the same time a morbid curiosity had her questioning if all Russians had a Peter this great or if it was just a vampire characteristic.

Searching her thoughts, she scrambled for mental purchase in a quagmire of lusty images. Back at university she had taken a vampire physiology class, only her professor had been timid, skipping over the interesting parts—like vampire sexual organs. Now she wished she had taken an advanced class or two, for knowing vampires' sexual habits and endowments would come in handy.

Jerking her eyes and her smutty thoughts away from the Prince, she said; "I will be more than happy to rid you of your ghosts free of charge, Prince V."

"Only ghosts, then? You can't help with anything else?" he asked playfully. He found it hard to believe that Sam Hammett was still resisting his will.

Sam stepped back twice, putting more distance between them. "Ghosts. I said ghosts."

He took two steps closer, lifted her chin with his finger. Her skin was very soft. He enjoyed the feel. He wanted to savor so much more of her silken sweetness, but this lying, luscious jade was playing hard to get, while he was just plain hard. "Well, we must be upfront with each other. Not knowing what's a lie and what's the truth can cause confusion. And you must call me Petroff."

"So, you'll allow me to work . . . ?"

"For now. We can discuss it further tomorrow—perhaps an early morning affair." But he dropped his hand when she quickly stepped back, jumpy as a newborn colt.

The Prince sighed. He knew she was extremely attracted to him, but that she was fighting the attraction; she was a complex woman with a mind of her own. Obviously, in spite of his good intentions their first meeting would not lead to a mating. He grimaced. He wanted her, this deceitful human; but sometimes a long journey could be more thrilling than the destination.

Sam smiled up at her host, giving thanks that she hadn't been booted out on her butt or brought within an inch of her life—or twelve inches of her dignity. Even though she was a hard-boiled preternatural pest controller, a nemesis to nasties everywhere and nobody's pushover or sure thing, she found Prince V. to be temptation on the fang, Rasputin's spell or not. But she had a company to save, and save it she would. Petroff Varinski would be glad he had hired her in the end—if not in the beginning.

Waving good night, she started for the stairs. Petroff watched her walk off.

"Where are you going?" he asked.

"To bed. Solo," she answered resolutely, continuing up the magnificent beige-and-ivory tiled staircase. Her body's subtle beauty, the tautness of her buttocks showcased by her faded jeans did not escape him.

"Just like that?" he asked. Those worn jeans fit her backside like a glove, like *he* wanted to fit himself to it.

"Yep, I've found that the shortest farewells are the best." And with that, she fled.

The Prince laughed. This woman wasn't quite Machiavellian, but her plot was devious. He should give credit where credit was due. Still, he wouldn't. He had caught the flash of triumph in her eyes when he agreed to let her catch his ghosts, and so while she thought she was winning, she had already lost the game. She just didn't know it yet.

No, Samantha Hammett had lost, and she deserved exactly what she was going to get. But he intended to seduce her before the truth was revealed in all its glorious colors and harsh black and white. The seduction, they would both enjoy. The betrayal, only he would appreciate.

Goldilocks and the Three Ghosts . . . and the Prince

Sam heard cursing the next morning, in both American and Russian. It didn't take her three guesses to know who was doing it. The Prince was up and royally pissed.

She continued carefully down the stairs, wondering how to deal with a cranky vampire in the morning; she rarely met vampires over six hundred years old and capable of being awake at that time.

Turning a corner, she saw his royal majesty stalking toward her. He was dressed in worn-out jeans and a pale blue sweater, which highlit the flecks of deep blue in his smoldering gray eyes. His expression was grim, no doubt due to the fact that he was wearing a partial painting of a can of tomato soup on his chest. The bright red oil was noticeably wet.

"Gives new meaning to the expression 'soup's on,'" she said.

He halted abruptly before her, his eyes narrowed. "I thought you were supposed to be some kind of big shot Bustin' professional. Why aren't you doing your job? That lunatic ghost, Andy, just attacked me! I don't even like tomato soup! I detest it!"

Deciding a poker face was the best response, Sam suppressed her grin. "I only got here yesterday. What do you think I am, a miracle worker?"

He arched a brow, his haughty aristocratic demeanor returning. "Excuses. Not much of a Paranormalbuster, are you?"

Prince Petroff hoped his words would make the woman mad. She had to feel as put out as he did. She needed to strain and toil to capture these ghostly phantoms infesting the castle. She needed to have her day start out the way his had, by being attacked by a crazy painter with a can fetish. Yes, Miss Samantha Hammett needed to be brought down a peg or two, needed to be taught a lesson—and he was just the instructor for the job.

Those were fighting words, as far as Sam was concerned. She forgot her amusement at the haughty Russian's dishevelment and snapped, "Greater men, spirits and demons than you have criticized me. And you know what I say?"

He watched and awaited her next words, noting how pretty she looked in the morning light. She had a great set of breasts; not too big or too small, just right.

"*This* is what I say," Sam retorted. Then, glaring up at him, she thumbed her nose.

It was a rather adorable nose, not too big and not too small, but just right. In spite of his ill humor, he grinned. "Take it back," he warned teasingly. "Nobody thumbs their nose at me!" But he was now reasonably optimistic that this grumpy Goldilocks would be sleeping in his bed by nightfall.

Sam rolled her eyes. "Who would dare, right? You don't think too much of yourself, do you? It's a good thing princes don't wear crowns these days, because yours wouldn't fit that swollen head. I think it's called megalomania."

He arched his other brow. "Is that any way to speak to your employer?" He knew he had scored a hit when he saw her wince. Good. She needed to be put in her place. Too bad that place wasn't under him. Yet, hope sprang eternal.

Sam sniffed and conceded. She needed this job, and she needed the Prince to be impressed with her work. She should be sweet-talking, not antagonizing him. Still, who the hell did he think he was—King of the World? He could use someone to bring him down out of his ivory vampire tower—or black wooden coffin or whatever. But she backpedaled anyway.

"Sorry. It's just that I majored in ghost, goblin and gremlin psychology. And I can be a grouch when I have to wake up early. I usually spend eight hours a night on the job, so mornings are mine to do what I want. Which is inevitably, sleep. By the way, I've been up since six this morning hunting your haunts. Unfortunately, these three wise ghosts are doing a disappearing act. Three hours later, and I have to admit that they have run me a merry chase. At least, Andy and Jules have."

She rubbed her forehead wearily. "I had Andy cornered and was making headway when I made a slight . . ." Sam hesitated, noting her employer's grim expression. "A very slight, *very, very slight*, miscalculation."

"How slight?" Petroff inquired.

In the abstract, Sam always felt that the truth was the best way to go in any given situation. Of course, most situations didn't deal with an obsessive-compulsive ghost. And she hated to tell the truth now, especially when she was the one who had made the blunder.

"I was talking to Andy about art and happened to mention that his work reminded me of Pablo Picasso's early work. Who knew that he would find that comparison an insult? He vanished in a haunted huff right before yelling 'Philistine' at me."

Petroff grinned. This woman was so cute discomposed. He was glad she wasn't decomposed, though.

"It's probably why he went off on a rampage and started to paint your chest," Sam went on feeling a slight twinge in her heart. Seeing the Prince's lopsided grin, she understood absolutely why women lined up for this devastatingly desirable vampire. She was also smart enough to know that whatever feelings she had for him had come on hard, fast and would likely be, lethal.

The Prince's grin faded, replaced by a tightening of his lips. He glanced down once again at his ruined sweater.

Sam sighed. If he didn't like the first bit, he really wasn't going to like what she had to say next. Pointing to the kitchen, she continued, "I got an urgent message from your cook. It seems that Jules is on the warpath again. Prince Varinski—"

"I told you to call me Petroff," he interrupted.

Conceding the point, she said, "You know, too many cooks in the kitchen . . . well, in this case, it seems too many cooks *spill* the broth. Your cook ended up wearing it. Let's go see if we can view the damage. Then I'll go back to shadowing the ghosts, Pete."

The Prince scowled at the Americanization of his name. "Not Pete. Petroff. It's a good, solid Russian name."

"Petroff's too stuffy," Sam suggested. "But if you insist."

Before Petroff could argue, she pointed to the kitchen. "You can follow me, in case you're worried about getting a pie in the face."

Swiftly she walked to and shoved open the door to the kitchen. Might as well get it over with quickly, she decided. But once through the door, Sam's mouth rounded in an "O". Forgetting momentarily that she was a good deal shorter than the Prince, she valiantly tried to block his view of a disaster that would terrify even Mr. Clean.

The mess was not too big; it was not too small—it was enormous. The two cooks had evidently both been working in this kitchen. One had apparently been trying to make eggs and ham; only, the eggs had been slimed, big-time. They were a bright lime green. Fortunately, the ham had caught a lucky break and been missed, but still, this ripped it for Sam. She had been hungry earlier, but no way was she eating green eggs and ham.

Goo dripped from the ceiling; the floor was awash in goop.

Sneaking a quick peek at the royally pissed Prince, Sam asked, "You're mad, aren't you?"

He turned to stare at her with an expression of high dudgeon. "Yes, Sam, I am." I cannot believe my own distress, I cannot believe this awful mess."

Cooked potatoes and stew meat were splashed across the black and white tiled floor and cabinets. Pots and pans were littered here and there. Splashes of wine and smashed grapes decorated the kitchen walls and countertops.

"I caught you were mad right off the bat," Sam said.

"Are you being flip?"

"Who me? No way. I'm not gymnastic. But you're kidding, right? Your nice new kitchen is a big mess, and I'm starving. That makes me mad, too," she said, hoping he couldn't read the humor in her eyes. Turning away before he could spot it, she couldn't help but grin.

The Prince's servant hadn't fared well in this cook-off catastrophe; Mrs. McCutcheon was now busy with a mop, and was wearing what looked like pieces of cooked carrot in her bun, along with a slathering of green slime.

"Yep, plastered by ectoplasm," Sam muttered, trying to keep the revulsion from her face. Being slimed rated right up there with having a tooth drilled without laughing gas. Of course, being slimed was just one of the many hazards of her job.

"It's horrid. Just horrid," the assistant cook Beverly complained, wiping the tears off her face along with streaks of stewed tomato.

Sam didn't know why the woman was upset; she hadn't gotten her hair slimed. But she patted Beverly on the back anyway. Some people just weren't up for ghostly visitations and such tricks of the trade. Sliming was generally one of the first cards a ghost played.

"I thought Jules would have had more class than to slime food. It's kind of like throwing your peas in the lunchroom in middle school," Sam remarked disgustedly. "He must be a real attention hound. Who'd have thought?" she asked the whole room.

"I thought *you* would. After all, aren't you the expert?" Petroff pronounced caustically, wearing the most exasperated of expressions.

She might have mouthed off, but she figured that the Prince had a legitimate beef—though his kitchen had little else left to eat.

On the sideline appeared a very leery Mr. Belvedere, his shoulders visibly shaking. He looked the color of old milk, as if his goose were about to be cooked. Reluctantly he faced Prince Varinski, his voice almost a whisper.

"I'm afraid Chef Jules was angered because I hid the wine. You see, he had already been drinking rather heavily, consuming a great deal of your stock, my lord."

The cook huffed, breaking in to say, "That stuffy, pompous Frenchman was angry because I was making soup. Imagine, that ghostly wino told me my soup was just plain blasé. I've won awards for it, mind you!"

The woman continued, clearly burning up. "He wanted to cook eggs for lunch! How foreign is that? Him, with his fancy spatula and fancy French ways. He had the audacity to scold me, telling me this isn't a soup kitchen. What does he know? Beans, that's what! He's stewed half the time on Claret. He's French and he's a ghost! Soup kitchen? Well, I never heard anything so silly in my life." Mrs. McCutcheon seemed to suddenly come back to herself, recalling who her audience was. "Begging your pardon, my prince."

Sam pursed her lips, keeping her mouth shut and her chuckles in. She wasn't going to laugh at the expression on Pete's face. She wasn't going to make a smart remark or find absurd humor in this kitchen catastrophe or even the carrots in the cook's hair. She absolutely would not make a wisecrack when she took another peek at Pete, who was wearing a can of soup on his chest. "Looks like the plat du jour, is soup."

Her words went unappreciated. No one laughed and Prince Pompous only glared, his slate gray eyes deepening to charcoal.

"Isn't it a lucky thing that my *girlfriend*"—he stressed the word—"has a degree in ghost psychology." He looked pointedly at her and moved close to put an arm around her shoulders.

"Really?" Rebecca McCutcheon asked, her face alight with hope. "I know you said you had some experience, but if you have a degree, then you must be a pretty smart cookie. Can you help us get rid of that puffed-up excuse for a chef?"

Petroff snorted, but Sam nodded. Tamping down her burgeoning desire, she ducked back. His close proximity, his embrace was too exhilarating; his smell was so fresh and invigorating that she could hardly stand it. In defense, she matched him sardonic look for sardonic look.

Turning back to the cook, she smiled a patently sweet smile, the expression she used to entice little goblins out from under beds. "Of course I will. I wouldn't want to let down my prince, now would I?"

Petroff snorted again.

"You make mincemeat out of him, dearie, that's what you'll do," the cook stated firmly.

Mr. Belvedere nodded. "Miss Samantha is a jolly good fellow, you know."

Sam smiled, then tilted her head to indicate the open doorway to the hall. "Pete . . . troff, I think we should discuss strategy."

The arrogant aristocrat held out his arm. "Whatever you say, sweetheart. Lead the way."

Outside in the hall, Sam stood uncomfortably while the Prince leaned against the wall. His expression was grim, his manner one of one royally outraged.

"You really aren't a morning vampire, are you?" Sam noted.

He scrutinized her carefully. "You really think I should be bright-eyed and cheerful after an employee orgy, a kitchen thrashed by a ghostly drunken chef, and a ruined wardrobe?"

Well, when it was put that way, Sam felt bad about criticizing him. "I know it hasn't been the best of mornings, or nights—" she backtracked.

"A terrible morning, really," he agreed. His lips looked so soft, and she wondered whose coffin he was sleeping in these days. Who was his current arm candy, and was she a sweetheart or a Tootsie Roll? Pete was everything she might want in a man and then some—except he was a vampire, and that did throw her for a loop or two.

"Right, you're right. It's been a really bad deal for you."

"No, it hasn't been good at all," the Prince went on. Last night and this morning might have been fun if she had been playing with him, rather than haunting the castle for those other haunts. "Nor fun."

"Look here, Pete, I am first-rate at what I do. The best. I have a ninety percent success ratio on the extraction and removal of ghosts. You can't beat those odds, and I'll get these ghosts. Don't you worry."

He smirked, as if he didn't believe her. Maybe he considered her a human pest.

"I'll work on both Jules and Andy to start. I know I can make headway with Andy this morning, now that I know what not to say. He may be a modern artist, but his heart is in the sixteenth century. He wants his art to be associated with the greats, like Michelangelo and da Vinci. He wants to make his soup can as timeless and elegant as da Vinci's *Mona Lisa*."

Petroff raised a brow, his expression one of disbelief.

Sam held up a hand. "I know, I know—soup cans weren't even invented during the Renaissance. Besides, I didn't say he could do it. It's just what he aspires to."

"Is this ghost psychology at its finest?"

"Yeah, it is. So just can your disbelief and remember I'm the professional. I know what I'm doing."

Glancing at the kitchen and then down at his soup-splattered shirt, he said tartly, "Are you sure? So far, all I see is a recipe for more disaster."

"I must be doing something right. Need I remind you that I didn't end up in my birthday suit with

Rasputin last night? And I'm not the one wearing paint on my sweater." As Sam fought back, she began to feel better. She was feeling light on her feet. She was dodging his punch lines with the grace of Joe Louis.

Petroff leered at her breasts. Smiling, he quipped, "But you could wear it so well. Mmm-mmm. Soup is good food."

Whoops, she might be down for the count if he kept it up. His perseverance was deadly, especially aided by a left hook like his smile.

Sam frowned, knowing full well when to retreat. Sometimes withdrawing from a fight left a person a leg to stand on. "You really are the fresh type, aren't you?"

The Prince shook his head in the negative, but a slight grin cracked the austerity of his features. "Well, I'm not canned."

Sam grinned back at him. Fresh was fresh, and a wolf was a wolf—even if this wolf was a vampire. "I warn you, buster, I pack a mean punch."

This time, Petroff's grin broke through completely. "Well, you can bring it when we picnic. And thanks for the alert, but I happen to like challenges. And sassy-talking females are my favorite."

"Let me put on my surprised face."

The Prince shook his head at her outrageousness. With a grin still on his face, he cocked his head to indicate the kitchen. "What about Jules? Do you really think you can manage to gain any rapport with him?"

"Is my name not Sam Hammett? Not to brag or anything, but I've done some top-notch work with some low-down ghosts. I'll manage Jules, and Andy, and then I'll go on to Rasputin."

Petroff shook his head. "I hate to suppress your natural talents, but I'll deal with Rasputin personally."

Sam blinked, incensed. *Nobody* did her work, although she did let her brother help out, and her uncle in emergency situations. Then there was that time when Larry the Leprechaun had chipped in. But that was neither here nor there. "It's my job, I'll do it," she said.

Petroff shoved away from the wall, his features rigid. "I will handle Rasputin myself," he commanded. "Being Russian, I understand him. Besides, he owes me a debt that I intend to personally collect."

Sam didn't like anyone telling her what she could do or not do, but something about the Prince's firm and rather loud conviction convinced her that she wasn't going to win this battle. Besides, she probably wasn't going to get paid for this job anyway, and so if her employer wanted to dispatch the mad, bad Russian Monk himself, more power to him. As long as it wasn't the Strakhovs.

"All right. You win. As they say, the client is always right."

"How quaint. Another American saying?"

"You bet." He gave her an odd look, and she swallowed. "I bet you always get what you want anyway."

His grin was wicked, his eyes dancing. "Yes."

"Well, that must certainly be sweet. But it's probably just because you're a royal pain," Sam added in a mutter.

"Did you say something?"

Oh, you heard, Sam thought waspishly. This Nosferatu was definitely too big for his britches—

although they fit him to a T, showcasing his tight butt and muscular thighs. "You know, it's guys like you who give creatures of the night a bad name."

"And you Americans have such a way with words. It almost makes me want to relocate," the Prince retorted mockingly. He walked off down the long marbled floor of the hallway, but eight feet away he stopped and turned back to Sam. "Dinner tonight is at eight. Don't dress . . ." He hesitated again, in both his step and words, just enough to give Sam's inside a heated quiver. "Up."

Then he continued walking. He refused to glance back. Samantha Hammett was quick-tempered and quick-thinking, but in a business she had no business being in. If she were his mistress, she wouldn't be staking her life on stalking the supernatural to stake them. And if luck were with him tonight, he knew exactly whose bed she would be in; only, she wouldn't be doing any sleeping.

Watching him walk away with lust in her heart, Sam decided that Prince Petroff really should be declared a masculine menace. Any female within walking distance was going to get her heart banged up seriously, if not downright broken into small gritty pieces. "Never give a sucker an even break— especially a vampire," she whispered, thinking hard about her uncle's words of otherworldly wisdom.

Sticking out her tongue at the handsome vampire's retreating back made her feel better, until she thought she heard his snicker as he disappeared up the marble staircase. Impossible! Vampires didn't have eyes in the back of their head; only goblins did.

"Well, wasn't that mature," she muttered. He really did heat up her emotions and bring out both the best and worst in her. Cursing her foolish fantasies of a feast of flesh—naked flesh, all his—Sam doddered distractedly in the direction of the south tower, where earlier this morning she had found Andy's stash of paints.

"Petroff thinks I'll roll over and play dead with him? Ha! Fat chance." Lust was lust. Just because she had never experienced anything as overwhelming as what she felt for this fornicating foreigner, Sam still knew where her bed was buttered. And tonight, she wasn't going to be anywhere near that particular vampire's coffin.

"Here's Lusting after You, Kid"

Sam wasn't anybody's fool. She knew life could be hard and a person didn't risk their heart until they absolutely had to take the plunge. She wasn't going to play Russian roulette with the vampire prince considering what the stakes were, she reminded herself as she made her way to the north tower for dinner.

As she walked under the stone archway, she stopped momentarily, taking in the understated elegance of the dining room and its occupant. Huge circular windows provided a breathtaking panoramic view of the coastline below. A small round table stood near the center of the room, with an intricate lace tablecloth of pristine white. On top was a golden candelabrum giving off a soft glow. Large floral arrangements of various hues were everywhere.

Standing by the buffet table, the Prince appeared the perfect gentleman, dressed all in black—the usual attire for the undead. He looked better than the food, and promised to show her a new meaning to the phrase *le petit morte*. But despite the flowers and his attractiveness, Sam was no innocent victim to be led down the garden path. Nobody had to knock her on the head. She could smell setup a mile away.

Frowning slightly, she mused that the male gender were all alike, whether human or vampire, seduction dominating their limited brains. For humans it had to be an evolutionary design, something ingrained in their DNA to keep the human race from becoming extinct. With the male vampire, Sam felt their desire for sex, sex and more sex had to be related to their taste for oral gratification. They mixed fornication and ingestion to heighten both experiences, like some humans did by smoking a cigarette after making love or after eating a meal.

Squaring her shoulders, she marched boldly into the room. Petroff's eyes reflected amusement as he studied her, then he clearly decided that the best offense was a strong defense.

"I must apologize for my behavior this morning. I'm not at my best when bested by a neurotic phantom," he stated. He could tell by her wary pose that she thought he had seduction on his mind. Smart lady.

She nodded, taking in how the Prince's smile transformed his features from ruggedly handsome to just plain gorgeous. "I see your afternoon batnap did you some good. Woke up on the right side of the bed, did we?"

He would rather have woken up atop her, but smiling devilishly, he shrugged. "Well, I did manage some sleep, though mostly I plotted ways to be rid of that mad monk."

"Any clever plans yet?" She stopped by the huge bay window on the east side of the room, a good four feet away from Petroff. The view was breathtaking—just like her undead dinner companion. "You know that he won't be a pushover. He'll fight dirty."

Petroff nodded. Walking over to the table, he poured a glass of wine for each of them.

Sam noted that his movements held an inhuman grace, were pure poetry in motion. She sighed. "Since you aren't wearing a soup can on your shirt or carrots in your hair, I would lay odds that you haven't run across Andy tonight—or Jules. And probably not Rasputin, since you're fully dressed," she added.

Petroff grinned, and let her wonder what he was smiling about.

She shrugged and leaned back against the window frame. "Yes, I hate to brag, but I'm one smart cookie." She grinned impishly, trying to downplay the chemistry between them. Chemistry she would have gladly studied if certain things were different. It was hard ignoring her body's urgings, which had first begun as whispers but were slowly growing to shouts. Soon she would have a hormonal riot on her hands. Better to give him the lowdown on what she'd found out.

"You don't have the worst spectral situation I've ever seen, but it's not pretty," she remarked, managing to drag her attention away from the Prince to find herself staring at the southern wall. A can of chicken noodle soup had been recently painted there, left open to reveal the chicken and noodles inside. Only, Andy had decided to paint it rather abstractly with the soup being a flaming pink with dark purple noodles.

Shaking her head ruefully, she commented, "Your Andy is rather paranoid."

The Prince raised an aristocratic brow.

"He's afraid of people stealing his work," she explained. Both Sam and the Prince glanced at the garish soup can on the wall.

"That's the straight dope," she continued after a moment. "It's why he paints on stone—so nobody can steal his work," she explained, grimacing at the artwork in question.

"As if any thief in his right mind would!" the Prince commented.

Shrugging, Sam nodded. To be honest, she agreed with his assessment.

"What about the galloping gourmet?" the Prince asked.

"My philosophy is to never give a ghost an even break. My take on Jules is that he's a crabby old chef with a penchant for disliking everything. He and Andy don't get along at all, since Jules hates the soup cans all over the place—he says that no real cook would even use anything in a can. He dislikes dull knives and don't get him started on microwave ovens. He feels they're the devil's design. Also, Prohibition. Jules can go on for ages about that time period in history."

"What's your take on Rasputin?"

"Dangerous, paranoid delusions of grandeur— and he's a sexual deviant. He's just plain evil."

"Well, thank you for your candor on my problems. I'm so glad you're having dinner with me," he added with a hint of a seductive edge. "I do so dislike dining alone."

Subconsciously Sam put a hand to her neck. She glanced back at the dinner table, and a sigh of relief escaped her as she saw two dinner plates and one steak—rare of course—on each. Sam had never been bitten by a vampire before, in spite of her oft-dangerous occupation. She intended to keep that the status quo. "What kind of guest would I be if I hadn't shown up? Especially after you've been so swell in hiring me and all."

"Perhaps an uninvited one," he said teasingly, amusement lingering in his smoke gray eyes.

"Jeez, Pete, what a lousy thing to say," Sam said. Before he could comment, she quickly added, "But I have good news and bad news. Nuts!" she exclaimed, bopping her forehead with her hand. "I always hate it when people do that to me. Good news, bad news—like anybody ever wants to hear the bad part."

"Do you always say the first thing that pops into your head?" Prince Petroff asked, noting that Sam looked flustered at her gaffe, but even more fantastic. Definitely very sexy. She looked good enough to eat all night, and he was suddenly starving.

"And second and third. Honesty is a virtue!" she said.

"Isn't that rather ironic, coming from you?"

Sam sniffed disdainfully. "I always tell the truth. Er, unless I don't," she added.

"I see," he remarked. "It's often easier to honor the idea of what's right than to act correctly. Honesty and honor are concepts this world still needs. And yet . . . sometimes lies are necessary. Now, let's sit down and you can impart your bad news first."

She nodded. "You looked like a man who would take the hard knocks first."

Sitting himself across from her, he said. "Life in Russia taught me that. It's a magnificently enormous country, with people whose hearts are just as immense. But it's always been troubled, plagued by outsiders trying to conquer. Yet all conquerors forget the spirit of the Russian people, which is as untamable as our wild steppes or our frostbitten Siberian landscape. We Russians show no mercy to our enemies or to any who try to hurt or dishonor us. You see, vengeance for us Russians is like breathing."

"That almost sounds like a warning."

He lifted his elegant hand, expertly sidestepping the issue. "Now, what would you and I have to be enemies about?"

Briefly Sam thought she saw his eyes darken, then the illusion was gone and he was smiling again graciously.

"Except, of course, in the age-old battle between males and females," he added honestly. "And that battle is to be tasted, savored, swallowed and digested. The journey is almost as exciting as the destination."

"I think we better skip this part of the conversation," Sam suggested. She knew a challenge when she heard one. But this was a challenge she couldn't win. She was his employee for the moment, and had nowhere near the experience this seductive bloodsucker had in affairs of the flesh.

"Coward," Petroff challenged, clearly enjoying the denial and desire he saw in her eyes.

"No, wiseguy, I'm just smart. I know a no-win situation when I see one. There's no way to win against a vampire prince, a playboy who has probably known enough women to fill Madison Square Garden. Besides, you can't have everything your heart desires."

"Who says?"

"Me."

"I see."

Revamping her strategy, Sam changed the subject. "You have an excellent command of the English language," she remarked sincerely.

He brushed the compliment aside. "I have traveled a great deal, and spent time in both England and America."

"While the Iron Curtain was up? How did you manage to leave Russia during that time period?" Sam asked curiously.

"With a great deal of caution."

Sam began to relax. She took a sip of wine, savoring both the tart berry flavor and the Prince's arresting gray eyes. "And now the Iron Curtain is gone, and you've moved here. Do you miss your homeland?"

"At times. But I travel back and forth. I like America for its uniqueness, and for the ingenuity of its people. A very independent people. This country is also large and very beautiful. But I do find some of the customs strange."

"Such as?" Sam was genuinely curious. She also loved hearing him speak, his slight accent giving the words a sexy spice.

"Sometimes I am watching television and I see people wearing cheese on their heads."

"Football games in the great northern states," Sam

acknowledged, grinning. Cheeseheads *did* look kind of funny.

"And New York. I like to walk around in New York and study people. Sometimes I see certain persons running around with bags and picking up their dogs' waste. Odd custom, that. Where are they planning to take it? I even saw a mugger accost one such woman, and he stole the bag!"

Sam snorted. "I bet he got the surprise of his life when he opened it. I wonder if he was caught. I'd love to see the judge's face when that came to court."

Petroff shared her smile a moment. "I also find American business odd."

"How?"

"I didn't invite you to this castle to do business, and yet here you are. I didn't invite you to remove my ghosts, but that's your plan. You *do* know I could have you arrested for trespassing. Were you even worried about that? Are you so reckless in your actions, or are you relying on your pretty face to save you?"

Sam gulped. "I look terrible in stripes, so jail time just wouldn't do. But you wouldn't send me there, anyway. In spite of your reputation, you really are a gentleman. I can tell. And my plan wasn't reckless, it was just good business sense. You have a bunch of ghosts you don't want, and I'm a Paranormalbuster!"

Damn, why had Prince Pete had to bring up her sneak attack now? The night had been going so well. She'd hoped to have him eating out of her hand by dessert—well, not literally, but at least to have stirred his interest enough to discuss his other homes and whether he had uninvited intruders at them.

"Why would you think I wouldn't have you arrested for trespassing?" he asked crisply, clearly surprised.

Sam shrugged. "You're too smart to get rid of one who'll provide a service free of charge. You've heard of my reputation, and you know I'm the best in the business," Sam returned confidently.

Her logic annoyed him, though it was correct. Prince Varinski did employ only the best, and he did prefer freebies. "Still, what you've done has given you an unfair advantage over the competition."

Tough taffy, she thought. What the competition had done to her had been unjust, unfair and unethical. Too bad she couldn't directly bad-mouth Monsters-R-Us. But clients rarely liked to hear the dirt on one business dished out by their competition—or rarely trusted it.

"Monsters-R-Us has been very busy lately," she hedged. Retaliating against the Strakhovs' own sabotage had been taking the Russian bull by the horns, but she drew the line at publicly calling them cheats or corporate crooks when it hadn't been proven, even if the shoe of sabotage fit; her father had taught her better business ethics than that.

"And you aren't?"

"You've just offended me. Triple-P Inc. has a lot of business. I just happen to be sharp enough to want yours too, to know how important it is, even though I'm swamped. Fortunately for you, I happened to have a short break, so I decided the best way to advertise was to show up in person and offer my services."

His eyes danced with amusement. "Well, I am

most willing to enjoy your expertise. I would bet a kingdom that you're . . . great."

Trying to backtrack, to protect herself, she added hastily, "I believe the client's got a right to know what he's getting."

Petroff did a slow scan of her body, sending heat flooding through her, and nodded. "Right now I can only imagine," he replied.

Flustered, Sam blushed. "Well, I am an expert after all. The consummate professional—always ready and willing." Seeing the hunger leap in his eyes, she wanted to curse herself for her awkwardness and stupidity. "I mean, ready and willing to trap ghosts and move them or lay them to rest."

She reached for her glass of water and quickly swallowed a sip. Jeez, it was hot in here. How much could a girl stand of one vampire hunk and his blatant sexual magnetism? She was only human, and he wasn't. That was the problem!

"*Laid* to rest. I'd love to see that. . . ." He trailed off suggestively. "Perhaps we can compare notes," he suggested, enjoying her embarrassment. "I would love to chat all about laying—or perhaps we could stage a demonstration," he added wickedly, watching her blush deepen from pink to red. How he enjoyed sparring with her! Just as he would enjoy making love with her. He reached for a glass of water and took a long, cool drink, wondering when the room had gotten so impossibly hot.

"Um, I don't think so. Laying a *ghost*"—she stressed the word—"is a personal job, between the apparition and the . . . layer."

"Such a shame. And I'd so wanted to learn."

Suddenly, Sam laughed. She was horny, the Prince was horny—but they were both going to bed alone. "Sorry, Pete, but I'm not buying what you're trying to sell. But if you ever get kicked out of the royalty business you should try selling ocean-front property in Oklahoma. You'd make a fortune."

"I'll keep that in mind," he replied, almost choking. Sam was a character. He forced himself to act normal. "And you? What would happen if *you* had to change jobs?"

She shook her head. "Not happening," she stated firmly.

"I've heard that Monsters-R-Us is fast becoming the number-one supernatural hunting and relocation company in America, and they're Russian-born. I must say, I feel bad not using them."

"Ha! That's a lie. Er, not that you feel bad, and not that they're Russian, but that they're number one. Puh-lease! They haven't been in the country long enough," she argued, her eyes narrowed in irritation. "Besides, I heard they lost a bunch of trolls on their last expedition. And trolls are fairly easy to capture if you handle them right and dodge all foreign flying objects." Nobody was going to compliment those shady sinister Stakhovs in her presence and live. Though, the Prince was already dead. . . . "Besides, I could tell you a thing or two about them. But I won't, being the fair-minded person that I am."

"Go ahead," the Prince urged coldly.

"Let me just say that the Strakhov brothers' business ethics make me look like Snow White."

From his comment, Sam knew the Prince still wanted to show loyalty to the Russian rat brothers.

For a vampire as meticulous and renowned for good taste, he obviously needed to learn a thing or two about who should deghost his domiciles.

"Why, what have they done?" he pressed.

"Skip it. It's water under the bridge—and not trolls. Besides, I promised to do this ghost removal for free, so why should you care who rids your castle of ghosts? As long as it's not costing you the big bucks—"

"Loyalty to my countrymen," he interrupted.

"Well, you're an American now, and you're better off with my services than those sneaky guys," she stated unequivocally.

"You sound like you hate them."

"Could we just drop the subject of the Strakhovs? It's too nice an evening to ruin."

Staring into her eyes, he seemed to see instantly that she wouldn't budge another inch. "All right for now," he conceded tersely. "Perhaps you'll enlighten me to the bad news you mentioned earlier."

Sam frowned and buttered some bread. "Jules went on the lam after his temper tantrum."

Petroff raised a questioning brow. "Was it lamb stew?"

She kept forgetting his Russian roots. He wouldn't know being on the lam from stuffed up the turkey. She herself wouldn't if it wasn't for Humphrey Bogart and her uncle. "Jules was a no-show," she translated. She put down her bread and held up one finger. "However, the good news is that Andy and I had quite an animated discussion. He's leaving tomorrow to go to London. Satisfied?"

Hmm, the Prince thought dryly. Satisfied? Not

with her sitting all the way over there while he was sitting here solo. "How did you manage that?" he finally asked, impressed in spite of himself. She appeared to be living up to her reputation.

Sam smiled, trying hard not to appear to be patting herself on the back. "I've gotta admit that Andy was a tough nut to crack. We talked all afternoon, and he gave me painting lessons." Sam now had a stack of Vegetable Beef and Chicken with Stars soup can paintings to carry back home—to her dumpster. "But I sold him by offering to get him an agent."

Slightly confused, the Prince asked, "An agent?"

"For his art."

"An agent for a ghost painter who paints soup cans?"

"You've heard of ghost writers? Well, there are ghost agents," Sam explained.

"Is the agent a ghost?"

Sam shook her head. "Nope. He's alive. Though he's a warlock. I've used him before when I ran across these creative types. The agent offers a wide spectrum of services for spectrals, so Andy will be treated fairly, and hopefully his career in soup can painting will take off. Who knows, one day he might be labeled the ultimate in commercial artistry!"

The Prince raised a disbelieving eye.

"Well, *vive le difference.* One man's soup may be another man's nuts. Andy's both. Either way, dealing with him was much easier than I anticipated. So . . . one down and one to go."

Finishing his steak, the Prince asked what she intended to do about the run-amok chef. As she explained, he snorted. But Sam did have talent, galled as he was to admit it.

"So, you're going to set up Jules with a cooking show on the Ghost Channel?" he asked. "You think that will be enough to tempt him to leave here?"

"Piece of cake. As soon as I can catch him when he's not throwing the stuff."

Petroff chuckled at her unpredictability. Such quirkiness! Not only did she know her business, she was inventive. That'd be hell on the competition. Which caused his smile to fade.

"You seem to know a lot about ghosts."

"Yeah, much ado about nothing, my uncle always says, but then I grew up with the Bustin' business. I can recall going to haunted houses with my parents when I was just seven or eight, wearing my ghost-busting sweatshirt. It was treated with Scotchgard to protect the fabric against Glaswegian ghosts. Clutching my protective magic amulet, I'd wander through the hallways—"

"I see you're wearing that same amulet now, no? You wore it last night. What kind of amulet is it? It looks German."

Sam nodded. "Good guess. Ban Protective, Inc."

He nodded. Everhard and Company had made his protective amulet. They also made jock straps. He figured that any company that could protect the family jewels against soccer balls or errant limbs could just as well protect the rest of him from ghostly enchantment or spells.

"You have one too?" she guessed, maybe from the look on his face. "Although I would imagine vampires are protected from most malicious mischief."

Her words caught him off guard. "Most, but not all," he said. "A very powerful ghost can overcome a vampire, if he doesn't wear some protection," he admitted with a small smile. Then he poured more red wine in their glasses.

"I'll admit to being surprised that you didn't know that fact, since you're supposed to be the expert on the supernatural. At least, that's what you keep telling me," he sallied.

The Prince's comment stung Sam's pride, but she didn't let on. "Expert enough to be alive and kicking at almost thirty," she growled.

"What is 'almost thirty'?"

She shrugged. "Not there yet."

He hated to admit it, but he had the sense she was going to last a lot longer than that.

Rasputin's Monk-ey Business

Romance was in the air. Damn that Rasputin, Sam thought as she gazed over at Prince Petroff. They had just finished their steak dinners and skipped dessert—or, rather, he had skipped dessert. She figured he was still hoping that she would be his cherry jubilee.

He was staring at her with a half smile on his face, his eyes smoky, smoldering, making her feel hot and bothered. If she were a man, she'd take what the Prince was offering. Of course, if she were a man he wouldn't be offering, and she wouldn't have these conflicts of interest with herself or even have this stupid conversation with herself, either. Sam shook her head in disgust.

"Cat got your tongue? Or are you nervous being up here all alone with me?" the Prince asked.

Shifting her position on the low-backed sofa, she determinedly touched her amulet. She would not be seduced, even if Rasputin was practicing his ghostly enchantments. Nor would she be just another notch on the Prince's coffin lid. No deranged, horny ghost would get her involved with an oversexed vampire; she'd overcome worse before.

"I'm not a coward, but I'm also not stupid. Being alone with an experienced vampire at night is not something a good girl finds easy."

He shifted closer. She inched away.

Petroff shook his head, amused. "So, my vampire powers worry you? In your line of business, I would have thought you well-used to dealing with the undead."

"Most of my business deals with the peskier, more petite creatures of the night, wiseguy. But I'm not in virgin territory here. I dated a vampire or two when I was young and foolish." To be honest, she had never been all that attracted to the walking dead; she'd been more in tune with hotter-blooded creatures like shapeshifters.

No, Sam had dated exactly two vampires in her life, and she had never gotten seriously involved with either. She didn't want to end up being one of them, more or less immortal. What could be worse than sleeping in tight spaces under a pile of mud? Or drinking blood, when she really didn't even care for tomato juice! And no way in hell was Sam going to live for hundreds of years without Hershey bars or chocolate-covered strawberries. That was just plain inhumane.

The Prince arched a brow in surprise. "You dated vampires? What happened?"

She laughed. "Now, I ask you: Do I look like the kiss-and-tell type?"

He looked both miffed and intrigued. "I wouldn't

have thought you to be a girl interested in being anyone's food," he said.

"I wasn't. I said that I had a date or two in college, not affairs with your nocturnal comrades. They took me *to* dinner, not *as* dinner."

"So it wasn't love at first bite?"

"No, definitely not."

"Unusual. They could have used their vampiric charms," Petroff said, intrigued. "Why didn't they?"

Lifting up the amulet from around her neck, Sam explained: "It's also bespelled to ward off Nosferatus' nefarious designs."

"So, you resisted their allure," he remarked slyly. "But then, you hadn't met me."

Dropping her amulet back into her sweater, Sam pointedly moved farther away. The Prince scooted closer. Like a wolf on the hunt, moving ever closer to his goal, his prey. He grinned in lupine delight. Sam inched against the sofa arm, a hand span between them. She gave him a look of supreme indifference, although she could feel her breasts standing to attention. He was the quintessential bat-ass lover.

"I've heard that you have known thousands of women," she said.

Petroff pulled back. "What is this, twenty questions? Perhaps I'm like you. I don't go for the old bite-and-snitch either," came his response, mocking her own earlier reply. He leaned in closer, reaching across the slight space between them, and ran one tantalizing finger over her slightly quivering lips.

Leaping off the sofa, Sam put a half-dozen steps between them. It was as if the room was closing in on her. The air felt electrified by his energy, and she was tempted, so very tempted.

"Well," she began, her heart pounding in her chest. "Somebody is talking. I've heard people say that if you eat a meal with a woman more than once she is expected to be the main course the next time you dine."

The Prince looked annoyed. "I'm surprised you believe everything you hear. I don't pay much heed to gossip. I'm surprised you do. I thought you said you were smart."

"Well, goody for you, not listening to gossip. But it pays to listen in my business."

The Prince narrowed his eyes in patent disbelief.

Sam narrowed hers right back. "My business success depends on listening when people blab. So I listen and even pay for information. And I listen to the best—demons most of the time. They're the best gossipmongers around, and generally correct. They have to deal with all those contracts for souls. They get a lot of weird wishes to fulfill—confessions almost. Kind of like a priest—except demons can't be Catholic. Still, the little buggers always know the juiciest gossip. They know heaps about vampires—especially royal vampires," she added.

The Prince was leaning against the sofa, elbow bent, his head on his hand as he listened. "Demons, eh? You appear to know quite a bit about them. Do you deal with many in your line of work?"

She shrugged. "My brother minored in devil deportation at university, so I've done quite a bit of reading while helping him with his studies. Fascinating stuff, if you're interested. Some of the best books are *How to go to Hell in a Handbasket*, edited by K. Reeves, or *Ageless Confessions of Serial Sinners*, compiled by Dr. Faust. And if you don't mind using a legal dictionary while you're reading, then D. Webster's book, *How to Beat the Devil at His Own Game*, is quite good, too."

She also had quite a bit of firsthand knowledge, since she had to dance with the devils on more than one occasion in her career. Fast on their cloven feet they were, which was one reason they were great at spreading gossip. They also did a mean tango, if you could stand their stinky breath—a vile and sulfurous odor she found intolerable. Demons also cursed up a blue streak when she sent them back to hell with her "Beam Them Down, Scotty" devil-vanishing kit.

The Prince was distracted once again from his pursuit of Sam's glorious body. Sam, with her odd but unique comments had a way of doing that: making him reassess her abilities. He found he didn't like this particular skill, as she was good at distracting him both sexually and mentally. He decided to go for broke: "Sam, I don't want to talk anymore about demons or ghosts or anything else that goes bump in the night. I want to talk about making love with you."

His words danced like the proverbial pink elephant through the room. There was a stillness in the air as Sam stared at the hungry need in his smoldering gray eyes.

"Business and pleasure don't mix," she finally replied, trying hard to listen to the voice of wisdom and ignore the voice of horny. She took a step back toward the door, a tiny step, but a step nevertheless. It

113

was one step down the road to sainthood—or at least toward keeping her principles and panties intact.

Petroff sighed as she gave him a Mona Lisa smile. "You do know that most women head toward me, not away," he said.

"I'm not most women."

"I believe I've noticed that."

Taking another step backward, she cursed her ethics. The Prince was everything sexy. But she had to be strong. "Uh . . . thanks for the meal. Maybe I'll see you tomorrow morning." And then she turned from the promiscuous prince, to make her escape by the skin of his teeth.

Quicker than she could say "Jack Frost" or "What the hell are you doing?" he grabbed her, turned her toward him, and his arms flew around her like bands of steel. Before she could open her mouth and put her adorable foot in it, he leaned in and kissed her.

The kiss was hot with possession. To Petroff it tasted of intimacy and of Sam, like a good fine brandy on a cold winter's night and a hint of sage honey; so golden, so sweet. His arousal stirred, and his hunger grew. She tasted as good as she looked.

The Prince's lips were soft, like sweet velvet, caressing her, making her want more, and as he deepened the kiss, Sam sighed into his mouth. Her longing was betrayed by both the sounds she made and by her body seeking his, like a hand seeking the warmth of a glove on a snowy day.

Grabbing his hair, Sam ran her fingers through it, transported to seventh heaven, though not ever having seen the first six. His hair was as thick and luxurious as it looked. She could do this forever. Would he let her trim it?

Boy, oh boy, did this vampire know what he was doing. His kiss was dynamite, and it was more than apparent he'd been around the block a time or two. Hellfire! He'd been around the whole damn world by the way he kissed, and that thought agitated her at the same time as she went all hot and melty inside.

Her sigh nearly sent Petroff over the edge. She had dreamed about just such a sound last night, dreamed that he had made her make it as she climaxed under him. Moving his hand to her breasts, he slowly began to massage, plucking at the nipples, feeling them harden underneath her sweater. He was fully tempted to take her down to the nearest flat surface and explore her completely in every position known to man, and possibly some that hadn't been invented yet; he'd always been an inventive male. His other hand slipped under her sweater and quickly unfastened her bra strap.

Sam was dissolving like sugar in tea, or really hot water. Waves of desire rode her hard. She was drowning, and she didn't give a damn. She was dissolving like a ghost could when angered, like Rasputin disintegrated last night after infecting the library with lust.

But then the windmills in Sam's mind finally began turning. *Lust . . . Rasputin . . . Petroff . . . Playboy . . . Sex with her client. Mind-numbing sex.* He would suck on her nipples and then on her neck. He'd bite her neck and her sweet, plump breasts. He would feast on her thighs and the sweet, hot haven in-between. She would be his midnight snack, his break-fast snack, and brunch. She would be—

"Hold it right there, buster," she warned as she shoved hard against his chest. No luck; she felt like she might have been shoving at a mountain. "I'm here to get rid of your ghosts, not raise your spirits."

Petroff sighed. He should have found her refusal irritating, but instead he found it refreshing. She was wholly her own person. She strained against his hold, wanting to be set free.

Fighting his instincts, he released her slowly, feeling a slight sense of loss as her heat moved away. "I have ghosts you need to put to rest. Let me just show you—"

Sneering she cut him off. "Nice try, bub, but I am *not* having sex with you."

He arched a brow.

"I mean it. I am not having sex with you," she repeated. "Read my lips." She wouldn't give him an inch or he'd take a mile. And while she might act the tough broad, her heart was just as vulnerable as the next.

"I'd rather kiss them," he replied.

Sam stepped away from temptation. "Boy, you just don't give up, do you?"

"Defeat's not in my dictionary," he agreed, and gave a simple shrug.

"Looks like we're at an impasse, then, because surrender is not a word I've ever used. Well, except just now. Besides, why should I fall for the slick line of a coffin-hopping vampire who's probably laid more pipe than all the plumbers in Pennsylvania?"

He was silent a moment. Finally, he said, "You certainly don't mince words, do you?"

She laughed.

"Well, good. I do so love learning these quaint American sayings." He looked away, clearly annoyed.

"You're just mad because you didn't get your way. But this is one woman who won't be dropping at your feet like a dead fly. I don't intend to be on your hit parade," she added as she took another step toward the door, which suddenly looked a mile away.

"It's hardly a parade," he corrected. "And what a romantic picture you paint."

"Romance has nothing to do with what you have in mind."

He stared at her. "Romance has *everything* to do with it. Come with me and I'll show you a world of sensual delights—and wicked fantasies. I'll make love to you like no one else ever has. That I can guarantee."

Rolling her eyes, she shook her head. "You and that ego of yours. How old are you? Did you ever meet Freud?"

In spite of his unresolved lust—his jeans were now two sizes too small—he laughed. "No, I'm afraid not."

"Well, I bet he would have had a field day with you. He'd need a field with the size of your self-love. You're a walking textbook on all that egomaniac stuff he wrote about. But it doesn't matter. I'm just not that kind of girl."

"*What* kind?" he asked.

"An easy lay. I'm nobody's beverage," she said resolutely. And with that, she headed toward the door.

"By all means, Sam, run away." Petroff halted her in her tracks with those provocative words, but he didn't press his assault. "If you need anything at all during the night—and I mean anything—give me a whistle."

Sam clenched her fists. No, surely not. Fate wouldn't be so cruel. This gorgeous hunk of a vampire watched Bogart movies and knew the lines? She glanced back at him, trying dismally to hide her shock.

"You do know how to whistle, don't you, Sam?" he asked impishly, flashing his sharp, beautiful teeth.

She stared at him. "What a crummy thing to say to a girl. If I had a stake—well, I'd whack you over the head with it." And then she fled.

Like a puff of smoke she was gone, leaving her flowery scent lingering in the room. Petroff sighed. This woman would never go gently into his bed. Still, he didn't want things gentle. And since he never lost, he'd have the Sleeping Beauty whistling Tchaikovsky before the week was through, and nutcracker or not, his canon would be accompanying her 1812 overtures.

Yes, We Have No Bananas Today

The next morning brought a new surprise for Petroff as he opened the kitchen door and found Sam with her head in the oven. He was curious to know what the Bustin' expert was up to now, since she wasn't the suicidal type and the stove was electric. He had to admit that he enjoyed the view sticking up in the air, her jeans showcasing her heart-shaped butt, temptation incarnate.

"Come out, come out, wherever you are," she said as she pulled her head out of the oven, her fingers tapping a beat on the kitchen counter. "I know you're here somewhere, Jules. No need to be in a snit. I'm sorry about the bananas." Sam stared at the cabinets in front of her and she opened them one by one. "Really, Jules, there's no need to sulk. Quit monkeying around and come back so we can talk. You know I sent Beverly to the store to pick up some bananas. Tons of bananas."

Grinning, Petroff asked, "What bananas?"

Sam jumped, turning to face him, her eyes nar-

119

row. "Don't you know better than to sneak up on a Paranormalbuster hunting for ghosts?"

"Apparently not," he replied with a grin.

She grinned back. "Well, a word of warning: Don't."

"I'll take it under advisement. Now, about those bananas . . ."

"You do know curiosity killed the cat," Sam teased. She poured herself a cup of coffee.

"When I find the cat, I'll be sure to warn him," he remarked dryly. "I came here to invite you to dinner tonight."

Sam nodded warily. He was watching her with more than a hint of hunger in his eyes, and the vampire would tempt a saint. She was many things, but not a saint.

"It needs to be an early dinner. Especially with Jules being difficult."

Cocking a brow, he neither agreed nor disagreed, asked instead, "Bananas?"

"Okay, okay. Jules was here earlier this morning. I thought, this is great, I can talk to him about the deal with the Ghost Network. Unfortunately, he was in the mood to make banana muffins."

"So, what's the problem?"

"Well, we have no bananas today." She added, frowning slightly, "I suggested blueberry. He took exception to my suggestion."

Glancing around the immaculate kitchen, Petroff asked, "How?"

Raising her eyes to the ceiling, she suddenly dodged. A cream puff pastry fell from nowhere, landing in her outstretched hand, squishing out some of its creamy filling.

"It's raining cream puffs?" Petroff stared, his expression solemn but his eyes dancing with humor. "His retribution is cream puffs? Rather sweet revenge, no?"

"What can I say? He must like me—or at least the castle, which is fortunate. But I don't think he's too fond of the cook or Mr. Belvedere."

"What's not to like?" Petroff remarked as he watched Sam drink her coffee and take a reluctant nibble of the pastry. "Ah . . . sweets for the sweet."

"I love cream puffs usually, but this morning I've already eaten seven. I truly hope he switches to sandwiches or pizza soon," she remarked wryly. She rubbed her tummy.

"So you've sent the assistant cook to the store for bananas."

"Yeah, a boatload of them, trying to bribe him. But he still won't rematerialize."

"Ah yes, ghost psychology," he remarked with a trace of sarcasm.

Sam growled. "Don't knock it. I use it a lot."

"I imagine you would, since your major in college was—how did you put it?" He looked amused. Holding out a hand, he smiled faintly. "Ah yes, the three G's."

She nodded. "Ghosts, goblins and gremlins. In my work, believe me, the stuff comes in handy. I also studied preternatural biology, though my focus was more on gargoyles, trolls, leprechauns, witches and warlocks. I have a minor in that. And I took several classes on vampire and werewolf physiology."

He cocked his head and studied her. She was much too pretty to be out chasing things that might cut her face and figure to ribbons, or might rip out her throat in a single bite. "Yours is a dangerous occupation. Didn't anyone ever explain the facts of life or death to you?"

Crossing her arms over her chest, she narrowed her eyes. "This should be interesting."

"Men are born to be strong. They're the ones conditioned to go off to fight wars and monsters, while women are meant to be soft, caring and patch men back together. Men and monsters alike need a soft warm haven to come home to, a soft warm breast to rest their heads upon after dealing with death and pain." His explanation was rational and made great sense, so why did Sam look like she'd swallowed a dozen more cream puffs?

Feeling as if a glass of cold water had been poured over her head, Sam narrowed her eyes into thin slits. The Prince's attitude was so backward-thinking that it had positively reached the Dark Ages. Of course, he'd probably been around at the time.

"You men tear it up and we women fix it? Your attitude could use some serious adjustment, Pete. You need to get with the twenty-first century here."

"I am who I am," he replied mysteriously, letting her feminism slide for the time being. "And you are who you are." He suddenly took her hand. "Why do you do it?"

"Do what?"

"Bustin'. I know it's a family business, but do you *enjoy* what you do for a living?"

Putting her coffee aside, Sam tried to explain her motivating factors in life, something both simple and complex. "Sometimes life just happens when you're living it; choices are made before you're born. Fighting tooth and nail with creatures that have bigger fangs and claws than I have can be tricky sometimes, but I use my head and experience, and I guess I've grown to love the adrenaline high. And I bust my gut to do a good job."

"But it's extremely dangerous. This isn't just dog eat dog. You're risking your neck for a business that could literally eat you alive!"

"Well, that's a drawback," she agreed. She thought a moment and added, "I think living life on the edge like this is part of the pull. I'm rarely bored, and worknights are never dull. Besides, my company has an excellent safety record. Nobody's ever died— except my parents. And that had nothing to do with Paranormalbusting, since a rogue Godzilla killed them when they were on vacation in Tokyo. Kind of ironic, isn't it?"

"I'm sorry for your loss," he said.

"It was a long time ago, but thanks. I loved them dearly and still miss them at times. Anyway, Bustin' isn't just all spills and thrills, I also get to help people. I'm kind of like the supernatural Terminex man. But I excel at finding supernatural pests a new place where they're wanted, which is extremely satisfying. Watching ghosts or gremlins find loving homes, or at least homes where they're not cursed or exorcised . . . I was born to this business. My earliest memories are of my parents traipsing about haunted houses or in cemeteries."

"Thrills?" Petroff echoed, grimacing as he recalled the state of his kitchen and his favorite sweater. "Ghosts can be a cantankerous lot."

"Depends on the ghost. Some spooks really are just high spirits. Others, the static ones, have a problem making contact—you know, projecting their image. With those guys you get a lot of white noise. It's strange, because most ghosts can manifest themselves A-OK. Like the ghost riders in the sky, or the specter that haunts Fort Phantom in Texas. And those nasty little spooks in Tombstone, Arizona. Only problem with those ghosts is that they have a western taste, spitting tobacco and beetle juice—not to mention their jangling spurs in the middle of the night. You try sleeping in any hotel in Tombstone after midnight with jangling spurs strutting up and down the hallway."

Petroff found himself grinning at the pictures she was painting with her words. "If I'm ever tempted to go to Arizona, I'll bring a soundproof coffin," he agreed.

She laughed and continued, encouraged by his interest. "I know a spook that has a thing for poultry. He keeps one around at all times and does a ventriloquist act called the Ghost and Mr. Chicken. Then there's this lady who is human, but her husband is a ghost. Well, they wanted to open a dance studio with both of them as instructors. Problem was, he was a newbie ghost and couldn't manifest himself. I sent him off to school."

"You did? Where?" The Prince fought a wave of hilarity. For someone with a balls-of-steel attitude in business, Sam's dry sense of humor was wonderful.

It was also clear that she loved her job—which was unfortunate.

"The City of Ghosts, where else?"

"Of course. How stupid of me not to figure it out," he teased. "Although, it's hard to believe that ghosts have cities now. Strange, that so many people who die can't find their way into heaven or hell."

"Yeah, and over seventy percent of those ghosts are male! That's why female spooks are at a premium. I can place a female phantom almost anywhere." She gave him a pointed look.

"Why is the percentage so high for men, do you think?" the Prince asked.

Sam grinned. "I was probably about twelve when I asked my mother that same question. I didn't really understand her answer then, but now I do."

"What did she say?"

"That ghosts were spirits who had gotten lost on their way to heaven and hell. They're mostly men because when did a man ever stop to ask for directions?"

Ninety-nine Bottles of Beer on the Wall—And One Wine Bottle on the Toe

After sending Andy and his art supplies on their way to London, Sam spent half the next day and part of the night playing hide and seek with the temperamental but sly Chef Jules. It wore her out. It also left her slightly tipsy.

She had tracked the crafty spectral from the kitchen to the north tower and back to the south tower, and just when she was about to give up, she'd discovered him in the wine cellar. The Chef had been Machiavellian in his negotiation, and for a short time she had been afraid that she was going to have to give up the ghost. Fortunately, Sam's spunk and mule-stubborn nature outlasted the galloping gourmet's jackass nature, and four bottles of wine later, she had her deal signed and sealed.

Out of the four bottles, Sam had consumed one. Her logical arguments had become increasingly illogical as the night wore on. Still, she managed, and in spite of the overwhelming problems associated with dealing with the grasping ghost, she had finally worked out a deal juicy enough to be worth the phantom chef's wily while.

You see, Jules confided that he'd always wanted to go to Paris, which was where his cooking show would be produced. He was quite happy that the Ghost Network's regular host was Casper, whom he had long admired. Jules had also been impressed with the large quality of the mediums who would appear in small guest spots to do a little cooking, like Allison Dubois, and there were also going to be guest spots by the deceased alumni of Saturday Night Live.

It was a sweetheart of a deal. Still, Chef Jules, the picky phantom, had demanded yet more. He was a tough poltergeist with an insanely overinflated self-worth. So with her Bustin' business reputation on the line, Sam had quickly formed a brilliant scheme that probably, seen in the naked light of day and without the wine's influence, would not be as brilliant as she thought: She'd conceded to Jules—actually, bribed him with—five cases of fine old wine from Prince Petroff Varinski's wine cellar.

It was a fact she would mention to Petroff later; much later. Like, maybe when the pompous Petroff was in one of his better states: absent. Or when hell froze over.

Still, she laughed out loud. She couldn't wait until the sneaky Strakhov brothers found out she'd ousted two tenacious phantoms from their Prince's castle. Oh yeah, she'd show those slimeball Strakhov brothers who was the number one ghost-getter in town.

Sam took a moment to enjoy her victory. After finally ridding herself of the greedy, grasping ghost chef, she lay back on a barrel of wine with a pinstriped chair cushion propped beneath her shoulders and head, and she began to hum. A bottle of Zinfandel was balanced on her big toe, sticking out like a sore thumb. Well, no, it was more like a sore big toe.

Choosing a song, she let rip. "Ninety-nine bottles of wine on the wall, ninety-nine bottles of wine . . ."

When she reached thirteen bottles, the cellar door burst open and in stalked the Prince. Pointing a long elegant finger at her, he growled, "There you are. I've been looking all over this monstrosity of a mausoleum for you. You missed dinner with me!" He was clearly angry at being stood up; his dignity was dented.

She didn't know it, but Petroff was also angry because Samantha Hammett wouldn't quit walking around in his mind. He enjoyed women and lovingly lusting after them. But that lust was reserved to short spells when he would see them, and it generally lasted only until the morning light. He didn't enjoy thinking about a female during his daylight hours. He needed his rest. He was a busy preternatural predator. But busy or not, the image of Samantha Hammett didn't care; she kept popping up in his mind like a demented fishing cork.

Sam wrinkled her nose. The Prince was not at his friendliest, and was using his North Pole voice. If she weren't so warmed by all the wine she'd consumed, she might feel a chill.

"You only want to eat with me so you can have sex with me after," she explained as well as she could with a bottle of wine in her system and a hiccup punctuating the end of her sentence. "Besides, I know vampires don't really need food all that much.

You just want to suck my blood. Have you sucked on . . . anyone else tonight?" Closing one eye, she looked him over. "You look well fed, all pink and rosy. In fact, if I were a betting broad—and I am—I would almost bet you weren't a va-vampire."

Petroff stared at her warily. "What are you mumbling about?"

"You're too dark to be vampire," she realized. "You have a tan."

He snorted derisively. "I have olive skin."

"Oh," Sam said. Another hiccup overtook her, then she gave him her best one-eyed pirate look, studying him like a bug under glass.

His wary expression faded as he finally grasped what he was seeing. Sam's lovely golden hair was a mess, and she was lying on a barrel of wine, her back braced by some sort of cushion. She was slurring her esses, and she had a bottle of wine balanced on her big toe. Sam wasn't just in her cups; she was in her casks. And he had evidence of her transgression in spades. "You're drunk!" he accused.

"Brilliant de-deduction, Sherlock." Hiccup.

"You're drunk on the job and you have a bottle of wine on your toe," he added judiciously as he came to stand by her side.

"Your powers of observation are a-astounding. Maybe you should be a spy. You could spy for America on the Russians. Or, as a Russian spy, you could spy on some other countries. But not on America. That wouldn't be American. And we wouldn't want that. Even though you're Ru-Russian, you do want to be an American, even if you are a spy, right? Can vampires be spies?"

"I believe you Yankees call this drunk as a skunk," Petroff said. Lifting his eyes to the heavens, he slowly shook his head.

"Ha! Skunks don't drink, they just stink. Hey, that rhymes. And I'm not drunk, merely in-intoximated," she said seriously, her prim demeanor belied by another hiccup. "Intoxicated."

Ignoring her, he asked, "Why do you have a bottle of wine on your big toe?"

Never at a loss for words, she answered, "I was ne . . . negoat . . . negotiating with Jules. You know what a sot he was in human form. Well, in ghost form that goes ditto. It took three bottles of wine for him and one for me to get him to agree to move. He's leaving tonight, three sheets to the wind."

Hiccuping again, she pushed her hair out of her face. "Probably he's already gone. Vanished. Gave up the ghost digs. Rode the old ghost train out of the castle. He tried to drink me under the table, but I foo . . . fooled him," she explained grandly as she pointed to the barrel she was sitting upon.

Petroff's lips twitched. Gesturing to her foot, he asked, "I'm a bit confused. You got him to go because you stuck a wine bottle on your foot?"

"Don't be ridiculous," she snapped, again slurring the *s*. "He told me his hobby was building those ship-in-the-bottle things. I said I could do it, too," Sam explained. She looked sadly at her foot with the large green bottle attached. "But I didn't have any b-boats."

Swallowing back a laugh, he had a flash of understanding. "I get the picture. You used your big toe in lieu of a ship. And now it's stuck."

"And now it's stuck," she repeated. "My gosh, you are bril . . . brellant. Oh, damn. Smart," she corrected as she leaned over to pat him on the shoulder.

"Even more than you know."

Sam grinned lopsidedly and pointed at him, missing by about two feet. "You should say 'thank you' and 'you did a swell job, kid.'" She hiccuped.

"Sam, oh Sammy," he admired. "You did a fine job of ridding the castle of two of the ghosts. If only you hadn't managed to get yourself plastered in the process."

"Oh, damned with faint praise! Come on, Petey, admit it—I did a fantastic, fabulous, fu-funking fine job. Oh, whatever! Now you'll want me to do any other critter removal you may need in the future. I will of course be de . . . delighted. I am the number-one Paranormalbuster in Vermont. Hell, the best in the whole northeastern part of the U.S.—maybe even the world!"

Hiccuping and smiling brightly, Sam patted herself on the shoulder and almost fell off the cask.

"Sam, you're good. But you're not *that* good. Monsters-R-Us is just as formidable," the Prince replied.

Sam's smile froze on her face, and she hiccuped again while shoving her hair out of her eyes. Those eyes flashed fire as she snapped, "Mea culpa, you lout. I have two ghosts down and gone, to your one in the hand—or should I say in your castle!"

Smiling enigmatically, he remarked, "While you were working on the chef, I hammered out a solution for Rasputin. He's also leaving," the Prince bragged, proud of the deal he had made with the appalling apparition, and also proud that the castle would now be ghost-free. Business was good. Life was good. All that could use a lift was his sex life. Well, not a lift, he thought wryly; Samatha Hammett managed to "lift" him just by breathing. Still, she was inebriated, and he didn't take advantage of drunken ladies.

Yes, he was relieved that the galloping gourmet, the bad mad monk and the atrocious artist were all gone. Of course, he was reluctant to tie up the loose ends too quickly if that meant Sam would leave tomorrow morning. He had sampled her Bustin' skills; now he wanted to sample her bustier skills.

"How?" She appeared all ears—well, and breasts and legs. Her curiosity was rampant in spite of her sluggish mental processes. "That malicious monk was the worst of the bunch."

"I promised to send him to the land of milk and honey," the Prince explained.

Sam looked confused.

"Not really milk and honey, but to his own personal paradise. A land of champagne, caviar and orgies. *Hollywood.*"

Sam's expression changed from perplexed to proud. "You're almost as smart as you're handsome!" she said. And with another hiccup out of the way, she leaned clumsily over and kissed him passionately on the chin.

Undeterred by her lousy aim, she added grandly, waving her hands in the air, "Nobody gets the better of Sam Hammett!"

Her second try had better aim: Her lips burned into his, making his heart pound like thunder. He could feel the beating of her heart, too. She tasted like berries and wine—tart and sweet and wonderful.

Kissing Pete felt wonderful. Sam ran her hands over his broad shoulders, thinking how safe he made her feel. He made her feel all woman—and horny as hell, if hell could get horny.

Sam had decided earlier to let the vampire make love to her. As she'd pleaded with Jules the wine in her bottle went down, along with her willpower. In her line of work, all she ever really had was the moment. If she was burnt to a French fry by a fire-breathing demon, killed by a lunging gargoyle or slimed to death by a plasm-pitching ghost, she would deeply regret not taking Pete up on his offer.

"Let's go to bed," she suggested as their kiss broke, feeling a connection that she had never before felt, a fierce compulsion to be all she could be for him. To share her thoughts and hopes with him and to hold him close and deep within her, giving of herself at the same time she received everything he had to offer.

He didn't make a move, only stared at her with grim determination.

"Where's all that seduction you've been throwing at me? Gone with the ghosts?"

"Let's get that bottle off your foot first," he offered instead. He wanted her desperately, but not drunk. He was ruthless when crossed, a hard, calculating man to do business with; but he didn't take advantage of women, even ones as adorable as Sam. Although, why he should consider her cute when she was got up to the gills, a deceitful wench wearing a big fat wine bottle on her toe, he couldn't quite figure out. In fact, he was stumped.

With a hard yank he jerked the bottle off her foot. A resounding pop filled the air and Sam screamed.

"Ouch! You big bully, you did that on purpose!"

"Of course I did. I had to get the bottle off," the Prince explained patiently, without any trace of remorse.

"Well, I won't go to bed with any vampire who hurts my big toe, even if his kiss knocked my socks off." And with those faintly damning words of praise, Sam closed her eyes and went to sleep.

Petroff picked up the sotted female, sighing as he realized what a hard day's night this was going to be. It appeared that Samantha Hammett was never going to go easy into any bed, let alone his.

Carrying her to her room, he pulled back the covers of her bed with one hand and gently deposited her on the mattress. Trying hard not to think about what he was doing, he removed her jeans. He sighed again.

Sam was short in height, but her legs were perfectly proportioned for her size and well muscled. She was very toned and fit. He bit his lip, his body at full attention.

This was murder: standing here staring at her luscious legs and the paradise between. Cursing softly in Russian, he unbuttoned the tiny pearl buttons and slipped her sweater off her shoulders. She was wearing a low-cut lacy bra in dark blue, which matched her lacy panties. Pale, rose-colored nipples peeked through where the lace was sparse.

Oh, she was beautiful, half-naked and he was hungry, horny and dying to do what a man did when a woman was dressed only in her underwear: unzip his Levi's and hump away.

But reaching for his zipper, he struggled with his conscience, damning both himself and Sam. He couldn't take her like this.

Sam woke up to see the Prince standing over her, his expression taut. She smiled sleepily. He was better than the Tooth Fairy and Santa Claus all rolled into one, and she could only imagine the gift he had for her. "You're pe . . . peeping."

He seemed genuinely offended, his voice harsh. "I'm not peeping. Russian princes don't *peep*."

Sam looked down at her half-clad body and giggled. "Looks like you're peeping to me."

"I wasn't peeping," he repeated huffily. "I was helping you undress. I reasoned that you would be more comfortable undressed."

"Imagine, a Russian vampire prince getting all hot and bothered about peeping." It had clearly wounded his dignity, and she regretted that. "Jeez, I'm sorry I accused you of peeping, and I'm sorry I fell asleep. But I'm not sleepy now." She yawned.

He arched a brow. "You drank too much. Now go back to sleep." His expression dark and hungry, he turned away. His conscience had won against his nether brain, and he was *not* a happy prince.

She yawned again, patting the bed beside her. "I don't want to be alone. I want you to make love to me. All night long. All through the night, and with that rather impressive bulge I see making a dent in your jeans, Peter." She grinned at her own silliness.

Unfortunately, the Prince didn't share her smile. It appeared that he was hard to make laugh. Well, he was at least hard.

"I told you time and again that my name is Petroff!" he warned grumpily, watching every move she made. His body was tense and aching.

"Peter, Peter, vampire feeder. Had a guest and couldn't keep her . . . satisfied." Sam giggled.

"Is this some kind of new American torture? You get drunk, ask me to have sex with you and then insult me with childish nursery rhymes?"

"What can I say? I'm a fun kind of girl." For a man who had been hunting her since the moment they met, his reluctance struck Sam as rather old-fashioned. It was sweet, but just plain stupid.

"Hellfire!" he said. "You're a pain in the ass and other more important regions. Besides, I thought you didn't get involved with your clients, mix business with pleasure." But if she jiggled her breasts just one more time, he just might forget honor and give her the most wickedly wonderful ride of her young life, his conscience be damned.

Sam shrugged, her hair falling into her eyes. She pushed it sloppily back. "You are technically no longer a client. The business is done. You are ghost-free as of tomorrow."

"Hmm. It would appear so," he agreed.

She stared at him, then asked softly, "Did you know you're a hunk? Even if you are undead. Every now and then I can still see some of the boy in the man and the man in the vampire. And I'm lonesome," Sam pouted. She pushed herself up on her elbows, causing her breasts to squeeze together, a feast for the eyes and mouth. She hoped the Prince was paying attention. With rapid movements made messy by her inebriated state, she patted the mattress beside her one more time.

"I don't take advantage of women," he said, his voice hoarse with need. "But I must admit, you don't seem as drunk as you were in the wine cellar."

She wanted him, but she was suddenly sleepy and a little bit dizzy. "I have a weird metabolism. Alcohol moves fast through my system. Give me a couple of hours and I'll be good as new. So if you come to bed now, you can wake me later with a surprise. How about it, Peter?"

He growled at the use of his name and the image she created with her hot little mouth. Still, he held his ground, searched her face for the truth. He could both see and smell her lust for him. The dizzy, unfocused look she was wearing earlier had receded. Now she merely looked tired.

She dropped back down on the pillows, opened the covers and sighed, "For Pete's sake, come to bed."

He almost shredded his clothes getting undressed. For Peter's sake he *would* come to bed. He grinned as he climbed in, then laid down beside Sam and pulled her close, holding her tight and breathing in her spicy sweet scent. She was again asleep. Glancing at his watch, he saw it was close to midnight. He would give her three hours and then she was in for the longest, hottest ride of her life.

All for Pete's sake. Wasn't Pete a lucky boy?

For Pete's Sake

Sam awoke to the silken glide of Petroff's tongue lightly stroking her own. He continued to kiss her expertly, stroking erotically, his hands reaching up to cup her breasts, his thumbs and forefinger plucking at her nipples. Sighing, she arched toward him, feeling his long, hard arousal alongside her thigh. His size had her pulling back and yanking down the sheets and blankets that covered them.

"What is it?" he asked, his voice heavy with lust as he stared down at her. The bedside lamp glowed softly, revealing his handsome features, taut with desire. He didn't want to ask, but felt obligated to make sure that sex was truly what Sam wanted.

Pulling the sheets past his hips, Sam glanced down at his erection; huge, hard, enormous. Gulping loudly, she blurted, "Wow, Peter. I can see you were certainly appropriately named."

Then she giggled, surprising him. Women did many things in his bed, but laughter was usually not one of those activities.

"Peter the Great. How true!"

Taking in what Sam was staring at, Petroff began to chuckle. This woman was a breath of fresh air blowing through the cobwebs of his jaded past. "It's just the luck of the draw."

She snorted.

Gazing down at her, he tweaked her nipples, loving their responsivity. He said, "I like your style, Samantha Hammett."

Before he could say more, Sam slid her fingers down his stomach and grasped him. She began a slow gliding motion up and down, which reduced his chuckles to harsh breathing.

"Now, who's had the last laugh?" she taunted smugly. But upon those challenging words, Sam was flipped on her back, and Petroff pinned her.

Again he took her mouth in a passionate assault, his caresses scorching her skin. His strong fingers slipped through the pale curls between her thighs, playing in the dampness he discovered there. He groaned. She trembled.

He kissed her neck, nipped it. She pulled back, warning, "No biting. No drinking!" No matter how in heat she was, Sam wasn't going to be anybody's after hours snack. Nor would she be their main course.

His eyelids were heavy, his features taut with arousal. At first he seemed confused by her words, but then he nodded abruptly and returned to torturing her nipples with his mouth, and his fingers played havoc between her thighs.

With the expertise of many long years and numberless conquests, Pete found the hidden spot now plump and tingling between her thighs. Skillfully he plucked and played until her head was thrashing from side to side, and her release built and built.

A rainbow of sensation took Sam, shooting her skyward as his hand worked and he bit down gently on her nipple. Screaming, she came apart, soaring to the stars in a burst of purple-white light. Petroff growled with pleasure at her passionate nature and hoarse cry of ecstasy, and quickly slipped on a condom.

Running her fingers over the powerful muscles in his back, she urged the Prince over her. He widened her legs, placing his heated flesh to her own, nudging the entrance to her wet, hot haven.

Feelings of primal desire urged him on. He wanted to mate with her over and over, to imprint his hold on her, to mark her as his territory. The thought brought him up short. He wasn't possessive of females and never had been; yet suddenly he knew that he didn't want Sam to be with anyone else. He didn't like the idea of another living or undead soul to know the spicy, hot splendor of her welcome.

Sam felt him move into her and winced slightly since he was so big. For a moment it was close, but he thrust gently, easing into her bit by bit. Lustily she sighed at the way his hugeness filled her in a way she had never been completed before. They were like two pieces of an apple that had been cut apart and were now placed back together, fitting perfectly. He was tender yet strong, and the look in his eyes told her that she was the only woman for him. He made love to her with a skill unsurpassed.

Suddenly she felt him slow, almost halt his wonderful thrusting. Moaning at the delay, Sam reached up and nipped his neck, and her hands massaged his taut buttocks.

Whatever control he had been practicing shattered. With a roar, he thrust hard, taking her breath away, stunning her. He felt so good inside her, so right. "Oh, more Pete. More." This man was the man of her dreams—even if he wasn't really a man but a vampire. She could fall in love with his charm, his haughty arrogance, his dry wit, his intelligence . . . and his great big peter. Not to mention the way he used it so skillfully, making her feel bliss—a word she had always known but hadn't really experienced before tonight.

He would have corrected her use of his name had he been saner, but all Petroff wanted at the moment was to ride Sam until they both expired of exhaustion. With a powerful rhythm he stroked in and out, in and out, thrusting deep and hard. Sometimes he kissed her, other times he nipped her neck. Sometimes he sucked on her nipples until she was screaming in pleasure.

At one long, deep thrust, her climax finally hit her like a freight train. She arched up, bucking, her head thrashing, and thoughts fleeing as she came apart; her body went limp from exertion and relief.

Feeling her inner muscles tighten repeatedly, Petroff let himself go too, his seed spurting, his climax powerful, shaking him. He felt weak as a newborn. Samantha Hammett was an incredible lover for such a devious female, and so giving for a woman wrapped in deceit; passionate, wild and so very, very hot. She was his kind of woman in many ways, but not the ways that counted for long term relationship. Which made him angry with himself and her. He wanted more than one night. He wanted many, many nights with her, but that was impossible since she was who she was.

His shout at the end sent Sam over the top again. Another climax hit her so hard that she bit her lips to keep from crying tears of joy and something more—a certain something Sam was afraid to put a name to. She wanted this promiscuous playboy vampire, in spite of her good sense and knowing that the challenge to keep him monogamous would be endless and hard-won. She would be challenged by some of the most beautiful women in the world for his attention. Yet, in spite of the difficulties he presented, she wanted him, even knowing that someday he would walk away and take her heart with him. It was stupid, foolish and downright scary. The Prince had hit her hard, fast and below the belt. But sighing blissfully, she hoped he would do it again.

Rolling off her, Petroff closed his eyes. Making love to Sam was an experience he wouldn't soon forget, if ever. He almost felt guilty. But then he forced himself to recall who she was: the spoils of war.

She rolled with him, ending up resting her head against his chest, all silken skin and hair. He raised his hand to touch her face, then stopped himself, fighting the urge to kiss her tenderly on the forehead. There would be no postcoital fondling, not with Sam.

Running her fingers through the dark hair on his chest, she remarked softly, "No wonder women chase you to ground. If you could be bottled and sold there wouldn't be an unhappy female in America."

He accepted her accolades, although he felt faintly uncomfortable at the soft glow in her eyes. Leaning over, he kissed her tenderly, but he remained quiet as guilt began an insidious crawl into his mind, his heart just now slowing down from the workout. "I think I just might be dead," he remarked.

"There's no might about it," she replied.

He laughed in spite of trying to distance himself from her.

"And I really appreciate you not drinking my blood while we were making love. I know vampires are big on that sort of thing."

The guilt Petroff was fighting suddenly struck him hard. He grunted. "Things aren't always what they seem. Don't you Americans have a saying, never judge a book by its cover?"

Sam ignored his words and his tone, because she was too busy examining his partially flaccid penis. Curiosity getting the better of her, she wondered if it would fit in her mouth.

Yes, but barely. She sucked and he grew hard instantly.

"What are you doing?" he managed to gasp.

She grinned up at him, lying between his thighs. "Come on. You're the expert. You tell me."

Petroff arched a brow, his guilt forgotten. "Round two for old times' sake?"

She licked him once, then added, "No—for Pete's peter's sake." Then she laughed as he lifted her above him and settled her tightly upon him. His last sane thought, as she rode him hard and without mercy, was that maybe her little Americanisms weren't so bad after all.

Beyond Hypothermia

Sam came awake with the bright morning sun shining in her face. Without opening her eyes, she stretched slowly, her arms high above her head, savoring her sore muscles and the afterglow of being sexually and emotionally satisfied. She had never had a night like her last, and she had discovered an amazing fact: Sex was better than chocolate. Who'd have thought?

She felt wonderful—both after last night and because she had done a first-rate job getting rid of the ghosts. Maybe now she could consider meeting the enemy Strakhov face to face. She couldn't wait to tell him how she had stolen business right out from under his big fat Russian nose.

And not only had she gotten a big account with all the Prince's many homes around the world, she had made love with a passion she hadn't known she had possessed. She was still tingling from it.

Yes, Pete was a very special vampire. For one thing, most bloodsuckers went with the old adage *If you got it, flaunt it,* but she had never even seen Pete flash his fangs. A toothy smile, yes; fangs no. And last night had been terrific, leaving her aware that she and the Prince had connected on a very emotional level. In fact, their lovemaking had been even more terrific because of that—magical, special, the best ever—because there had been no serious biting or blood loss. Her and Petroff's souls had communed. For the first time in her life, Sam felt cherished.

Comparing other lovers to Pete was like comparing a broken down pickup truck to a Ferrari. He made her feel utterly female and impossibly special. Yes, indeed, he himself was better than chocolate.

Finally managing to open her eyes, she saw that her prince was gone. Patting the pillow beside her, she felt the blue silk. It was cool. Pete had been gone for more than a few minutes then. She frowned slightly, feeling slighted. Still, if he had left her bed, he obviously had business to attend before he had to go to ground and the sleep of the dead. And yet she had hoped for a morning wake up call: one more round of hot, lusty sex.

Climbing out of bed, she winced at the muscles of her thighs and in between. Those muscles hadn't been used in over four years.

Stepping into the shower, she hurried through the motions of washing, dressing just as quickly so she could find Pete and see his morning-after expression. Was he feeling sated and content? Was he edgy, the bite of sexual tensions urging him to spend the morning in his coffin in spite of the work he'd had scheduled for today? Did he feel guilty sleeping with a human who wouldn't let him drink her blood, and an ex-employee? Did a man like Prince V. ever feel guilt? Most vampires didn't.

Sam stuck her head into the Prince's bedroom, which was undisturbed. Next she tried the library, but no sign of Pete was to be found. Hurrying toward the kitchen, her heart beating fast, she fought the urge to skip with undiluted joy. She wondered what her uncle and brother would say about her dating a corpse? Hopefully she could convince them that she was happy, and that Pete was really quite lively for someone who had seen both the Franco-Prussian War and the French and Russian Revolutions.

Sticking her head into the kitchen, she found that Pete wasn't there either. Spying Mr. Belvedere in conversation with the cook, Sam explained eagerly, "I'm looking for Pete . . . Petroff. Do you know where he is?"

Mr. Belvedere smiled. "Prince Varinski left early this morning," he said.

Stunned, Sam felt her mouth drop open. It was like she had taken a sucker punch to the gut.

"Did he leave me a note or anything?" This couldn't be happening to her. She had finally found love—at least, she'd thought that was the feeling she was experiencing with Pete. She couldn't believe he would hurt her like this, not when she had been busy spinning daydreams in the shower. Now her freshly spun dreams were cobwebs, ashes and nightmares. Why had he left without saying anything?

Mr. Belvedere shook his head. "Prince Varinski said that his business here was finished, and that he had an emergency." The butler beamed and congratulated Sam, "And may I say how happy we all are for your help in getting rid of those atrocious ghosts? We think you're amazing. And the Prince agreed. Yes; you were quite efficient in the way you managed to rid Mandelay of two of its unwanted guests."

Sam gulped. Pete—no, Petroff—had abandoned her without a word of farewell; no rose on her pillow or even a lousy good-bye kiss. No asking to see her again. The affair had ended without a bang or a whimper. Well, she was thinking about having a whimper.

Her stomach was churning and her heart hurt. Yeah, she thought sourly, she should have been smart about the whole business, knowing better than to go to bed with such a promiscuous playbat. She should have expected this long sensual trip to paradise would end up nowhere, and she should have kept her jeans zipped tight.

Willing her face to remain expressionless, she nodded to the butler. She couldn't let anyone know how Petroff's defection had wounded her. Logically she knew their time together had been short, but the heart was a strange master, and it felt what it felt and loved who it loved, whether that occurred in three days or thirty years.

"I'm sure the Prince will call you as soon as he's able—he's such a busy vampire. But since you're his girlfriend, I imagine he'll be giving you a call sometime soon. He mentioned that you had a tiring night last evening, and that you needed your beauty rest."

She winced at Mr. Belvedere's words, guilt eating

at her like a parasite. She had never been his girl-friend, and apparently never would be.

"I see," she said, and she did. She had given herself to him in joy and affection, with possibly the first stirrings of true love, and she had been cruelly rejected. No wonder he hadn't drunk her blood. She'd thought it was in consideration of her feelings, but rather it appeared the playboy prince hadn't wanted that close a connection. So much for their supposed communion of souls. He had made her into a one-night stand, three words Sam hated with a passion.

Using up her remaining self-control, she kept her face stoic though she was becoming aware of a pulse slamming somewhere in her temple. It was as if someone was repeatedly knocking a hammer there.

Trying to seem nonchalant, she smiled the smile of a wax dummy, thanked both the cook and the butler for their help, and explained she would be leaving. Scenes of Humphrey Bogart forcing Ingrid Bergman to go away with her husband in *Casablanca* flashed through her mind. She added; "I'm leaving and not looking back."

Packing her bags in haste, she left Mandelay behind in a cloud of dust, driving fast and furious, tears stinging her eyes. She would never forgive its bloodsucking lecherous leech of an owner—even though, in this case, she'd been the sucker.

No, she certainly wouldn't ever forget him; not since he had used her cruelly with nothing more on his mind than a quick pump in the night. How stupid of her to think that she was different, that he might actually care for her. Sam Hammett, master of her emotions, who generally kept a tight rein on her sexual urges, had ended as what she had never wanted to be: another notch on Prince Petroff Varinski's coffin lid. She'd give him the cold shoulder next time she saw him if she ever did!

As her car rounded a curve in the graveled road, Sam felt a chill bone-deep within her. She started to shiver. Oh yes, she was beyond hypothermia.

Oh, the Places Sam Would Go!

It was a Saturday; no better than the day before, no worse, Sam thought as she looked out of the large-framed kitchen window, waiting for the ham to fry in her skillet. Across from her family home on Mulberry Street, kids were playing in the park. Two houses down, Mrs. Horton, the block's official busybody, was probably working on her list of who was naughty and who was nice. She was always trying to hear who was. She and her best friend Mrs. Fishe would be discussing it, giving everybody a good grilling while they used binoculars to survey the parking lot of Sam's uncle's bar. Mrs. Horton and Mrs. Fishe knew what everybody drove, and they loved to see if one car, or two cars, red cars or blue cars would still be in the parking lot on Saturday or Sunday mornings.

Sighing, Sam realized it was just another Saturday morning like a thousand other in her life. One hour following another, each without a phone call from a one-night-standing dirty rat of a vampire.

Almost one whole week it had been! "Six days,

over one hundred and forty-nine hours and no telling how many minutes, all with Prince Petroff Varinski being a no-show," she complained to the empty kitchen.

Sam had not only fallen off cloud nine after their glorious bout of lovemaking; she had crashed to earth in a large splat. After being splattered, she had quickly congealed into a slumping grump, and then slouched into what she regrettably called "the waiting place." Waiting for the phone to ring. Waiting for Petroff to realize what a fool he had been. Waiting for her heart to start mending a little, and waiting to hear that remarkable raspy voice with the Russian accent.

"What a sap I am! An easy sap!" For boy oh boy, had he given her the royal brush-off. She grumbled, wondering how she could have thought that a vampire who had more shoes under his coffin over the years than Wal-Mart kept in stock could ever fall in love with her. How could she have hoped that the places she would go with Petroff included a happy flight off into the sunrise and a coffin for two. No, that was something only a knucklehead would believe in, a vampire fairy tale.

And there'd been no check, either. Well, she told herself, she hadn't really expected a check. After all, she was the one who'd told him that her services of ridding him of his hurtful phantoms were free, meant to showcase her talents. Still, she couldn't help picturing the proverbial check in the mail. It seemed to represent his acknowledgment of her business service, since he was obviously ignoring her bedroom service.

"I did a great job of removing his ghosts, and

quick too. What a cheapskate. For somebody who's really rich ... A real gentleman, vampire or not, would have sent a check, flowers, made a phone call—something," she griped, scowling ferociously at the coffeemaker, which only gurgled back.

Not one word had Sam heard from the womanizing vampire. For years she had ignored the various talk shows that spoke and complained about men, as did her friends, but it appeared that every female who had ever been dumped was right on target: The male species were all alike, and they all had two faces. Men wanted to acquire, but once they had acquired, they often wished they had not. The innocent victim—usually a female—always got a shock treatment. And now Sam saw that vampire males clearly had the same unattractive characteristics as human males. When it came to lovemaking, love-taking and getting the hell out of Dodge—or out of Mandelay castle as the case may be—they were all the same: no good.

Rubbing her forehead, she grimaced. She'd had another one-night stand once. The galling incident had happened around six months after her parents' death, when she'd been a naive nineteen—a *stupid* nineteen. She had met the man in Scotland while clearing out a nest of nasty gargoyles in a small hamlet. The gargoyles were worse than ever, and in full rutting season. There wasn't anything more dangerous than a cranky gargoyle in rut.

While Sam had been scouting out the gargoyles' numbers, this man had been documenting the rutting for the *BaCall Scientific Journal of Preternatural Mating Rituals*. The two of them had developed a friendship, talking and walking together for over a week. Romance had been in the air, despite or perhaps because of the coupling gargoyles. Sam had gotten all misty eyed. And to the accompaniment of some gargoyles' rustling wings and mating cries, Sam had been seduced.

Unfortunately for the budding romance, the next morning Sam discovered that the lying jerk had a wife he'd forgotten to mention. The betrayal hurt, although her heart wasn't really broken. Still, she had been pained and felt guilty for years. To this day, she cringed when she heard the cry of a gargoyle in rut, though that might be because that wasn't a particularly nice noise, anyway.

Regrettably, Sam was experiencing one-night stand syndrome all over again. She felt used, abused, angry, humiliated, guilty and worthless—as a female and as a human. She was alone and lonelier than ever, and all because of a too-big-for-his-coffin prince who obviously felt she was beneath him, the lousy leech.

Yanking her frying ham out of the pan, Sam sat down at the table and poured herself a glass of juice. Deep down, she felt like grabbing the nearest stake and marching back to the Prince's palatial home in Dodge and shoving it somewhere the sun didn't shine. She'd stick him in the heart, but she was no longer sure he had one.

She had done a bang-up job at ridding him of his lousy ghosts. She had done an even banging-uppier job of making love with him. Their souls had met on some distant plane, but that plane had apparently gone down in flames.

"We should be hot and heavy right now," she muttered to herself. It wasn't often a man and a woman—or even a vampire and a woman—could touch each other's souls. "Instead all I got was a Wham, Bam and No Thank-you, Ma'am!

Ham in hand, Sam heard the scuffling of tiny feet. She wrinkled her nose. Sure enough, the ham smell had awakened her pet goblin. Damn! Now she would have to make the breakfast her pet, Zeuss, loved.

Reaching into the refrigerator, she pulled out some eggs and plopped them in a skillet, making a moue of distaste at their forest green color. Although it wasn't as unappetizing as the lime green of ghost slime, it still wasn't pretty.

"A breakfast food should be brown, tan or even red, but never green," Sam criticized her pet.

Zeuss hopped onto the counter with his little yellow feet, his white tongue flicking in and out as he made little purring noises. Goblins were much like cats, except they walked on two legs and their fur was varying shades of green and gold. Today Zeuss had on his top hat, making him look like a character out of some weird children's book.

Turning the eggs, she spoke to him like a person, although his understanding was much more along feline lines. Still, she wanted to keep his attention. Zuess loved and adored her when she was feeding him; when she was not, she was pretty much on her own.

"I feel like the greatest dope alive, and I've never taken an illegal drug in my life! I laid my emotions on the line for that vampire. I want to wash him right out of my hair, but I can't seem to. How could I get involved with an overblown, oversexed, callous client?"

Zuess yawned; his little rainbow-colored tongue flickered in and out.

Petting her pet, Sam continued her list of grievances. "It's just my lousy luck that I had to pick a loser for love in the game of life. I bet that stupid unprincipled Prince will give the rest of his paranormal pest problems to the Strakhov brothers, too. I battled with that smashed grapes of wraith chef and the appalling artist apparition, and all my hard work and risk will be for *nada*—zip. A big, fat zero. And what do I get for all this? A cracked heart."

Shaking her head at her maudlin thoughts, Sam picked up the newspaper, eyeing again the notice she had seen earlier that had sent her blood pressure skyrocketing. Prince Varinski was giving a party tonight, for various friends in high places—jet-setters, vampire bats and other nocturnal creatures—and she obviously and quite pointedly hadn't been invited. This, coupled with the ignominy of being unpaid and a one-night stand, was the proverbial straw that broke a woman's back.

A slow grin spread across her face, and a crafty little plan began to form. Nodding her head at Zeuss, she vowed, "I'm going to crash Mr. High-and-Mighty's party. And there, I'll tell the Prince of Batasses just what I think of him."

Sam picked up her glass of orange juice, raising it in a toast. Her goblin in a hat squawked. "Here's to plain-speaking, and to the place I'm fixing to go. I'm going to knock that arrogant vampire for a loop!"

Her pet goblin had finished his meal, and he merely looked bored and rolled over onto his back. Well fed and satisfied, he went immediately to sleep.

"Got what you want and you go to sleep? Just like a man," Sam snapped.

Then she stalked out of the kitchen with grim determination—the determination of a woman with revenge on her mind and in her sights. She had a hundred dresses to try on, and at least two hours of hair-styling; she was hauling out the big guns for this finale, and she didn't mean ogre pistols!

Walking Tall, but Feeling Low

Sam crashed the Varinski party without anyone being the wiser. Once inside the massive house, she went with the flow of the crowd, noting the elegant décor. The walls were filled with paintings by such renowned artists as Van Gogh, Monet and El Greco—no soup cans here. Champagne seemed to be the beverage of choice, as waiters and waitresses in black and white uniforms distributed tray after tray of Cristal and caviar.

Guests were dressed in varied attire. Old money and politicians assumed the conservative look, with dark suits and club ties, while their wives dressed in vivid hues, adding enough rocks around their necks or fingers to finance a third-world country.

The undead crowd dressed differently. The men wore flamboyant capes and were garbed entirely in black, while the female vamps strutted about in varying degrees of undress, with bright and gaudy plumage; some even wore animal fur sewn around their low-cut necklines and knee-high boots. Others wore wispy feathers, which served as bodices or backs for many of their dresses. Sam guessed it was kind of a Vampires in Vermont theme. For such a beautiful species, they really had appalling taste.

Sam had chosen a black, off-the-shoulders cocktail dress, and had twisted her hair into a complex design on the back of her head, with a few curls about her face and neck. The only jewelry she wore was her protective amulet, tucked tight into her dress, and a silver cross ring on her pinkie finger. She didn't want to be upfront and in the vampires' faces with a cross around the neck, but she also wasn't stupid enough to leave home without one—especially when this was a party full of bloodsuckers.

All in all, even with a broken heart still slightly bleeding, she was walking tall—all of her five-foot-five height. Her pride might be in tatters, but no one at this party had to know, most especially not that pompous Prince of Bats.

Tension filled her as she mingled among the crowd, searching for Petroff. Planning to tell him off in a room full of people was one thing, doing the deed quite another. Still, Hammetts were not cowards. And Petroff definitely deserved a piece of her mind—and boot.

Suddenly the crowd parted and Sam saw a tall, dark and handsome man. He had a smooth forehead, which seemed to melt into dark gray eyes, eyes so dark they were almost black. His hair was a deep ebony, with hints of silver at the temple, very straight and short, barely touching the collar of his black silk shirt. His face shape and strong aquiline nose reminded her of Petroff. Perhaps they were related, as there was this faint resemblance. It was also obvious the man was no man, but a vampire: his pale skin, masculine beauty and the gliding way in which he moved.

He smiled at her, revealing only the tiniest flash of fang, his dark eyes interested and alert. He stared at her. Sam felt like he was assessing her clothing, and then her without her clothing. Yep, he was definitely a relative of Petroff's, as they both shared that presence which screamed *Beware! Proceed at your own risk*. Sam would give him a wide berth. She certainly didn't need to meet another pain in the neck Nosferatu.

The vampire suddenly grinned, amusement filling his eyes. He nodded at her arrogantly, and Petroff appeared, sauntering up to join him. Soon both were staring intently in her direction.

Tearing her eyes from the unknown vampire, Sam stared at Pete. Her eyes narrowed. His expression was completely blank, and there was no penetrating the deadpan mask. Was he shocked that she had crashed his party? Was he irritated to see her? Was he even now thinking about their night together? Did he regret, even the tiniest bit, not having called her?

Nicolas Strakhov had noted his cousin's preoccupation and, turning around to see, he had spotted Samantha Hammett not five feet from him. Her expression was cold and distant, her jaw muscle knotted. She matched him hard stare for hard stare. He wondered if she had determined his deception.

Sam kept staring at Petroff, while managing to maintain a slightly mocking smile on her face. She glanced back and forth between the two men, felt her heartbeat speeding up, racing; something was definitely up.

Suddenly, the unknown vampire clapped his hands. "Attention, everyone. I have an announcement to make," he called out above the lively din of the crowd.

The room stilled as if by magic. People strained their necks to hear. Sam stood rock still, her insides beginning to heave. She was supposed to be a tough, no-nonsense businesswoman, yet her hands were shaking like crazy. Something was up, and it was big; she felt it in her Paranormal bustin' gut. And she probably wasn't going to like what this big, bad vampire had to say.

"I, Prince Petroff Stephan Varinski, have invited you here tonight to meet my cousins, who not too long ago moved from my mother country of Russia here to Vermont," the vampire explained. His voice was deep and mesmerizing.

Sam felt as if she were going to throw up. She had made a colossal mistake, ignoring the old adage, *Never judge a vampire by its coffin.* Dumbstruck, she flinched, almost certain what would come next. And this was no simple case of mistaken identity; Strakhov had played her like a violin.

The previously unknown vampire—the *Prince*—pointed to two men standing near the large marble fireplace, and he announced grandly to the room, "My cousins Gregor and Alex Strakhov." Then, turning back to look at Sam, he held up his hand and placed it on the man Sam had thought was Prince Petroff Varinski. "And this is my cousin Nicolas Petroff Strakhov, one of the owners of Monsters-R-Us." There was a general sound of welcome and goodwill.

After a moment, the Prince led Nicolas over to stand in front of her. He said, "And you are Samantha Hammett. I've heard quite a bit about you. Did you have some refreshment?" He motioned to the table with beverages.

"Boy, you sure don't believe in pulling your punches, do you?" Sam asked, her voice a bit shaky. There was a strong thread of anger sharply woven in, too. So, the vampire prince had heard about her? Just what had he heard—intimate details of the boudoir, or how she had helped clean up his haunted home? Glaring up into amused eyes, she felt safe betting on the first. She felt like screaming and punching everyone from Russia in the nose.

"You live up to your reputation—and more. Your beauty," Prince Varinski stated sensuously, "Well, my cousin did not do you justice. You are even more beautiful than he claimed."

Strakhov looked irritated at the Prince's words, but Sam felt numb, devastated; she tried to keep her expression blank. She had been in scary situations before, and dangerous ones as well. Embarrassing situations weren't new to her either. But through all her triumphs, all through her mistakes and failings, she had never slipped up so bad. Now she felt as if she had fallen into a bottomless pit, a remorseless pit where she would keep falling forever into a dark oblivion. She had been savaged, and not by a preternatural creature. She'd consorted and slept with the enemy. And worse . . . she had fallen in love with him.

Nic saw Sam blanch white—paler than some of the vampiresses stalking the room. A shallow triumph coursed through him; Sam had been the woman who had sabotaged his business, and who had tried to steal his cousin's patronage away; tonight the sly schemer was getting her just desserts. And yet, even though he didn't trust her, disliked her for her ruthless ambition, a tiny part of him felt like reaching over and pulling her into his arms to offer her comfort.

He mercilessly quashed the feeling. Sam Hammett was nothing to him but a foe now vanquished. He didn't care that she was the same passionate, giving woman who had screamed his name in the night while he brought her to climax after powerful climax. Resolutely he would forget that she was the very same clever female who had outsmarted a pair of pesky ghosts without breaking a sweat. Determinedly he would ignore the fact that she was the same sassy sweetheart who had both made him angry and ecstatic all in a matter of minutes. Nic frowned at her. She was not who she seemed or what she seemed.

"I believe you know my cousin Nic quite well," Prince Varinski remarked, his eyes twinkling.

Sam dug her fingernails into her palms, trying to will back the tears threatening to fill her eyes. She wouldn't cry in front of these ghoulish men; she was made of sterner stuff than that—at least she hoped she was. "I get the picture. You two are cousins." Turning to Nic, she squeezed her fists tighter. "Your name is Petroff," she said, glaring at him, her eyes wet and liquid.

His tone mocking, Nic responded, "On my mother's side the non-vampire side of the family. I was named after Prince Petroff here. He is my great-great-great, etcetera, uncle." He motioned with a tilt of his head to his cousin.

Prince Varinski laughed, the sound like a shard of crystal, beautiful yet cutting. "Nic, my boy, no need to make me *that* old. I may be a dinosaur, but I'm not yet a fossil."

Nic laughed, too, but Sam remained frozen in utter mortification. Anger began to tinge her cheeks, and she glanced from one man to the other. They were both devastatingly handsome, with thick dark hair and beautiful gray eyes. But Prince Varinski was much paler than Nic.

She wanted to kick herself. She should have realized that a true vampire would not have had the tan Nic sported, or have resisted biting her at least once in the height of passion. Her expression full of pain, she glared at both of them.

Trying to play it tough, she remarked to Nic, "Good party. Are they here for your eulogy?"

"I'm not dead," Nic remarked.

"Yet," Sam said furiously. "The night's still young. So don't count your chickens!" Her eyes were grim, the threat of dire consequences flashing in their depths.

"Chickens? Why would I count them? Besides, I don't have any," he stated coldly.

She glared at him. "Forget it. You're too un-American to understand."

"Ah, another one of your quaint sayings. We have one in Russia: When winter freezes the flower, it's time to quit planting seeds."

Sam looked confused, which pleased Nic mightily.

"Yes, my Russian saying makes as much sense as your does. So accept defeat gracefully. You've been bested, and I've won."

"Over my dead body," Sam argued valiantly, ignoring the fact that she faced a wall of enemies. "But then, it wasn't my body that's supposed to be dead! Silly me, *you* were supposed to be dead—or rather I thought you were one of the undead. Just call me a sucker. But at least I'm not a bloodsucker like I thought you were. Dumb of me, really. You certainly don't have the charm or the supposed Nosferatu prowess in bed." She added, spitting the words out as if they were hard stones, hoping to wound him, "I had heard rumors of course about vampire sexual ecstasy, but after we went to bed together I figured they were only tall tales. You know, vampire myth and all. I mean, you were good, but not great."

She saw his eyes darken, so before he could refute her, she added acidly, "Which really isn't the point, is it? You led me to believe that you were a vampire. But you really aren't one. You were pretending to be your cousin. You led me on!" Sam was out of breath by the time she finished her list of heated grievances.

Nicolas Petroff Strakhov controlled his anger. He knew Sam had been over the moon with his lovemaking, so the saucy little Tartar had no complaints on that score; he could still hear her screams when she climaxed. He should show her scorn, but her fieriness had turned him on, reminding him of what had attracted him at Mandelay.

"Assumptions can be such a bore," he remarked, though his mind whirled. Sam was so adorable when roused in anger. Magnificent really, with her flashing blue eyes and pert breasts thrust out combatively. He wanted to have sex with her right now, though that was nothing new; he had been fighting his feelings for her all week, his hormones haunting him. With Sam, a kiss hadn't just been a kiss, and a sigh wasn't just a sigh. He had gone so far as to pick up the phone two nights ago to give her a call, but a gremlin emergency had luckily occurred. After chasing the vicious little vermin all night, he had been too tired to even think of sex—and almost too tired to think of her sweet face.

"You went to your cousin's to clear the house of ghosts, and when you found me there you ran roughshod over me," Sam accused, her heart breaking into a million tiny pieces.

"Funny the way things happen, isn't it? It's a mad, mad, mad, mad world out there," Nic replied mockingly.

His two brothers walked up on either side of him. Both were curious, and both were well aware of the tension between their vampire cousin, their older brother and this short, blond female. They had also been briefed about what had occurred at their cousin's castle with Nic and Triple-P Inc.'s owner.

"Funny, what some people will believe," Nic went on, rubbing more salt into Sam Hammett's bleeding wound.

"You *let* me believe it," she accused, wishing the ground would swallow her whole. Unfortunately, there were never earthquakes in Vermont. "Lying, cheating, ensnaring imposter! Of course, I should know better than to expect anything different from a double-dealing Strakhov!"

Alex and Gregor gasped with outrage, but the real Prince Varinski only smiled with tolerant derision.

Nic suddenly felt that maybe Sam wasn't as cute anymore, not standing there insulting his proud family name. Speaking slowly, he made his voice soft; some might have thought it tender, but it wasn't. "Perhaps I should have told you the truth when I first met you, when you were pretending to be my cousin's girlfriend. Or perhaps I should have told you while you made the offer to service the castle free of charge, trying to steal our client. Which would you have preferred? Just when should we have gotten into our discussion on ethics?"

Sam snorted, and anger made her see red. "You wouldn't know the word *ethic* if it bit you on the neck. You and your sabotaging siblings are a public nuisance. John Q. should beware!" Switching her hostility from Nic to Prince Varinski, she snapped, "Oops, that's *your* thing—biting people on the neck. Strakhov here just sucks them dry." She felt very cold and very alone, standing solo against this iron curtain of Russian tyranny. Alas, it seemed that the Cold War had never really ended.

Her back so rigid she felt like it was made of steel, her eyes bright with tears and anger, Sam continued: "The history of the world is the struggle between the selfish and the unselfish, and you four take the whole rotten cake."

The Strakhov brothers looked at each other in confusion, wondering why she was suddenly spouting off about dessert.

"Yes, you and your sleazoid brothers come into my town and try strong-arm tactics to take my clients! I guess phrases like *fair play* and *common decency* don't apply to you. You try to ruin my business!" She almost shouted the last, standing face to face with Nic Strakhov, on her tiptoes in her high-heeled shoes and sticking her finger in his face. "Peter the Great? Ha! You're nothing but an impersonating prick!"

"And you're nothing but a lying, scheming seductress! I would call you a whore, but honesty forbids me. You offered your company and your body free of charge!" Nic spat the words like they were poison. "You thought to charm, seduce and entrap me with that lovely little body of yours, just like you entrapped those two ghosts. But nobody tricks a Strakhov, even if they think they're tricking someone else!"

Always being one to step up and admit her mistakes, Sam winced, but there would be no difference after doing so; her world was already spiraling out of control. "I might have been stupid and gone to bed with you, but you seduced me with a capital S! Besides, I was still tipsy with wine. There'd be no other way I'd rush into bed with your Russian-into-bed self."

It worked. His mask of indifference was replaced with rage, grabbing her by her shoulders, he snarled, "You wanted me as much as I wanted you. Want me to repeat the invitation?" Letting go of her, he motioned at the crowd around them. "I'm sure everyone would like to hear how easily you fell into my arms like a ripe tomato."

"That's plum!" Sam growled. "A mistake I'll never repeat! Going to bed with you was the worst mistake of my life! How was I supposed to know you're a depraved imposter? In fact, I bet you'd hump anything with two X chromosomes!"

"Well, all's fair in love and war," Nic snarled, his gray eyes smoking, his hands clenched into fists. Sam could almost see steam coming out his nostrils. "And this, my scheming jade, is war!"

Gregor placed his hand on his brother's shoulder, fearing Nic might attack the lovely, red-faced blonde. She looked too innocent to be the scheming cheat that he'd heard. In fact, Gregor didn't believe it.

Glancing out of the corner of his eye, he noticed Alex's arrested expression, his slightly hunched shoulders. Gregor shook his head. Something was rotten in Dodge, and he would bet it had to do with his brother's inane practical jokes.

Rubbing a hand over his eyes, Gregor turned back to Nic and Sam. He couldn't help but watch the feuding couple in fascination, stunned to see his elder brother carry on this way in front of an audience. Nic was a cold, hard man, given little to public displays; his anger was generally hidden from his foes. When he struck, he struck silent and deadly, his aim quick and devastatingly accurate. Tonight Nic was impassioned, fairly shrieking, which meant this female Paranormalbuster had grabbed him by the heart—or lower.

"I'm not surprised it's war!" Sam retorted.

"Definitely war, and you were the spoils," Nic repeated, throwing off Gregor's arm.

"Why, you stupid, sabotaging stooge! Someday you're going to regret the way you treated me. Maybe not today, maybe not tomorrow, but soon, and for the rest of your life. Why, I bet you don't even know when the Fourth of July is!" Then Sam turned and marched off, not bothering to waste time with good-byes.

The three brothers and the Prince watched the angry blonde storm off, the guests parting before her like the Red Sea for Moses. Nobody but nobody wanted to mess with this Paranormalbuster.

"The Fourth of July?" Nic said after a moment, his temper beginning to cool. His respect for Sam had grown. She had taken an impossible, mortifying situation and not only faced it with sheer determination and a rigid backbone, but she had also left on her own terms. She was one in a million, and he wanted her. But . . . "Isn't the Fourth of July on the fourth of July?"

His cousin the Prince could barely nod, shaking as hard as he was with silent laughter.

The Young, the
Dead and the Practical Joker

Carefully studying his elder brother's face, Alex frowned; Nic still hadn't taken his eyes off the doorway where Samantha Hammett exited. Although he was a prankster and usually more interested in stirring up trouble than paying attention to deeper emotions, Alex had seen the flash of regret cross his eldest brother's usually stoic features. Nic never regretted anything. But then, Alex had never been around Nic and a female who generated such blistering heat. The air around the two had fairly sizzled with sexual attraction. Obviously his brother wanted her with an intensity that was shocking. Alex could even smell Nic's need, making guilt creep up on him again.

At first, sabotaging Paranormalbustin' Pest Pursuers Inc. had seemed like a fine prank, creating confusion among the enemy. Alex had even anticipated their retaliatory strikes. However, it had taken three sabotaging strikes before they'd retaliated, and Alex had been thrown off. When they struck, it had been with brutal efficiency, leaving Alex in a big, smelly mess. Literally. Nic had been gloriously furious, almost as furious as Alex at the time, since Alex had temporarily forgotten his part in the feud.

No, Nic would never have approved of his actions. He despised cheaters, liars and any who played dirty. Corruption and sabotage were words which brought out the fighting side of Alex's brother, and so after her retaliation, Samantha Hammett hadn't stood a chance.

Only now, after the damage was done to both parties, Alex recognized the intense attraction between the two. Which was unfortunate. Nic wasn't getting any younger, and he needed to take a mate and have kids. This female, as unlikely a choice as she was, was the only one who had managed to stir Nic's deepest emotions. Which meant that Alex had kicked his elder brother in the teeth by playing his stupid tricks.

Shaking his head at his folly, Alex knew his big brother was going to be very angry with him when his part in the war between their two pest-punting companies was revealed. And Alex valued his hide. Still, as a Strakhov, fraternal honor weighed heavy on his shoulders—along with a healthy dose of fear. Yes, Nic was formidable when irritated. When angered he was a great, bad beast. And yet, Alex had no choice: Strakhov honor was at stake. He was doomed, and he tapped his big brother on the shoulder.

"Nic, I need to speak with you."

Nic glanced at his youngest brother, noting the tightening of Alex's features, smelling the faint whiff of fear. "Yes?" he asked cautiously. Whenever Alex wore this look of contrition, he just knew he wasn't going to like what the kid had to say.

"Outside," Alex suggested.

The two brothers walked outside together. The eyes of most of the women in the room followed their progress with predatory interest, but the two Strakhovs were lost in their thoughts and remained unaware. Beneath a large maple they halted, and Alex began his rather reluctant admission.

"You know how I hate to lose . . . ? And you know how I always love a good practical joke, even sometimes when they aren't that practical?" he began.

Nic stared at his baby brother, his expression almost as shadowed as the outdoor lighting. No, Nic mused darkly, he wasn't going to like this at all.

"I thought it would be funny to sort of set up the competition for a fall or two—or three or four," Alex went on, feeling like a young pup who'd peed on the rug.

"What did you do?" Nic asked, getting an inkling of what his brother was about to say. Rage began pounding in his temples.

"Um, the Hammetts didn't start the Bustin' war. I did. I'm the one who sabotaged them first. And it took three incidents before they took action to get back at us," Alex explained, guilt written all over his attractive face. "It seemed like a good idea at the time. Funny, you know?"

"A good idea? Funny? Boiling you in oil is a good idea! Hanging you from the rafters by your thumbs is a good idea! Starting a war with another monster-

removal company—that's contemptible! Where is
your honor?" Nic shouted, wanting to knock his little brother into the dirt and stomp him to dust.

Nic felt horrible. The deception, his deeds, his
words—he was suddenly regretting deeply all that
had happened, and even sooner than Sam had expected. She hadn't been truly guilty of anything except trying to promote and protect her business
against a competition that was unethical, ruthless
and corrupt. No wonder she had used the tactics she
had! No wonder she disliked Monsters-R-Us so thor-
oughly, and the Strakhov brothers. Some bad eggs
had pushed the hard-boiled Buster into a corner,
and she had fought back the only way she could.

Glaring at his brother, Nic felt his admiration for
Sam grow again. She was truly a force with which to
be reckoned. Her Beethoven, those trolls . . . Leaving him and his brothers in the shit . . . At the time
Nic had been enraged beyond belief, but looking
back he suddenly found her method of sabotage creative, intelligent and ingenious; he could only approve. Not to mention the way Sam made love: with
all her heart and passion.

"Robho! How she must hate me," he muttered.

Alex was watching his brother carefully, feeling
guilty and foolish and, he hated to admit, a bit faint-
hearted. After their parents had died in a fire, Nic
had been the father figure. He was the presence always looking over the brothers' shoulders, the one
to dole out praise or discipline. The discipline, Alex
had often felt, was dished out unfairly, as he'd had
an advanced sense of humor.

"You do know, Alex, that you're not some young

pup anymore. Your actions have consequences. You need to grow up. What you did wasn't funny. It was unethical and cruel. You could have gotten Sam hurt or killed by sabotaging her efforts in pursuing and entrapping paranormal pests. You know how dangerous and deadly our job can be; all we deal with are creatures with long sharp claws and even sharper teeth! It must be even more dangerous for a short female, even if she does think she walks ten feet tall," Nic growled. He began issuing curses in every language he knew. Sam could have been killed!

"Where are your protective instincts? The female of any species is the weaker sex. You were raised better than that!" he continued furiously, his eyes smoldering. Of course, he had to admit Sam wasn't exactly weak.

"Look, Nic, I'm sorry. I didn't know you were going to go panting around after that Hammett woman." At Nic's black look, Alex added resentfully, "I mean, she's pretty, so I can see why you're in heat—"

"I'm *not* in heat!" Nic stated emphatically, his gray eyes in flames.

Alex was tired of being yelled at, and his own anger was starting to rise. "The hell you say! I can smell your lust from a mile away. And she's just as bad as you are. You know, we don't live in a glass menagerie here, Nic. You guys are like two cats on a hot tin roof—jumpy and snarling because you aren't in bed together. She wants you bad, brother."

The last comment made Nic's rage recede a little. He knew very well that Sam desired him, even if she would deny it until her face turned blue. Even his youngest, common-sense-lacking, practical-joke-playing brother could tell.

Who would have thought after that mortifying troll incident that Nic would be the one with bridges to mend. But then, Sam was his own personal street-car of desire.

Grabbing Alex by the scruff of his neck, he explained roughly, "You and I have an apology to make."

Oh, boy! Alex realized. It was worse than he'd thought. The love bug had bitten Nic, and the world was ending. It had to be, because his eldest brother never apologized.

Ripley's Believe it or Not

Before Nic and Alex could reach the door to his cousin's spacious home, Prince Varinski and Gregor halted their approach. An unknown werewolf was with them who, though in human form, was still recognizable as a shapeshifter from his slightly wolfish odor and his wolflike brown eyes. He had thick eyebrows with only a scant half inch between, givng him a predatory look.

Nic could tell from the expression on his cousin's face that something was wrong. Petroff's usually amused features were taut and drawn.

"What's happened?" Nic asked.

Prince Varinski gravely shook his head. "You remember my old lover, Natasha Barrington?"

Nic nodded. "You and she were quite an item during the Russian Revolution—and for many years afterward."

Waving his elegant hand, Prince Varinski said, "She's a beautiful vampire with a heart of steel, quite irresistable."

"Has something happened to her?" Alex asked.

"No. To her sister, Jessie Barrington," Prince Varinski explained. Turning to the werewolf he added, "This is William Ripley. He brought the bad news. Jessie has been killed in a most unusual manner, and Natasha is requesting our help in finding the creature responsible." The Prince's black-gray eyes were flashing. No one attacked and killed the undead without stirring up a whole nest of snarling, fangy vampires. Retribution would be brutal, quick and deadly.

"When did this happen?" Nic asked, already knowing he would help track and destroy the murderer.

William spoke up. His voice was deep and gravelly, with a faint hint of southern Tennessee. "Last night. We found the body early this morning. I'm a good friend of both Natasha and Jessie, have been with their nest for years. It's hard to believe Jessie is gone."

"I assume she wasn't staked?" Alex asked curiously.

"No. Nothing human did this," Ripley replied. His voice was harsh. "We found her naked and turned to stone. There was no magic dust, and no hint of any kind of spells on the body or in the air."

Alex gasped. Gregor looked thoughtful, pondering the facts of the case, while Nic also remained silent, his mind racing. He tried to make sense of this amazing story. Ripley said no magic was cast, and Nic would take him at his word, since a smart werewolf could sniff out bad magic at least ten feet away—a lucky attribute, since most truly harmful spells had to be personally administered. That would place an attacking witch or warlock in close proximity, certainly closer than ten feet, and within striking distance; he would leave a trace.

Concentrating hard, Nic tried to imagine what could kill a vampire in this way. After all, he reasoned, killing a vampire was very much a risky endeavor, since all undead had already died once and did not go gently into that good morning. Vampires were a tough and tenacious lot, skilled hunters, diplomats and deadly warriors. Whatever had turned this vampire into solid stone had to be another supernatural creature. But the only creature Nic could even think had such power—besides a queen witch or a king warlock—was a monster extinct for over eight centuries.

"You're certain Jessie didn't have a spell cast on her?" Gregor asked, his brows furrowed.

"Positive," Ripley snapped, irritated that his word was being questioned. "No spells. Just little Jessie Barrington, stone cold and stone dead."

"What do you think, Nic?" Prince Petroff questioned soberly.

"What I think, I don't believe. It's not possible. The only creature that could turn someone to stone has been extinct for a long time—before you were even born into the vampire world."

"Nothing's impossible," the Prince remarked. Twice tonight Nic had surprised him: First, with his obvious interest in Samantha Hammett, and now with his obvious frustration at not knowing who or what was Jessie's killer. "We'll leave in two hours, and take my jet to New York. I'll go and begin clearing out my guests."

Nic nodded. Two hours would give him enough time to see Sam and apologize.

Interrupting his cousin's thoughts, Petroff cut slyly in, "By the way, do you think you could use that Hammett woman's help in hunting and tracking this monster?"

Alex and Gregor looked affronted, but Nic looked intrigued, which made the Prince smile. He hid it. Nic was growing old; the years were passing him by, flashing onward in the blink of an eye. But his cousin had a succession to fulfill, and a duty to produce other sons. No, Prince Petroff wasn't the only other member in the royal family line.

"I believe I *could* use her help," Nic agreed. "Come on, Alex, we have a lady to see." Suddenly his body was alight with an inner fire, and his crafty mind was already working on how best to get Sam to comply.

Opening his mouth to protest, Alex stopped as he took in his brother's firm determination. Giving a sad shrug, he resolutely followed Nic into the house.

Outside, Gregor stared speculatively after Nic. He couldn't help but wonder why his eldest brother was obsessed with Samantha Hammett. After all, she was a cheat, unethical and untrustworthy. Of course, at the party sparks and words had flown. If Nic was truly interested, then Gregor could only wait and see.

As his cousins disappeared inside, Prince Varinski threw back his head and laughed. If Nic didn't end up with Samantha Hammett, then he'd be a dead man. It was too good to be true.

Noticing the Prince's wry amusement, William Ripley asked, "What's so funny?"

With a cynical smile, Petroff answered simply, "Ripley, you just wouldn't believe it."

Everybody Goes to Rick's—
Including Vampires,
Werewolves and Whatevers

Another Saturday night at her uncle's Casablanca club, Sam mused, noting that there was a steady flow of traffic through the old worn doors of the place. The usual traffic, the usual suspects.

A smoky haze filled the air, along with the scent of liquor and beer. The décor was old-fashioned and pictures of the great movie stars of the forties hung on the wall. The club's twenty-foot bar was old, weathered and made to endure; fashioned from cherrywood, its red hues were hidden by the hazy atmosphere. Scars lined its surface, along with a thousand stories of heartbreak, depression, jealousy, hate and joy.

Sam loved this place, loved playing in it. The ambience was straight out of its namesake film, and it seemed to her that in the Casablanca club her music took on a quality of timelessness. There had been an age where a man was a man and a woman was a dame, and that man gave his life for his woman, if he loved her. It had been an age of beautiful women with fashionable, form-fitting clothes and elegant hairstyles.

Those women gave their all for their man, and loved passionately, were gloriously alive in their love even if it was foolish. When Sam played here, she couldn't help but resent that the forties were long gone.

Yes, even if lovers and moonlight would never go out of style, the old romances of the forties and fifties just didn't play in today's world. It might still be the same old love story, but the rules of the game were entirely different. In the twenty-first century, a girl was lucky to get a guy to buy her a cup of coffee without some kind of sexual overture, and most monsters nowadays ended their sentences with propositional claws. A girl could forget chocolate candies and flowers, but a second date meant breakfast privileges. Respect seemed harder to gain than ever, and there were fewer men worth giving it to.

Sam supposed deeply passionate, romantic love had slipped away sometime in the eighties, when money, money and more money took precedence. Women had become as hard as men to survive. Being a mother, wife and provider took the romance right out of the soul, and females had become tired to death of the neverending realities of life. They'd seen life put paid to their fantasies.

Today when a woman met a man; she was lucky she didn't get mugged—either at gunpoint or sneakier means, where she'd end up supporting him. Women might have come a long way, baby, but they had lost something in the process. No one put them on a pedestal anymore; rather the world had knocked them off, and men weren't looking to pick them back up. No, self-reliance was the watchword of the day, and old-fashioned romance was forgotten.

"Take Nic, the promiscuous impersonator," Sam muttered to herself. "All the good guys have gone and rode off into the sunset." They sure weren't returning to Dodge. Her heroes were dead, faded from sight. The age of innocence was gone, except for when her music touched a corner of it, and for a few minutes the feelings of the forties and fifties were coaxed back to life here. Ah, the smoke-filled Casablanca bar.

Leaning back on the piano bench, Sam stretched out her fingers. She'd been playing for half an hour, ever since she'd given that less-than-stellar performance at Prince Varinski's party—the real Prince Petroff Varinski and not the lying betraying snake named Nicolas Strakhov.

Although there wasn't a cowardly bone in her body, tonight's devastating drama had unnerved her, wounded her deeply. She felt like she'd gone ten rounds with a two-ton dragon. Not wanting to be alone tonight, she'd hightailed it over to her uncle's bar, got a hug from her uncle and Rick, the other owner, a stiff drink, and had sat down to play. At least in here there were others like her; all shared the dark, the pain, the solitude.

Playing the piano helped, although she felt her heart oozing red like a leaky catsup bottle. She hurt.

Her pride.

Her dignity.

Her heart.

As her fingers swept the keys, Sam squeezed her

eyes closed, shutting out the tears, remembering Nic's kiss. She would always remember his kiss. The world might always welcome lovers, but it was the woman who paid the bill when all was said and done.

How could Pete, whom she now knew was Nicolas Petroff Strakhov, have done this to her? "Such a long, dumb name," she muttered as she played, her guts churning. How could a man who had made love so beautifully, so passionately, and who had taken her soul to a place in heaven, how could he turn out to be the jerk of the century? Not only had he tried to ruin her family business and steal her clients, the fiendish imposter had stolen a piece of her heart, ruining her for all other men.

Words—big, fat ugly words kept spinning in her brain so fast that she was worried she might snap. Those words beat against her brain, trying to escape. "Bamboozling betrayer . . . licentious liar . . . imposing imposter . . . depraved deceiver . . . fraudulent fake."

Sam closed her eyes, trying to keep the not so pleasant thoughts at bay, along with her tears. She never cried at sissy stuff like having her heart trampled on, or her pride ripped to tatters like an unpopular flag.

Again, her music filled the smoky haze over the general din of talking customers and the noise as they joked, quarreled and played pool, balls knocking together with a loud thump.

"As Time Goes By" sprang from the old piano as Sam forgot herself. The haunting music reached out into the smoky gloom of the bar, and many of the customers leaned back with drinks in hand and listened. At the mellow, sad sounds of the piano, pool players took a break and stood with hands on cues, listening and remembering a time long gone.

Eyes closed, intent on forgetting her troubles and woes, which all began and ended with the capitals "N. S."—that was how Nic first saw her in the bar.

The Uninvited

Nic watched Sam play the piano like she was born to it, the music melancholy yet intense. Staring hard at her, he realized that she had great talent, and an amazing ability to transport the listener into her emotion.

His brother stood shifting anxiously beside him. "Come on Nic," Alex prodded. "Lets get this over with."

Nic almost smiled; his brother had never liked to apologize, even as a kid. He nodded, and the two forged ahead.

Before she opened her eyes, Sam could feel Nicolas standing near her. She didn't know if it was his musky scent—the smell of old-growth forests in autumn—or his heated, forceful presence. Either way, the ignoble impersonator was here, somehow having managed to blindside her once again.

Snapping her eyes open, she proudly kept the surprise out of them, giving Nic a look that should have caused him to drop dead on the spot. Too bad it didn't, she thought snidely.

"Are you alright?" he asked politely—too politely for a man who had ground her pride and heart into the hard-packed dirt beneath his feet.

"A lot worse than a second ago," Sam snapped, wearing her heavy but dented armor of pride. "Did you come here to gloat?" Giving him a cold-blooded glare, she switched her attention to the man by his side, his younger brother. The man was not as compelling as Nic and his hair was a lighter shade of black but—a fact she hated to admit—Nic was devastatingly handsome. "I see you've brought your cohort in crime with you."

Alex's eyes narrowed. He realized this frost-ridden, acid-spitting female was not going to forgive his brother easily. Fate was a fool, Alex decided then and there. All the years of his life, he had watched Nic being chased by females, discarding them as casually as he changed clothes. Now fickle fate had fixed Nic up with this one. What a frigging farce!

Seeing Sam's resolutely disdainful expression, Nic knew he had quite a mountain to climb to get back in her good graces. But then, really, what could he expect? With her unflagging pride, he was going to have to use all his powers of persuasion—which were quite considerable, if he did say so himself. Hopefully he would have her eating out of his hand before the night was through.

"You left the party before I could introduce you," Nic said, gesturing to his brother. "My youngest brother, Alex Strakhov."

Sam grimaced, her lips drawing into a taut line. If Nic thought she was going to spout niceties, he had another think coming—not after the sucker punch he'd given her.

At Sam's glaring silence, he continued: "My brother Alex has something he needs to tell you." He didn't like her being mad at him, although he understood her anger. The hurt in her eyes bothered him immensely.

Nudging Alex, who was trying to look innocent and was being as silent as Sam, Nic began to lose patience with his brother. "Alex?"

The tone of Nic's voice was all the warning Alex needed. "I came to apologize."

"What for? Did you pretend to be some vampire you weren't? Did you lie to some woman without a regret in the world? Did you heartlessly ignore her, after seducing her ruthlessly for your own pleasure? Are you a sneaking saboteur?" After her short little speech was finished, she felt proud. She still wore a smile on her face, when all she really wanted was to deck the callous cad and his knucklehead brother.

Alex looked to Nic for help but Nic merely scowled. Playing matchmaker for this hardheaded pair was not going to be a stroll through the countryside, even if the air was fairly charged with the rampant lust the odd couple generated. Of course, this tough-minded couple seemed oblivious to what was obvious to him, and to anyone within smelling distance. "Miss Hammett, I don't know how to tell you . . ." Alex hesitated.

"Just spit it out," she remarked sourly.

"I was the one who sabotaged your company. Not Nic. Not Gregor, just me. And without my brothers' knowledge."

Sam stared at Alex, judging the truth of his words. "So, you're the one who's been playing dirty pool?"

Alex looked confused. "I play pool, but I wash. Oh! Cheat? I don't have to," he corrected indignantly.

Sam shook her head. "You men and your notions of honor. You won't cheat at pool, but you will sabotage a business rival?" she retorted coldly, giving him a hard stare into the depths of his soul. She didn't know if she liked what she saw. Pete's baby brother was crafty, but spoiled and conceited. "So you're the wiseguy that came up with the idea to run the competition out of town. Is that right?"

Alex nodded. "I'm sorry. I shouldn't have done it. It was beneath the Strakhov name."

"You got that right, buster. You *shouldn't* have done it. Fair play is fair play!" Sam declared adamantly. Then she turned her attention back to Nic. If he thought this apology was going to cause her to dance with joy, he was suffering from delusions of grandeur.

"How long have you known about this?"

"Right after you left, my brother told me what he'd done. I too wish to apologize for any hurt my family has caused yours," Nic apologized sincerely. "To use an American saying, I have come to mend fences. I'm terribly sorry."

"If you think this squares us, buddy—well, you're dead wrong," she warned frostily. "I wish I'd never laid eyes on you." She wasn't going to let him touch her fences or any other part of her ever again.

Nic frowned. Sam had every right to be angry, but apologies came hard for a Strakhov. The least she could do was accept them graciously. "Perhaps this will help," he said formally, and he pulled a check from his jacket pocket and handed it over. "This is for ridding my cousin's castle of ghosts. For a job well done."

Reluctantly Sam took the check, making sure her fingers didn't touch Nic's. So, the check wasn't in the mail, it was in Nic's pocket. As she took a peek at the amount, she had to fight her urge to gasp. She glanced back down at the amount, stunned. Trying hard for nonchalance, she tried not to gape at all the zeroes.

"Better?" Nic asked. His voice held a hint of mockery.

"Hardly. If you think money buys forgiveness or good manners, you've got a screw or two loose. But then, I forgot. You're a man."

"What the hell does that mean?" Nic asked.

"An all-out idiot."

"Look, Sammy," he snapped, more than just irritated at her peevish temperament. "We came here, hat in hand, to say we're sorry, and you act like you were given another insult."

Pocketing the check, Sam stood up from the piano bench. She shook her head in anger. "No, the insult was when I went to bed with you, my arch business rival and enemy, while believing you to be someone else entirely. I don't like you, and I don't trust you and your sneaky brothers. With good reason it seems," she added harshly, including Alex in her withering stare. The Strakhov brothers, Mean and Meaner, had kicked her insides out.

"Distrust is no longer necessary. You have your check for a job well done, and our apologies. What more can you want?" Nic asked, his jaw muscle ticking. He glared at Sam. "I know I'm in the wrong, and I'm sorry." He had already apologized, something he just didn't do, since he was rarely wrong. He wanted Sam and she wanted him. They made love like magic, and the desire flaring between them was a wildfire. Why couldn't she get over her feminine sensibilities and be practical? They could still have a very long affair, could share their lives and lovemaking, and even their work. He wouldn't mind throwing a few jobs her way, as long as he went along to protect her.

"For somebody smart enough to fool me, you sure can be stupid," she said.

Nic growled. "Are you going to keep dropping these little insults, or tell me what's wrong?" She was starting to make him angry. Another Russian would accept such a heartfelt apology, he felt sure, but this stubborn American wanted more—it was always more with these Americans.

Slapping her forehead, she glared at him, amazed that anybody so handsome could be so utterly without a clue. "You mendacity-ridden jerk, do you go around lying so much that you can't remember what you've done?"

"Generalizations, Sam, are the refuge of a lazy mind. Be specific." Nic wanted to shake her, hard, then shake her with some lovemaking. He wanted her to scream for mercy from his ardor, though he would be certain to show her none. He'd make love to her until they both expired from ecstasy.

"You want specific? I'll give you specific," Sam repeated acrimoniously. She began to count on her fingers, so angry she was lost to her surroundings, unseeing of the crowd of interested barflies that was beginning to form around them. "One: You told me you were your cousin, the Prince, so I slept with a man I thought was someone else. Two: You masqueraded as a vampire playboy who seduces anything in long or short skirts, so I broke both my rules about bedding the undead and womanizing males. Only, you aren't a vampire, but a human pretending to be a vampire related to you. The only thing honest about your performance that night was that you *are* a womanizing playboy, and a one-night stand man. Three: You made love to me, then vamoosed without a thank-you, without a phone call, with nothing, making me a one-night stand—and I hate the hell out of that!" Sam practically shouted the last as she poked Nic hard in the chest.

Undeterred by his surprise, she continued. "Four: You and your devious brothers have the nerve to apologize. But not for any of that. You ditched me, you dropped me like a hot potato, and now you want me to forget and forgive? Fat chance!"

Nic's lust was stirred even more as he watched her. Breasts heaving, her eyes sparking with blue fire—he wanted badly just to grab the Paranormalbuster and hold her curvy, busty little body next to his own. She was so magnificent that she must have some Russian blood somewhere in her, Nic decided as his eyes devoured her.

Cocking his head, he shook it, agreeing with part of her assessment. He had been devious, deceitful and devastatingly seductive. But he'd had good reason: he thought her his archenemy. Yet even when he thought her the foe, a crafty crook, a beguiling Buster who used her sex to gain favor, he still had wanted her again and again and again. She was a fool if she'd thought of herself as a one-night stand. Sam the Frito-Lay: You could never have her just once.

Now she had been wronged by his family, so he owed her a debt. But that only meant he could have his cake and eat it too, as Americans said. And as the humor of the situation suddenly got to him, he broke into a grin.

"I'm truly sorry, Sammy. Up at the castle I thought you were my enemy, so how could I reveal who I really was? I was angry, and rightfully so since it took me a good two days to get rid of that troll dung. I thought you sabotaged us first. But you were never a one-night stand. Never. I was going to call you, in spite of myself."

Sam rather liked the sight of the arrogant Nic Strakhov eating crow. Almost as much as she'd liked watching him pelted with troll waste. "Yeah, right," she mocked. "I waited for that call. You never made it." But after the words left her mouth, she felt like smacking her forehead again. She sounded like she really cared if the rotten rat of a Russian called. Just because she'd waited by the phone for a week like some lovesick sap, hoping each time the phone rang she would hear Nic's voice—It meant nothing, nothing at all.

No, she wasn't a woman to be used and abused by a prancing, pride-driven Don Juan of the Paranormalbusting world. If only she could keep reminding herself of that as she stared at the heat shimmering in Nic's smoke-colored eyes.

"Be generous, Sam. I've had a rough, busy week," he began, raising a hand to stop her rant. "I was going to call you." He invaded her personal space, placing a hand on her arm and filling her senses. "Do you think I could forget what we shared?" he asked huskily. "Impossible. You're unforgettable, that's what you are."

The crowd around them parted to reveal Uncle Myles, who brushed up beside Sam and looked Nic and Alex over carefully. "Is this who I think it is?"

Sam nodded, and Myles reached for the gun hidden under his bartender's apron. He jerked it out. With a sigh, Sam quickly retrieved it from her uncle, explaining to the Brothers Grim, "It's not loaded."

"Not loaded?" Alex asked, confusion evident in his voice. "Why carry it then? When trouble comes, it comes fast."

Nic remained silent, staring at the curiously dressed Humphrey Bogart imitator. In his opinion, Sam's uncle looked much more genuine than even those sideburn-wearing Elvis imitators with their rhinestone bodysuits.

"Why not?" Sam replied cryptically.

"Want me to bust his chops for you, sweetheart?" Myles asked. "A doll like you shouldn't have to mix with scumbags like this."

In spite of her anger, Sam almost laughed. The expressions on the Strakhov brothers' faces and her uncle's eccentricity were too much. "No. I appreciate it, Uncle Myles, but it seems like you'll have to rearrange their faces some other night. They're here to apologize."

"Heard of me, I guess. A little too tough for you wiseguys?" Myles asked the Strakhovs.

Nic nodded, his face a mask. "Yeah. I've heard all about you. You could run rings around me in detective work. Besides, I don't want my face rearranged. Sam likes it the way it is."

Myles looked pleased that his reputation was so widespread, but Sam's expression turned sour.

"In fact, since you're here as head of the family, I'd like to ask for your help in persuading Sam about a job I have," Nic went on, even though he knew Sam was really the undisputed leader of the family business. But he didn't think shmoozing the old man would hurt. In fact, noting Sam's petulant attitude, he might need to have the old fellow on his side.

Continuing, he explained gravely, "There's a serious supernatural mess in New York. I need Sam's assistance. My cousin Prince Varinski will of course pay her well."

Sam looked shocked, but Myles smiled cheerfully.

"Haven't you heard that familiarity breeds contempt?" Sam asked caustically. "Oh, wait—in your case I already feel that way."

All three men ignored her, and her uncle remarked, "Run it by me from the beginning, big guy, and don't spare the details."

Five minutes later Nic had Myles's promise to deliver a reluctant and sassy Sam to the airport in forty-five minutes. A lesser man might have been discouraged by her coldly polite acceptance, but Nic knew better; behind her disinterested face beat the heart of a hunter.

Yes, Sam would want in on the business of finding out who had stoned the vampire Jessie, or his name wasn't Nic Strakhov. (And it was!) She might have a chip on her shoulder right now, but he would have days and nights of her company to help her get rid of her anger. After all, he wasn't a paranormal problem-solver for nothing; he was used to getting rid of the unwanted, and he would exorcise Sam's unwanted anger. Although she might not be eating out of his hand right now, he wasn't discouraged by her bristling attitude. He had a way with women, always had. They adored him. So being the charming playboy he was, he would just turn on his continental charm and seduce Sam right back out of her paranormalbustin' pants and back into his bed.

Nic laughed. Sam might not be easy, but she would be had by him and him alone. New York, New York. If he could make it with her there, he could make it with her anywhere.

New York—the City of Monsters that Never Sleep

"I can't believe I'm here with you," Sam remarked rudely. The plane had landed, and they were riding in a chauffeur-driven limousine to the site of the murder.

Nic smiled grimly. Sam had sat with William Ripley on the plane, ignoring Nic. However, when they were getting inside the limo, Nic had practically pushed the werewolf away and snagged the seat next to her, crowding her against the door. "You've heard the old saying, keep your friends close and your enemies closer," Nic remarked calmly.

"Is that what you are doing?" Sam asked, her Bustin' boots longing to stray—with her in them. Anything to get away from Nic and the other occupants of this car. A sleepy Alex was on the other side of Nic, while Ripley sat across with Prince Varinski facing her. The *real* Prince Varinski, she recalled again.

Frowning slightly, she couldn't believe she had been so ditzy as to mistake their identity. Seeing Nic and the Prince together, she conceded the size of her failure. While Nic was arrogant and self-assured, the Prince fairly oozed with royal hauteur. Prince V. wasn't just lordly; he was imperial. He was the King of the Hill and top of the creep heap. The arrogance was probably due to centuries of vampire inbreeding, Sam decided snidely as she elbowed Nic.

"Move over," she growled.

Nic leaned close and whispered, "No way, sweetheart. You're not my enemy anymore, so I'm keeping you close because you smell good and look better. You're beautiful, you know."

"Want my advice? Go back to Russia with your love," she advised coolly.

Smiling down at her, Nic shook his head. "I don't think so. You're too alluring to resist."

Sam opened her mouth to protest, then shut it quickly. Nic was being like any other man who wanted someone who didn't want him, only more so. Besides, sometimes the best defense was to remain silent and keep your foe guessing. Nic was a tricky fellow, trying to flatter her out of her anger. But it wouldn't work, since she was wise to the wiseguy oaf. No way was Nic going to get back in her good graces again—or her underwear.

"Your charm and beauty make me speechless," he went on, his tone wickedly sensual.

"As I always suspected. You're showing your true colors, Nicky," Prince Petroff remarked. "It appears you're a rank sentimentalist." Varinski shot Nic and Sam an amused look, the same one he had been giving them on the plane.

His amusement grated Sam like sandpaper on skin. Evidently Prince V. thought he knew some big secret about her, which irritated her to no end. Even on the jet, during the debriefing on the murder, the Prince had retained this politely amused smile. And Sam wasn't some Kewpie doll or stand-up comedian brought here to entertain the haughty Russian aristocrat.

Nic edged closer, so Sam scooted away, trying not to make a scene with so many eyes watching. Instead she ignored him, which he chose to take exception to; he shifted his weight, his thigh touching her leg. This time she scooted so far away that she was wedged into the door handle—not a comfortable position.

Glaring at him, Sam couldn't help but notice his two hundred pounds of pure male beauty, all trying to soften her up. She shut her eyes, recalling remorsefully that even though he might be two hundred pounds of hot raw man, he was still grade-A prime jerk.

Leaning back against the seat cushion, Sam decided to ignore everything—the amused Prince, the brutish Ripley, the rowdy Alex and the randy Nic—and concentrate on New York's preternatural pest problem. A woman petrified was more than bizarre. Nothing alive and kicking in this century could turn a woman to stone. True stonings only happened on college campuses. Otherwise it had been since Greek and Roman times—although maybe also as late as the thirteenth century, when there had been two unsubstantiated cases of women being reduced to rubble. Spontaneous stonebustion, it was called.

Carefully but quickly she had read the research papers done on such creatures to cause petrification, but in her opinion they were too vague to be helpful. Could an almost prehistoric creature be alive and well, running around New York City? If so, the beast would be the find of the twenty-first century. She would be famous for capturing such a creature; not to mention raking in a lot of dough at the monster's removal.

No. It was impossible. Even though William Ripley had reassured them on the jet that no black magic was found at the murder site, Sam didn't have to be a diviner to believe that a Lei-line queen witch or a king warlock was at the bottom of this mess. Only Lei-line royalty, which was basically earth witchcraft, could summon this kind of power. The king and queen of the Lei-line coven—and maybe their two prince sons and one princess—had the right type of heritage to do the kind of damage to a human body that had been described. Sam reasoned that it *had* to be the covens doing this foul deed, since the alternative was just too unbelievable for a practical, hardworking gal like herself to contemplate.

"Sam, we're here," Nic said.

She looked outside. They were at a typical brownstone, New York style.

Nic took her arm as she climbed out of the limousine. "Are you going to behave yourself?" he whispered.

"Behave?"

"Play the consummate professional," Nic advised, his face a blank.

Like a furnace blast, blood rose to her face. "I *am* the consummate professional. It's you I have doubts about." She said the last while jerking her arm out of

Nic's hand, and stomped up the front steps. She'd show him professional; she could out-professional Nic with her eyes closed. Once she was at the murder scene, she would switch to job mode and forget her ire at the double-crossing creep. "Professional? Ha! My family has been finding monsters before you were even a gleam in your father's eye!"

Inside the brownstone, Sam calmed down, placing duty before her anger and taking note of her surroundings. The rather plain façade of the building was not reflected on the interior. The furnishings were extravagant and pricey; she recognized many as they bypassed the formal living areas and went straight for the stairs to Jessie Barrington's bedroom.

On the bed was a naked statue, back arching, nipples pebbled, caught in what looked like a smashing orgasm. Only the big finale; the climax as it were, had been the vampiress being turned to stone. Talk about hardcore sex, Sam mused darkly, appalled and yet horribly fascinated at the same time.

The expression on the petrified woman's face was one of both pain and pleasure. No *le petit mort* for this beauty; no little death, though she'd clearly been rocked.

Talk about being stone-faced, Sam thought. How humiliating to be caught for eternity with her pants down. Then, realizing what she was doing, she quickly berated herself, feeling ashamed for making jokes about the dead. She supposed it was a defense mechanism against the cold hard reality of death.

Taking another long look at the bed and nightstand next to it, she noticed a bottle of vodka, half-finished, with two glasses. Jessie and her lover had apparently been drinking before sex. Smirnoff on the rocks.

Stepping forward placed her directly by the bed-side. A faint blush tinged Sam's cheeks, embarrassed as she was by the intimacy of the body's pose with Nic and Alex in the room, along with the Prince. Petroff had lost his amused look; his expression was dark and his eyes hooded.

Taking a thoughtful poke at the body, she wondered if Jessie Barrington had been a hardbody before. She definitely was now.

Looking up, she met Nic's eyes and said, "There's no magic in the room." It was the first thing she'd checked, as black magic always left a whiff of sulfur, and other spells left their own kinds of dark vibrating energy. "No spells. Jessie here was turned into a rock on this bed, and no witches or warlocks did it."

Alex went to stand next to Sam, letting out a long whistle. "Will you look at the boulders on her! She had some body. What a damned waste!"

Nic shot his brother a disgusted look, while Prince Varinski hissed, his long white fangs flashing. "Jessie Barrington was a close friend of mine. If you weren't my cousin, I'd rip out your throat," he snarled.

Alex jerked his head up, clearly chastened by the scolding.

Sam sympathized. "Look here, Prince V., take it easy. We all know Alex has a big mouth. He's a real paranormal joker. But take it from me, he didn't mean anything cruel." Gesturing to the body on the bed, she continued, "This is a horror you don't see everyday. We're all mad and shocked, and humor is the outlet a lot of people need in a situation like this. I've seen it a hundred times. No disrespect to the dead intended, but don't get your cape in a knot."

Both Nic and Alex looked surprised at Sam taking up for someone who had played such devious practical jokes on her, but they were also surprised by the wisecrack Sam made about Petroff's attire. Generally Prince Varinski dressed like a human, but the man did have a fetish for capes, wearing them whenever he could. His Dracula complex was something Nic and Alex had teased him about for years.

The Prince acknowledged her, nodding once as his fangs receded. Then, glaring at Alex, he warned, "If you find you must say something like that, please do it outside."

Alex nodded, relieved that he and his cousin were not going to get into a fight.

Ignoring the last echoes of the family fireworks, Sam began a methodical search of the bed, looking for evidence as to what might have done this foul deed. She had her suspicions, but they couldn't be right, could they?

Nic joined her, searching under the bed, while a chastened Alex, an enraged vampire prince and a quiet Ripley, who had just entered the room, watched. Ripley stood stoically, his eyebrows drawn so tightly together they looked like one long black line. He really needed a wax job, Sam mused abstractedly; then she turned her attention back to Miss Marble.

Under the silk pillows, Sam found a dark hair. Since the female vampire was a sandy blonde—Sam had noted the picture on the nightstand—the hairs weren't hers. She also found a few scales and grimaced as she picked them up with tweezers.

Holding the tweezers up for Nic to see, she dropped a few scales into his hand. Nic shook his head in grim amazement, his eyes wide.

"We need to roll the body," she said.

Nic complied with her request, easily rolling over the hundreds of pounds of solid rock. Sam watched in amazement, thinking that Nic must work out daily to be able to handle so much dead weight without breaking a sweat. She suppressed a shudder of desire.

Examining the woman's back, Sam was thankful that Jessie had worn her hair short, because she found what she was looking for on Jessie's neck. Even after seeing it with her own eyes, she still had trouble believing. But the rock solid evidence left no doubt as to who or what had perpetrated this crime.

Ripley moved forward, staring hard at the two large fang marks on the back of Jessie's neck, just below the hairline. "It looks like a bite, but it's too big to be a vampire's, and a werewolf would have torn the skin more."

"It's a serpent bite." Sam opened her hands to show them the scales. Then, pointing to the claw marks on Jessie's lower body, she added, "Claw imprints. They resemble the claws of a lion, but are a bit shorter and thicker."

"Impossible!" the Prince argued, his voice filled with disbelief and horror. Nic gently replaced Jessie's stone body to its original position on the bed.

"When you rule out the impossible, all that's left is

the possible," Sam quoted. That was wisdom from her favorite literary detective, besides Sam Spade.

"That's right," Nic stated grimly, facing his cousin. "She was bitten by a Meduse, a gorgon. Hard to believe, but true."

"A Meduse?" Ripley asked in confusion.

At that moment, the sound of voices and footsteps approaching interrupted their discussion. A few seconds later, Sam felt decidedly less feminine as two drop-undead-gorgeous female vampires walked into the room. Escorting them was a short but well-muscled vampire with long dark hair pulled back in a ponytail. He would have been extremely good-looking if he didn't have beady black eyes. In human years he looked about twenty. In lived years, who knew?

The taller of the two women, a honey blonde, was statuesque with pale eyes the color of amber. The shorter had a knockout figure, perfectly proportioned, and was beyond pale with tiny freckles covering her face and shoulders. She had hair the color of copper, hair clearly natural because that color didn't come out of any bottle—although the Irish vampiress could really have used a different haircut. A cut that maybe feathered more about her face, Sam thought as she brushed her fingers through her own loose hair, hoping that it didn't look too windblown.

Studying the extremely pale redhead, she reflected a moment that she had never met an Irish vampire before, although she had known quite a few leprechauns. Those were short charming fellows with a ready laugh, but were terrible employees. Always off to see what was over the next hill. And on rainy days, forget it.

The Irish vampiress glided up to Nic and kissed him on the cheek, and Sam decided then and there that she didn't like her. The hag could forget any hair tips that might otherwise have dropped her way.

"Hello, Nic," the sexy redhead said. "It's been a long time since I've seen you in our neck of the woods."

Not long enough, Sam thought, keeping her irritation hidden behind a mask of cool disdain. The redheaded vamp was trying to vamp Nic with her odious charms.

"Forest. Nice to see you, too," Nic replied, eyeing the rather spectacular cleavage on display with the dress. "Let me introduce you to Alex, my little brother, and Samantha Hammett."

Forest smiled at Alex flirtatiously, then turned to Sam and deliberately shot her a mean smirk, her dark green eyes shining with malice. The expression revealed a hint of very white, very long fang.

Ha! Sam thought. Those two-inch fangs didn't scare her at all.

Nic motioned with his hand for Sam to step closer. "Samantha, this is Forest O'Day." Gesturing to the short male vampire and the tall blond female, he added, "And this is Boris Van Winkle and Natasha Barrington, Jessie's sister."

Boris flashed a big smile, with plenty of tooth, while Natasha merely nodded. She turned back to stare sadly at what was left of her sister.

"Sam is helping us out on this case. She owns Triple-P, Paranormal bustin' Pest Pursuers." No one seemed particularly impressed by Nic's introduction, Sam noted peevishly.

"Let's go downstairs and discuss what we have learned so far," Nic advised, taking Forest by the arm.

"So, you know what did this to my sister?" Natasha asked, her voice filled with equal amounts of hate and sorrow.

"Let's take the discussion downstairs," Petroff Varinski repeated. He'd noted the extreme pallor of his old lover's face, which was really pale even for a vampire.

Feeling like last night's cold pizza, Sam followed the others downstairs, taking one final look at Jessie Barrington's corpse as she muttered, "Hold on to your hats, ladies and vampires, because we have a rocky road ahead." Then Sam walked out of the room, singularly alone and feeling it.

The Rocky and Van Winkle Show

Downstairs, Prince Varinski seated himself next to Natasha, petting her hand from time to time in a gesture of comfort. Boris Van Winkle sat on her other side, his hand possessively caressing the vampiress's knee.

Alex and Ripley stood by the huge black-bricked fireplace, their moods betrayed by the restless energy with which they shifted from foot to foot.

The moment they had entered the room, Forest had pulled Nic down beside her on a small sofa. Next, the vampiress had entwined herself around him like a snake, Sam observed hotly, noticing immediately that there was less than an inch of space between him and the viperous vamp. She undoubtedly wanted to sink her fangs into him; it was so obvious, Sam wished herself oblivious to the tacky seduction.

More the fool, she, Sam decided disgustedly. Let Nic break the Irish vampire's heart and take her to the heights of heaven, only to let her fall back to earth with a big fat splat, like Sam had done. Let the slinky Forest O'Day get lost in the wood.

Sam narrowed her eyes at the cackling couple. Nic seemed to be enjoying all of the overdone attention, and right now the vampiress was running her fingers along his collar, playing with all his silky, thick hair. Natural hair, because Nic didn't wear any hair gels, like the overmoussed Forest, whose front bangs were a little stiff. Rolling her eyes, Sam regretted that she even cared how Forest the sex kitten was eyeing Nic, like he was a tasty piece of chocolate that she intended to devour.

Narrowing her eyes in derision, Sam watched Forest flutter her eyelashes, a flirtation that had gone out of fashion with the Civil War. Of course, Sam judged, Forest was no sapling; she was more an old growth, because it was obvious the vampiress had seen at least two centuries, maybe more. How could Nic be interested in an older woman *that old*? And he'd warned her about being professional, while all the time his eyes were glued to this client's cleavage. Professional, my ass, she grumbled silently.

She had the sudden urge to shout "Fire, fire—run, Forest, run," then sit back and watch the vampires all fly to the front door in fear of their overindulged lives. It was a cruel thought, and it made her smile secretly since she had gumption to do it. Unfortunately, she also had the smarts to know better.

Natasha Barrington's words interrupted Sam's criticism of her competition—competition Sam wasn't willing to yet admit was competition.

"I just know Jessie would die if she knew she was immortalized in grey."

"She'd be petrified," Forest agreed. "Jessie should have been changed into marble or gold, not something as mundane as rock."

"She was such a beautiful creature, all fire and light. Now she's stone cold dead. We'll never again share the thrill of shopping for a good bargain on coffins, or drink human martinis at sunrise after a night of raunchy sex," Natasha mourned, her eyes filling with scarlet tears.

Listening to Natasha's grief, Sam was very glad that she wasn't a vampire: coffin hunting and human martinis were not her thing. In fact, the only thing she had ever liked about a martini was the glass. And the olive. The drink tasted like hair tonic.

"We'll never again turn into bats and harass the tourists around the Brooklyn Bridge. Jessie had such a sense of humor. She used to love hearing the tourists scream when she got tangled in their hair," Natasha continued, her litany of regrets growing.

Monster memories, how sweet, Sam thought snidely. Jessie's humor sounded a little twisted. Messing up people's hair was just plain rude, especially since tourists didn't have their regular hairdressers to help them!

Turning her face to Prince Varinski, Natasha spoke: "Now tell me, who killed my little sister?" Her voice was devoid of any humanity, causing Sam to shiver in her chair by the fireplace.

"A Meduse—a gorgon," Petroff answered somberly.

"A *Meduse?* I thought the term was Medusa?" Boris said, his tone doubtful.

Nic answered this time. "The Medusas were from

Greece originally. They're also known as the three gorgons, cursed by Athena because the youngest sister had an affair with Athena's lover, Poseidon. What's not commonly known is that they had a brother, who also was cursed. His name, Meduse."

"But I thought Medusas were all hideously ugly, with snakes for hair," Natasha said; then she resolutely shook her head. "You're wrong. Jessie wouldn't be caught dead with anyone even average-looking."

What a fractured fairy tale, Sam mused wryly. And what shallow bloodsuckers. "The oldest recorded versions state that the gorgons were all very attractive people, and that they would only turn into snake-headed creatures with red bulging eyes and long claws when their emotions were aroused. It's the venom from the bite of the snake that causes a person to turn to stone."

"That's mythology! These creatures weren't ever real then, were they?" Forest asked. Her tone was dismissive, her face conveying her scorn.

Nic broke in. "As real as you and me. There were sightings and deaths attributed to the gorgons until the thirteenth century. Then history goes quiet. I thought, like everyone else, that the gorgons were extinct. Not any longer."

"I thought so too," Sam threw in. It earned a smile from Nic, a smile Forest took exception to. She ran her fingers up and down his silken sleeve, her long red fingernails making a slight scratching noise on the fabric. Sam wanted to punch her lights out, or at least find an ax to chop her down to size.

She said instead; "The evidence doesn't lie. And

unless I miss my guess, we have a serial stoner here. Have you heard of any similar deaths?" Inside she was seething. She knew a stone-dead woman when she saw one, and also knew that no black magic was involved. First Nic had unfairly questioned her professionalism, and now this half-dressed bimbo bloodsucker was questioning her Bustin' ability. Sam was used to her word being taken for granted. She'd years of experience and was considered an expert by everybody who counted.

Natasha glanced at Ripley, who shook his head. Boris answered: "No, we've heard of nothing suspicious in this way, no deaths where people are turned to rock."

"On the jet, Ripley explained that Jessie was dating somebody special. But Ripley didn't know his name," Nic mentioned, his gray eyes probing.

"Since I was her close friend, I know his name," Forest replied, smiling seductively into Nic's face. "Nero. But I don't know much else."

Sam couldn't agree more. The Irish vampiress was nothing but a big, fat snake with oversized breasts and fangs. Fuming at the woman's overt play for Nic, she added hastily, "Nero? He has just one name, kinda like Cher?"

Forest swung back around to face her, her red lips twisting in a sneer. "She met Nero at a Goth bar. Jessie had a couple of dates with him. He gave her a beautiful ruby ring, and she was in love. They hadn't had sex before their last date, which was last night. I don't know what he looked like or his last name. Although, I'm positive he was a supernatural creature—Jessie was rather adamant about never dating humans. So limited in their . . . abilities." Forest's smile was smug as her gaze swept up and down Sam's body, then dismissive as if Sam were nothing more than a bug on the carpet. It really didn't surprise Sam; apparently Forest was also a bigot, with humanity being beneath dirt-nappers like herself.

"Yeah, I guess vampires don't have to take Viagra to get a nice hard stake in the action," Sam retorted sarcastically, matching the venal vampiress look for look. "Anyway, which Goth club did she meet this Nero guy at?"

Forest shrugged, causing the spaghetti strap on her right shoulder to slip, revealing even more of her abundant cleavage as she ran her fingers down Nic's muscular chest. When she went for his leg, Sam debated briefly on whether she might not just go ahead and knock the vamp's block off, but though she longed to tug the Irish hussy's dress back up and pop Nic one in the kisser, she maintained her stoic expression. Stupid Nic didn't seem to realize he was this vampiress's intended breakfast of champions.

"I think it was that American one—American Gothic. They have some hot hunks there, though not as hot as what I'm sitting by tonight," Forest remarked. Licking her lips she whispered, "Do you taste as good as you look?"

Nic wouldn't be all male if he didn't respond a little to that blatant invitation. He smiled at her wickedly, noting from the corner of his eye Sam's chagrin.

"Probably better," he commented softly, but just loud enough for Sam to hear. Then he added in a more professional tone, "Did Jessie and Nero go to any other places?" His eyes began to sparkle as he now had a place to start tracking his quarry—and also he loved the expression on Sam's face. Sam thought she was being nonchalant, but she had too much passion to carry it off. Right now she was glaring at Forest, clearly despising the fact that the Irish vampiress was all over him.

Normally Nic would have been interested in a vamp this gorgeous, but he had Sam on the brain. She was what he wanted in bed, naked and hot, and her jealousy was only firing his lust. If he wasn't careful, he was going to get aroused right here and now, thinking about Sam.

"Besides American Gothic, Jessie hung out at Bram Stroker's Bar and the Breed Club," Forest said, her tone oozing seduction. "Every vampire who's anybody goes to Bram Stroker's Bar. It's all the rage. And every elite supernatural shows up at American Gothic sometime or another."

Sam shrugged. "So we know now that Nero hangs out at Goth clubs and picks up supernatural females, but we don't know what he looks like," she said, trying hard to ignore the nymphomaniac vampire. Who'd known Nic would be into corpses, even if those corpses had to-die-for bodies and lovely red hair with too much mousse. And why hadn't she brought her paranormal pest kit, inside which she had an assortment of razor-sharp stakes and a bunch of nasty tricks and treats for monsters?

"I think he has long black hair and violet eyes," Natasha piped up. Everyone turned to stare at her.

"How do you know this? I thought Jessie hadn't said much to you about him?" Ripley said.

"I'm pretty sure I saw her with him briefly on the last night they met. At least, I think it was him. He was beyond handsome."

"Why do you think it was Nero?" Sam asked.

"Because Jessie loved beauty, and this was a beautiful male. He was assuredly the best-looking person in the bar. And the bar was American Gothic. I left soon after, and then Boris and I went out of town for a few days," Natasha admitted regretfully. "I can't believe I was in the same club as my sister's killer and I didn't rip his heart out!"

"When was this?" Nic asked cautiously, aware of the vamp's fragile state.

"Last Saturday."

"Okay. So now we have a place to start tracking," Alex announced. "And now the bigger question: How do we kill this monster?"

"An interesting thought. No one has run across a problem like this in centuries," Prince Varinski mused, his expression thoughtful.

"Perseus cut off Medusa's head with a golden sword," Sam mentioned, wishing she had a golden stake to use on Forest. Talk about being unprofessional, she griped silently, hoping that Nic and the vampiress wouldn't decide to copulate on the small sofa in front of company. Wrinkling her nose in disgust, Sam hatefully wished that Nic wouldn't be able to get a woody. If the vamp sent Nic up in flames, she certainly wasn't going to put the Forest fire out. The doof, the doof, the doofus was on fire? She didn't need no water, let the mothasucker burn!

"Like many Greeks, the gorgon will have an Achilles' heel. Probably his head. So, I imagine the golden sword theory is best if we listen to mythology. I wonder where we can acquire two or three such swords?" Nic spoke up, trying to ignore Forest's continual carnal caress. The enemy they were soon to face was dangerous, deadly and crafty—a tough combination to beat. But this kind of adventure was the kind he liked best, as gargoyles, goblins and ghosts were a little tame. Nic loved to pit his wits and skills against an evenly matched adversary. He had never lost yet; nor would he, since his cousin, his little brother and Sam's lives all possibly would depend on his skill.

"I can supply those swords by tomorrow night if all goes well," Prince Petroff volunteered.

"And I'll do the research to make sure we're on the right track to killing him," Sam offered. She didn't like killing supernatural creatures, but some were just plain monsters. And a serial stoner was one seriously heavy bad guy.

"I'll help you," Nic remarked casually.

Sam shook her head, no. She knew that it wouldn't do at all if he came with her. They would just end up arguing or kissing. Either way, she knew she wouldn't be able to keep her mind off the gorgeous jerk, and she should be studying the ancient texts.

"You, Alex and Ripley need to visit the Goth clubs and talk to the bartenders before the regular crowd gets there. Between the three of you, you should be able to get that done before prime time. Ask around and see what you dig up. Do a little spying. See if you can't help pinpoint where Nero's lair is located."

Nic began to argue. "There are only three clubs!"

Sam frowned. "Three that we know of. There might be more. Besides, you guys might want to check out Greek restaurants in the area."

"Greek restaurants?" Alex asked.

"The Meduse is probably homesick for good old home cooking," she explained.

"That's stupid," Forest said. She didn't like Nic's interest in Sam, and it was obvious.

Nic frowned. "No, Forest, it does make a kind of sense. The Meduse won't feed from his kills; he kills for pleasure. And he eats like humans do. I imagine Greek food would tempt him—a piece of home. Who doesn't like a Greek omelette?"

Natasha spoke up, her fangs flashing as Prince Varinski put his arm around her shoulder. "I don't care how you do it, just get me his head on a pike."

"Don't worry, darling, we'll take care of this for you," Petroff promised. Then, glancing at Boris and Forest he added, "We need to go to sleep soon and sleep till dusk. We'll need all our energy for this creature. It's time we go to the hotel."

The Prince stood. "Everyone needs to use extreme caution. Especially the females of this group. We're up against the unexplainable. So, take care and, must importantly, beware of Greeks bearing gifts."

Saved by the Elevator Bell

The drive to the nearby Transylvania Hotel was passed with conversations highlighting the plan of action for tracking the Meduse and destroying it, but emotions were running high. Pulling up to the building, Sam observed its austere beauty. Located at Transylvania Ave. 6-5000, the exclusive hotel had been built for the sole purpose of catering to vampires and shapeshifters. There were no windows in the rooms from floors one to seven, and every room was fitted with an elaborate coffin. Inside the mini-bars were bottles of blood. And mirrors where everywhere. (In spite of vampire lore, the undead could not only be seen in mirrors, they gloried in their good looks. After dying and coming back as one of the Nosferatu, a human's looks were enhanced. An ugly person could become pretty; a pretty person could become a Helen of Troy.)

From floors eight on up, the Transylvania Hotel had installed large windows with ornate wrought iron balconies, completely caged in but providing the much beloved view of the sky—a necessity for any self-respecting shapeshifter. Heavy steel doors led in and out of each room, which werewolves or other more violent shapeshifter species couldn't break or claw through. Bouncing balls, old shoes and live mice were provided for entertainment.

Inside the elegant hotel, Nic firmly took Sam's arm. Eyeing the others with a look of stern warning to stay put, he turned back to Sam, holding her firmly. "I'll escort you to your room. We're on the same floor."

Glancing at the others' expressions, Sam could tell she wasn't going to get any help from them. Saying a gruff good night, she reluctantly allowed Nic to lead her to the elevator doors.

Stopping at the lift, he glanced down at her, his expression intense. "I've wanted to be alone with you. No interference. We didn't get a chance to talk on the jet since you almost broke your neck sitting by Ripley. And at the Barrington brownstone, there didn't seem to be an appropriate moment."

"So, you've decided to strong arm me?" she asked pettishly. "Subtlety must not be your specialty."

Tapping her foot, Sam wished the elevator would hurry up and arrive, because she needed to get away from Nic before her control slipped. She couldn't let him know how much he affected her.

"Come on, Sam. Give me a break."

"Give you a break?" she asked in outrage. "Nuts! I knew you were no good for a woman when I first laid eyes on you. I really knew you were no good when you seduced me in three days. I'm not easy!"

Nic studied her flashing blue eyes, and crossed his arms on his chest. "Your point?"

"I'm not finished yet, buster!" She had barely stepped up to the plate and already she was swinging. "I really, really knew you were no good for a woman when you let me experience your expertise. Finally, I recognized you for the hardheaded heartbreaker that you are when you added me as just another notch on your bedpost and left without a word! You ditched me, plain and simple. Despicable."

"I was going to call, Sam, but things got in the way," Nic said, hiding the anger that was burgeoning deep within him. Women didn't criticize him; they made love to him.

Nic didn't even know why he cared what Sam thought of him. Yet he did. Each time he saw her, the ache in his groin increased and his possessive nature wanted to take her in front of God, the bellboys and any other creature in the vicinity. She drove him crazy faster than anyone he knew, and made him so mad that he wanted to walk off into the sunset, never to return—but only if she came with him.

"Ha! You guys are all alike. You never call after a one-night stand," Sam argued heatedly. Then, realizing what she had implied, she frowned, adding too quickly for Nic to get a word in edgewise: "Of course, if a man called after a one-nighter then technically it wouldn't be a one-nighter, but a one-night stand with a little extra. Not much better, but still something. Something you didn't do."

"This is all hypothetical bull and beside the point. We were discussing you and me. You weren't a one-night stand Sam—never that."

"No? You didn't write, call or come by. I'd say that really clinches it. You know something, Nic, you made me feel on top of the whole supernatural world when you made love to me. Then you made me feel like the Queen of Dunces by letting me know just how little I meant to you. You made me feel used and sleazy, and no one does that."

"What can I do to make it up to you?"

Tapping her foot impatiently, Sam complained, "This has got to be the slowest elevator since the dawn of time. Think you can manage to get it to open?"

Nic was frankly thankful for the elevator's slow descent; he needed all the help he could get, even from simple machinery. "I never meant for you to feel stupid. And I love it that I made you feel special."

Poking a finger into his chest, she retorted hotly, "Liar! I know what you're thinking. You think you can sweet-talk me and I'll cave like a Jell-O mold. Well, Mr. Big Shot Strakhov, I know what I know, because of what I know. I also knew what you thought, but you were way off base about what I thought. Think! You're the equivalent of Russian rat poison to a woman like me. I demand respect. I deserve it! I'm nobody's plaything. I'm not something to pick up when you're horny and then shove back in the corner when you want to get on with your regular life."

The elevator doors finally clanged open. "Now shove off, Petroff, Pete—or is it Nic or Nicolas? Just what in the hell am I supposed to call you?" Sam taunted.

She stepped inside the gold gilt elevator, but Nic followed, not wanting to be left standing outside

BUSTIN'

with his hat in hand. Punching floor nine, he turned back to his red-faced quarry.

"Call me anything, anytime, Sam, and I'll come. Or just whistle."

Shaking her head, she replied in a clipped tone, "That line is a cliché. Go bother some other unsuspecting sap and stay out of my hair."

"If I'm annoying you now, you're really going to get annoyed shortly, because I can't leave you alone. I wish to God I could, but I can't. You're like a fever in my brain—and call me Nic," he finished, his voice lowering at the end. Logically he knew she had every right to feel betrayed and angered by his actions, but enough was enough. Why couldn't she accept his apology and go back to the way things had been at the castle, particularly in bed? This was new territory for him, and he was finding himself up in the air on how to deal with this Bustin' temptress with her bad temper. "I know you have every right to be angry, but—"

Sam interrupted snidely, ignoring the warm spicy scent of him in the closed quarters. She could also feel the heat waves coming off his body, burning in more ways than one. "Give the guy a gold star!"

Nic reached and pulled her into his arms. He would kiss some sense into her. Or at least he would try.

Leery of his quick moves, and of the feelings his kiss might engender, like making the earth move, Sam put up her dukes. "You try it and I'll pop you right in the old kisser."

Dropping his arms, Nic sighed. "I remember. You have a mean right hook."

227

Sam nodded. "Tell me, Nic, how does a guy like you get to be a guy like you? You talk a good talk, but you're all hot air."

Nic hit the emergency button, halting the elevator on eight. He leaned in close, his breath on her neck. "Oh, honey, I'm a lot more than hot air and you know it."

"Ha! Since I've known you, you've sabotaged my company, lied to me, pretended to be someone else, left after a night of wild, hot, wonderful sex with not so much as a good-bye—a night I thought was extremely erotic and rare. I thought you did too. But you fooled me so completely that you should go to Hollywood, because the role you played that night was Oscar material."

Placing his arms on either side of her shoulders, he pinned her, glaring daggers. "I had a damn good reason at the time, or at least I thought I did. I believed you'd sabotaged my company, and now I've apologized like a man. Take the apology like a woman!"

Sam blinked twice. His words made her angrier, but his nearness was confusing her with his virile sex appeal. He made her feel like she was flying, like her feet were eighty feet off the ground.

Her Uncle Myles had once told her it took a big man to apologize, that she should always accept. The problem was, her heart, pride and femininity had been wounded. The least Nic could do was beg, crawl on his hands and knees.

Shoving hard at his chest, she shook her head. "You're just horny and you think I'm easy."

"Oh, come on, Sam! Be fair. There's nothing easy about you."

Reaching behind her, she fumbled until she felt the switch and hit the emergency button, releasing it. Nic stepped back.

"I started to call you a dozen times. I had my fingers on the phone, but I thought you were the enemy."

"And you only sleep with the enemy once, is that it?"

"Not in your case," Nic answered savagely. He was irritated, sad and going to go to bed alone tonight. One look at her face showed no miracle was headed his way, either.

"Sam, I care about you. Even when I thought you were my enemy. It made me angry at myself, but I couldn't help it. I care for you, and believe me, I don't say that too often. I also want you. I want you desperately, like a starving man hungers for a bite of food."

Nic's intensity was too much for her, and she had to look down at the elevator floor. Her body ached from needing his body joined with her own. Foolishly she wanted him like a drowning woman wants a lifesaver; he was everything male, magnificent and macho. He had rung her bells over and over that night they had made love, until all she could do was almost faint from the pleasure. She'd floated away on the clouds of the most earth-shaking orgasms she had ever experienced. Still, her sanity and self-respect were hanging in the balance, making her aware that it was time to downplay all the sex stuff going on in the cramped space. "Look, Nic, I never discuss love on an elevator."

Dragging his hands through his hair, he cursed in Russian. The elevator doors slid open with a ding.

"Saved by the bell," Sam said. Leaping out of the elevator, she hurried down the hall to her room.

Nic followed like a dog after a very tasty bone, talking to the back of her head. "You'll forgive me, Sam. You're just as hot for me as I am for you!"

Inserting her card into her door, she muttered loudly, "You can apologize up, down and sideways. You can apologize until the cows come home, but mad is mad. And that's me right now."

Shoving the door open, she quickly reached into her purse, pulled out two quarters and threw them at Nic. "Now go call somebody who gives a damn." And with those words, she slammed the door in his startled face.

American Gothic

There were over eight million stories in New York City, most of them not pretty; but the gorgon story was downright ugly, and looking for that extinct Greek monster, who was not extinct, in a city of over eight million people, was like looking for a needle in a haystack. A needle that could turn you to stone.

Sam had known from the very first that this was going to be a tough case, a dangerous case, maybe the worst of her life. It would be a case to tell her grandkids about, a case to be written up in the *Unusual Monsters Scientific Journal*, a case she might not survive. But then, that's why she got paid the big bucks, she admitted as she walked up to the American Gothic Club, where she was meeting Nic and the others.

Along with her research today, she'd been thinking over Nic's apology. It had been a nice apology as far as apologies went, even if he hadn't gone down on his knees and begged. There was also a lot of sexual chemistry between them. She would cut him some slack, she decided reluctantly.

Patting down the sides of her French braid and straightening her skirt, she glanced up at the outside of the club. The facade was painted a deep scarlet, with various black paint decorations, and it looked rather like Andy the ghost had somehow won the bid for this particular paint job. On one side of the club, gold American graffiti was prominent with words such as "Fangs feel great" and "Call Vlad for a good suck." Sam shook her head, paid the cover charge and walked inside.

The American Gothic Club took its theme from vampire movies of the sixties and seventies. There were five-foot paintings done on black velvet of the various Draculas and werewolves of that period, such as Frank Langella, Christopher Lee, Lon Chaney and Jack Palance, and Bob Kelljan and Robert Quarry, who'd done the popular 1970 Count Yorga vampire series—true vampire and werewolf Americana.

Inside, the club was dark with fluorescent purple and blue lights. The ceiling was black but had glittering dots, which looked like stars and a blue moon. All the décor was definitely out of the sixties, with black shag carpet and couches and chairs done in vinyl the color of spilled blood. Sam thought it was very campy and, evidently the crowd did too, since the club was full.

The band was great, too. They were playing sixties and seventies rock and roll. Right now they were playing a Rolling Stones song, while various supernatural species mingled with humans on the dance floor. Sam grinned at the song; the Stones were a particularly appropriate soundtrack for hunting this killer.

Spying Nic and Alex at a corner table next to several trios of dancing clubbers, and noting that the encroaching Forest wasn't around, she hurried over, eager to tell them what she'd uncovered. She was also curious to discover if they had made any progress investigating Nero in other Goth bars and Greek restaurants.

Since she was cutting Nic some slack, and since she couldn't see Forest through the threes, Sam grinned at Nic and slid into the seat across from him, noticing just how handsome he looked tonight in his dark blue shirt and faded jeans, which fit low on his hips. He was an American girl's dream, even if he had a Russian anatomy.

"Guess what I found?" she blurted before they even had a chance to say hello. She leaned her elbows on the table. "Gorgons can hibernate like certain species of desert frogs. The frogs hibernate for decades as they wait for a good rain. Well, so do gorgons. I mean, the gorgons don't wait for rain, but they can actually hibernate for centuries. And a gold sword will definitely kill the Meduse. It's his Achilles' heel. Well, his neck is. I found the original curse and how to stop it: Death. Beheading by a solid gold sword." Sam fought down her growing excitement.

Nic's eyes were bright with interest, and even Alex remained quiet.

Hurriedly Sam conveyed her other findings, the words bubbling over like a brook in a flood. "You can also stab the Meduse in its human form, in the eyes, and that will slow him down. With most super-natural creatures it's the heart, but not the Meduse. He has a rocklike substance his heart is encased in, so it can't be touched without a jackhammer drill or some serious hammering and chiseling." Her grin grew even bigger as she waited for her pat on the back; she'd spent over eight hours in various libraries around New York City, deciphering extremely difficult foreign passages. "Believe me, those old texts were Greek to me, but I managed."

Before either Strakhov could comment, Forest appeared. She walked up, slid her arms around Nic's neck and bent to kiss his cheek.

Sam's grin fled. She didn't flinch outwardly, but inside she was seething. Once again she had gotten nary a thank-you-ma'am, while Forest stole her thunder with a blatant siren's seduction. Narrowing her eyes slightly, Sam focused on the vampire's dress—or rather, what little there was of it. The vampiress resembled a teenaged rock star who'd forgot to put on her skirt.

Yes, Forest definitely stood out. With her red mini-skirt and knee-high black boots, and her see-through black lace shirt, the sultry underdressed vampiress made Sam feel like a true ugly American. Forest looked like sex on wheels, and Nic would be dining in if he didn't show some sense.

He was currently leaning toward Forest, giving her the once-over, as his eyes came to rest on the large nipples barely covered by her black lace shirt. The man was a fool, a darn carnal fool. But then, what could Sam really expect from the Russian rat? Certainly no American justice. Her poor unhappy heart was being batted around like a baseball, and watching her ex-lover—the key word being *ex*—fawned and drooled over by Miss Melon Breasts with Fangs was not a pretty sight.

The redheaded vampiress was certainly getting Sam's Irish up, and Sam wasn't even Irish, rather a mix of German and English, she reflected crossly. She wished the Irish trollop would go fawn over an American gigolo or someone, *any*one, just as long as it wasn't a white Russian she went home with tonight.

Slamming her glass on the table a little harder than she meant, Sam watched Forest slide into the seat next to Nic. Her hand caressed his arm, those wickedly long fingernails scratching the smooth material of his shirt. Nic glanced at Sam, shrugging his shoulders in a gesture of appeal that had a hint of little boy about it. Yeah, right, Sam thought tersely. Nic was about as innocent as a wolf on the prowl. And he was already lurking deep within the Forest.

Chin on her palm, Sam gave Nic a faint smile, as if she could care less what he was doing and with what. If he wanted to date a vampire, get drained dry, go beyond the pale, more power to him.

Nic managed to hide his grin, noting Sam's expression. His Paranormalbuster was not a happy camper. He wanted to laugh, but instead he addressed himself to Forest. "Sam was just telling us what she uncovered." Turning back to the slowly stewing Sam, he added, "Petroff said the swords will be ready by midnight." Then he winked.

Sam stifled a colorful comeback. "What if we run into the Meduse before then?" she asked tersely.

"Are we supposed to just let him go, or become the next monuments to his invincibility?"

"I guess we'll cross that bridge when we come to it, as you Americans say," Nic replied.

His slight Russian accent was sexy. Way too sexy, Sam despaired, for that villainous vamp vixen was still sitting next to him, lapping up his presence like a cat with cream.

"Tomorrow night will be better for our hunt. Petroff and Ripley will be able to join us, as well as Boris and Natasha. Our cousin is still working with his craftsman on the swords," Alex volunteered.

"Where are Boris and Natasha?" Sam wanted to know. She took a sip of her drink, looking over the rim of her glass to scan faces in the crowd. She had expected the pair to be here tonight.

"Setting up Jessie's memorial service," Alex answered.

"And Ripley?" Sam asked, inching to slap Forest's hand, which was possessively patting Nic's arm.

"Using his nose to sniff out some leads," Nic replied. He was enjoying Sam's jealousy—a jealousy she tried to conceal, but somehow couldn't quite manage.

"Sniffing out leads?" Sam said, then found herself feeling stupid when the others laughed. "What's so funny?" she asked.

"Ripley's a *werewolf*, Sam," Nic explained, his eyes bright with humor—and something else, something Sam couldn't interpret. "I thought you knew. After all, you keep telling me how you're such an expert on supernaturals." Nic's tone was clearly amused, his eyebrow quirking.

Sam began to fume. First Nic made her a one-night stand, then he let the hussy from hell slink all over him, and now he was adding to his list of grievous sins by insulting her professionalism? What a louse!

"Sure," she snapped, both hands planted firmly on the table. Glaring at Nic and Alex, she growled, "What? Just because the man is hirsute, I'm to automatically assume he's a wolf in sheep's clothing?"

Alex almost choked on his drink.

Nic snorted, while Forest started giggling. "Humans," she said. She clearly meant, *What are you going to do with them; you can't live with them, and you certainly can't live without them as a food supply.*

Seeing the brief flash of hurt before Sam tightened her expression, Nic backtracked. "Sorry, Sam. You're right. We should have told you. You don't have any problem working with werewolves, do you?" He waited patiently for her answer, his gray eyes curious.

Leaning across the table, Sam stared daggers at him. "As long as he's housebroken and doesn't bite, I have no problem with the guy. And I guess it goes without saying that Forest would be at home with the dogs."

All three reacted differently to Sam's words. Forest laughed outright, glancing from Sam to Nic expectantly. Alex looked everywhere else. Nic looked pissed off, his mouth suddenly a grim line.

"How bighearted of you, Sam, being willing to work with the fur challenged," he said.

"Oh, lay off. I didn't mean it like that." She was indignant. Who was he to be pissed at her? He was the one at fault. In fact he was so at fault that if he was California he would have fallen off into the ocean.

"Sure—some of your best friends are werewolves," Nic agreed sarcastically, steadily holding her gaze.

Obviously having a vampire for a cousin made Nic a bit touchy about supernatural creatures. "No. But one of my good friends is a witch, my brother has dated a werelioness and I have a goblin for a pet." She wasn't a preternatural bigot, she was just choosy. And if she tended to prefer men who didn't try to sip your blood like fine champagne, or men with more wit than hair, that was her business!

Leaning toward Sam, Nic studied her with a new intensity she found unnerving. She remarked tensely, "Not meaning to change the subject, but I am." Ignoring Nic's odd huff she continued, "I think I know where the Meduse might strike next."

Nobody asked where with bated breath. Sam narrowed her eyes and pursed her lips, but Nic just continued to stare at her strangely. He took a long sip of his Rolling Rock beer. The silence stretched into a minute, until Alex finally asked the big question: "Where?"

"The Statue of Liberty." Sam waited for everyone to make the logical connection. They remained silent, however, staring at her with varying degrees of disbelief.

"Well, the Meduse is really into statues, you know. He finds them arousing. And you can't get bigger or more womanly than the lady herself."

"You mean, he'll go and look at her like a porn magazine or something?" Alex managed to ask, his voice a little shaky. He was clearly suppressing laughter.

Sam nodded.

Alex cracked up. Nic snorted in disbelief, and Forest was staring at Sam like she was the stupidest human alive—which in her opinion was saying something.

"That's an usual ideal, Sam. Original, even," Nic added when he saw Sam flinch.

"It's a great idea. There's no lady larger in the good ol' U.S.A., and without question she's the prettiest. She makes Philadelphia's Liberty Belle look cracked and tawdry in comparison. So, that's where I'll be tomorrow night—a front row seat at the Statue of Liberty," Sam said through clenched teeth. She glared at Nic. "Go ahead and snicker. They laughed at Galileo, Peter Venkman and Victor Frankenstein. I'm glad to be in the company of giants."

Forest hooted with laughter, for once forgetting her sex-kitten image.

"You can't go charging off into New York City at night by yourself," Nic said. "It's dangerous and deadly. You know it's an urban jungle out there, filled with all kinds of lethal creatures. Even *without* the Meduse hanging around," Nic added.

"Oh, give me a break. I'm free, proud, and a member of the World Bustin' Association. I'm not afraid of no gorgon. And heck, if I were a gorgon, I would find that statue sexy." Seeing the disbelief in their eyes, she opened her mouth to tell them that she had also found an obscure reference to Medusae having an affinity for large stone, copper and marble statuary. And the bigger the better. The perverted monsters liked nothing more than to have intercourse with hard, cold humanlike statues. And none of this modern art stuff for them. They might be perverted, but they had traditional taste.

Before Nic could say more, Alex put in his two cents: "I'll go with Sam."

She kept her mouth closed tight, narrowing her eyes at Nic, who was still smiling at Forest. See if she would mention finding that really old book at the library and the odd reference it held—the strange reference about the statues sculpted by Michelangelo and da Vinci that had met with a really scary fate. The gorgons had gotten their rocks off by having bizarro sex with them; the sculptures had been destroyed and the world had lost another David or two. And how do you think the Venus de Milo had ended up looking how she did? Well, let the oversexed vampires and the underbrained Nic figure it out for themselves.

Nic started to argue with both his brother and Sam, but Forest got there first. "Let's dance, Nicky—now." Giving him a come-hither look, she pulled him to his feet.

Glancing over to note Sam's reaction, Nic hid a smile. He could almost see the steam jetting from her ears. Taking a quick peek back at Forest, he could see why. The Irish vampiress looked ravishing tonight, although a little wooden. Yes, for all her fine looks, Nic just couldn't seem to see Forest as a threat to his feelings for Sam; she was all bark and no bite.

"Sure," he replied, glancing once at Sam as he led Forest to the dance floor. It would be better to let her cool down.

"What a creep," Sam muttered as he left.

Alex looked amused. "Nic, a creep? What will he think?"

Sam drew her attention away from the gruesome twosome and gave him a dirty look. "Not Nic. Forest. Boy, that lady is a tramp."

Alex started laughing again, wiping his eyes.

Sam ignored him. "Nic's no creep. He's just a lecherous, oversexed and rutting Russian. He's also pretty dim-witted when it comes to figuring out the psychology of a gorgon. Lucky I'm here."

Alex laughed even harder. The course of true love was certainly not running smoothly for his big brother. "He'll be glad to know that he's not a creep—and that you're jealous."

"Oh, drop it, joker boy," Sam snapped. Nobody said she was jealous, not without getting a fat lip in the process. Lucky she was acting the lady tonight, or Nic's little brother would have trouble sipping for a week. She instructed him testily, "Give me the lowdown on those clubs and Greek restaurants."

Alex stopped chuckling. "Okay. You were wrong about the restaurants, but some of the bartenders at the Goth clubs think they might have seen him. Those at the Breed Club, the Resident Evil Bar and Club Dread all remembered seeing a male supernatural with Jessie who fits Nero's description."

"When was the last time they saw him?"

"Last night, here."

"Damn! We missed him."

"I know," Alex grumbled. "But we'll get him yet."

"Get who?" Forest asked, walking back to the table. Daintily she sat down in her chair, running her fingers through her shoulder-length copper curls. Her mini-mini skirt sliding up almost to her waist, Sam noted nastily. Nic remained standing, watching Sam.

"Who else? The gorgon," Sam retorted. "Where have you been? Planted in la-la land?"

Forest took her time answering. Pointing a long red curved fingernail at Sam, she suggested with pure ice in her voice: "Watch out, little human, I don't like being insulted."

"Then don't hang around," Sam shot back. Yes, her Irish was up, as well as her English, her German, and her dander.

Alex snorted. Nic suppressed a grin, knowing that he really shouldn't find Sam's insults humorous. After all, Forest was a vampire, and an enraged vampire could wipe the floor with a human. They often did, cleaning up any blood they might have spilled while drinking, sort of like some people use bread to sop up steak juice. Still, Sam was made of sterner stuff than most mortals, and Nic enjoyed her jealousy. And she *was* jealous, she cared about him far more than she wanted him to know.

The Irish vampiress struck fast, latching on to Sam's arm with terrible strength, knocking over her drink in the process. "I don't like being given instructions. Especially not by a short and stupid mortal whose lifespan is growing shorter by the minute."

Grimacing in pain, Sam retained a half grin. She knew she had to. Never let them see you sweat: Her parents had drilled that into her as a child. Supernatural creatures thrived on fear and pain, and Sam wasn't about to give this venomous vamp the thrill.

Jerking out a cross she had hidden in her jacket pocket, she pressed it down on Forest's arm. Immediately the Irish vampiress's skin began to smoke.

"Short maybe, human, definitely, but stupid, no way,"

Forest jerked back her scorched arm, her fangs extended. She hissed at Sam, "You're stupider than I thought!"

"But you aren't as tough as you think you are," Sam wisecracked unwisely. She ignored Nic's nervous expression.

"You'll pay for this, you malicious miscreant!" the vampiress howled, cradling her arm.

"No, she won't," Nic broke in harshly. "We are at serious business here, and you provoked her."

Sam agreed. "We have better things to do than trade insults all night. I get enough of those from Nic," she said. But she was pleased as punch that Nic had taken up for her.

Before Forest might launch herself across the table, Nic staunchly placed both hands on the woman's shoulders, suggesting firmly, "Forest, remember that Sam was invited here by the Prince of New York, New Hampshire and Vermont. Prince Varinski wouldn't like it if you attacked her. She has Petroff's protection as well as my own."

Then, dropping his hands from Forest's shoulder, he grabbed Sam's hand and pulled her to her feet. "Let's dance, Sammy." He gave her no chance to object.

"The name is Sam," she protested, tugging slightly on her wrist. Forest gave her a look that would have sliced her to ribbons if it was a blade, then stormed off in a huff, her red miniskirt barely covering her fast-moving bottom.

"I'm really not in the mood to dance with a devil," Sam spoke up as Nic led her to the floor.

"Tough."

On the dance floor, the band was playing an old Chicago tune; "Colour my World." Glancing over Nic's shoulder, Sam couldn't help letting her feminine side enjoy a victory; Nic had taken up with her and Forest was stomping upstairs to the bar area of the club!

"That's some playmate you've picked out for yourself," she said snidely.

Nic only smiled.

"Better watch your neck, your back and anything else that gets in the way of those snapping fangs," Sam remarked, secretly savoring his closeness.

"I'm a grown boy. I can take care of myself."

Sam snorted. "You're not as smart as you think, buster. You're not as tough as you think. You may be good-looking and all that, but good looks don't cut it with a fang-face."

"I happen to like fang-faces."

"What, you want to end up sharing a sepulcher with some nasty Nosferatu? Funny, I didn't take you for a sucker."

"I think I'll manage."

Sam couldn't stop herself. "You may not realize it, but you're heading the way of the uneternal big sleep by letting her hang all over you."

"She's beautiful, sexy and none of your business," he replied, stoking her jealousy. She was hot and bothered; her lips were in a pout, her pink, ripe lips, making him ache for a taste. She pushed against his chest, but Nic didn't release her. She felt too good in his arms.

"Are you always this charming, or did you take piss-women-off lessons?" How dare the rotten rake flirt with both her and Forest! He couldn't have that birch and her too; only he was too dumb to recognize that fact.

"You know, you're adorable when you're mad, Sam. It makes me want to kiss all the spit and vinegar out of you."

"I don't think that can be arranged," she replied angrily. His face was just inches from her own, with its dark smoldering gaze daring her, challenging her. But he had used and abused her, and he didn't deserve for her to give him the time of day, much less a kiss. He could have all the vinegar he wanted, though.

"Too bad. We could have a lot of fun."

"Ha!" Sam knew it wasn't her best comeback, but she was again thinking of how hot and honeyed Nic's kisses were; how much she wanted not only his lips, but also wouldn't mind another in-depth history lesson about Peter the Great. She stifled a groan.

"We can have a lot of fun, Sam, if you let us."

"In your dreams. I won't sit through intimacies with liars, betrayers, or one-night standers."

Nic stopped dancing and held her at arm's length. "You better walk easy around me, Sam, and learn where to draw the line. I'm prepared to give you some leeway because of our past, but don't insult my honor anymore. And for the hundredth time, you're not a one-night stand!"

"Don't threaten me, Nic!" she snapped.

"Don't push me, Sam, or you're gonna end up on the floor with your skirt around your head." Nic stared at her, smoldering. Oh, how he wanted Sam— here and now! "You want to make a scene in the middle of a vampire bar?" His eyes were glittering with the red-hot glow of desire; this feisty female roused his passions faster than anyone he had ever known.

"You know, buster, somebody needs to teach you a lesson."

"Who's going to do it?" he asked smugly. "You?"

"You bet. I'm the one wearing the boots that are going to kick your Russian butt right back to Vermont."

"Sounds kinky. Let's go," he replied. He wore a wicked grin, a lady-keep-your-knees-together grin. "I'm all yours. I know you want me."

Unfortunately, before Sam could punch Nic in the gut or let him have a piece of her mind or boot, Ripley interrupted them. "Outside, now. There's been another stoning."

First-rate Dicks

It was a night for detectives, Sam mused dispiritedly. Where was Columbo when you needed him? Sam had always felt that there was something comforting about Columbo's old trench coat and sad-faced dog look, just like Monk's ever-ready handy wipes. But they were on their own, no help to be had.

Sam, Nic and Alex followed Ripley to the back of an alley on the corner of Baker Street and McCallam. Wearing only a short skirt and a long sleeve blouse, Sam certainly felt the nip in the air. But the chilly night winds were not what had frozen the woman on the ground.

Moonlight filtered down, revealing the body. Sam studied it. This victim was marble hard, and death was death no matter how a person bought or paid for it.

"Yep, it's murder," she said stonily. She didn't need to be Leonardo da Vinci to figure out that the gorgon had struck again. And if they didn't catch him soon, there would be a new exhibit of female stationary gracing the sidewalks of New York. She doubted the Met would approve of the competition.

The woman lay with her skirt hiked up, her face frozen in pain and ecstasy for all time—just a stoned throes away from a big city that didn't care.

Shaking her head, Sam remarked, "The NYPD Supernatural Task Force will be stumped." How could they suspect a mythical monster that hadn't seen the light of day for over eight centuries? Would they realize a gorgon was getting his rocks off by turning women to stone? "Will they even believe us?" she wondered aloud.

She and Nic were between a rock and a hard place, like running a gauntlet blindfolded or walking a tightrope in high heels. She doubted the NYPD Supernatural Task Force would help them; more likely they would just slow things down. Even their best detective, Rockford, with his meticulous files, wouldn't be able to deal with this murder case. And CSI couldn't get blood out of stone.

"I doubt it," Nic replied. His eyes narrowed in rage; nobody deserved to die like this.

"The task force also won't know the weapons to kill a Meduse. They sure can't go after him with Remingtons or Magnums."

"You're right. We shouldn't involve them yet," Nic agreed, sniffing the air and surveying the crime scene.

Picking up the victim's purse, Sam found crackers and a wallet inside, along with other detritus. The lady's name was Harri Kenny. "Human female, five foot seven, one hundred and forty-two pounds and thirty-one years of age. Well, at least we know who killed Kenny. You don't have to be a psych to figure it out. What a tragic end to a life cut short. Dammit! We've got to stop Nero. This woman needs to be avenged," Sam said.

"We will, Sam, we will," Nic vowed. He was closely seconded by Alex, whose usual good spirits had vanished with the night's gruesome discovery.

Ripley had been sniffing the air, and he remarked, "The Meduse doesn't leave any scent. Strange, but I can't get anything from either the victim or this alley."

Sam frowned. A werewolf had a better nose than a bloodhound. "You didn't get a scent at Jessie's place either?"

Ripley shook his head. "The Meduse must have some kind of spell protecting him."

"Probably the de-scenting spell. Costly, very costly. And it only makes things harder for us," Sam complained, shaking her head. She pulled a card out of the dead woman's wallet, noting it was a pass card. "The victim works for Dragnet Industries, a business that goes over to Asia and captures dragons for domestic use here in the U.S.A. She's also a card-carrying witch. The Cagney and Lacy Clan."

"Dragons for domestic use?" Alex asked curiously.

"Yeah. Dragons are used for controlled crop burning in the midwest, and of course nationwide at funeral homes. Cremation."

Nic tapped his foot, his expression grave. "She wasn't exactly born a supernatural, but she did work for a more magical industry and is a witch. She was also blond. I wonder what else about her drew the gorgon?"

"She's got great breasts," Alex volunteered. "So did Jessie."

Sam narrowed her eyes and nodded curtly. "Thank you for telling me. Thank you so much. Now if you come a bit closer, I'll put my fist in your eye."

Nic sighed. His brother had always been a breast man. He himself preferred the total package—a package very much in the shape and size of Sam Hammett.

"I can't believe the gorgon struck again so soon," Ripley muttered, voicing everyone's thoughts.

"Three nights and he's struck again. That's bad news," Nic agreed. Looking back at the sidewalk to where a few Goth-costumed clubbers were walking by, he noted, "It's a pretty public place to be getting his kicks in killing. He must not be afraid of capture at all."

"Or John Q. Public. It appears that Nero's certainly not sitting around fiddling while we roam," Sam added hotly. She summed up her conclusions: "He comes out of nowhere and starts stoning women. This is the second victim we know of in three days. Usually a serial stoner works up to his killing. It usually takes months. Yet we have two occurrences in less than a week. You don't go from crawling to running. No, there must be other bodies that we know nothing about."

Sam glanced at Nic, who was rising from examining the corpse. His stance was taut, his body weight evenly distributed; he stood on the balls of his feet, ready for the rocky path ahead.

"If there were any other murders, we would have heard it through the paranormal pipeline. Petroff has good connections. So do I," Nic remarked as he glanced back down at the victim. "But I tend to agree with you, Sam. This hunter is skilled and unafraid. Maybe he just got to New York and his other kills are elsewhere—maybe the West Coast or Europe."

"You aren't as stupid as you act, Nic," Sam remarked. "Congratulations."

Alex hid his smile behind his hand, while Nic merely stared at her. After a moment he said, "Well, isn't this a Hallmark moment?"

Turning her back on the brothers grim and grimmer, Sam headed back toward the club. Over her shoulder she called, "Just one more thing. I'll check my West Coast contacts tomorrow. Since you guys have friends in Europe, you can check there."

"Where are you going?" Nic called out. He was irritated that the sight of her curvy, swinging hips could almost mesmerize him. She was dynamite in that short blue skirt, dynamite ready to go *bang*. Which was entirely the wrong train of thought. There was a big, bad monster loose in New York, and he was lusting after a maddening menace with a big mouth.

"I'm going to *bed*," Sam said. Then she stopped and turned. "But that's not an invitation. Now be sure you dispose of the body properly; NYPD Supernatural just isn't up to it." She started briskly walking, trying to escape the cold night air and the hovering chill of death.

Nic watched Sam go, his insides smoldering. Noticing that his little brother was avidly watching him watch her, he frowned. He shot Alex a hard look. "Don't press your luck, buddy. Just keep your mouth shut."

For once Alex took his eldest brother's advice.

After a moment, glancing back down at the woman in rock, he asked Nic, "What do we do with her?"

"What would one normally do with a stone statue of erotic nature?"

"Take it to a quarry?" his younger brother guessed.

"Nope. To an art gallery specializing in erotic art," Nic explained, and they rolled the corpse in a blanket Ripley had procured.

"Got one in mind?" the werewolf asked.

"Yeah, the McCloud Gallery."

"Ah. I know it. I'll take her," Ripley volunteered.

"Okay, but while you're there, check and see if there's any more life-sized art like this. Maybe someone else has the same idea as me for getting rid of murder victims," Nic advised gravely. He turned. "Alex, you and I have to make those calls pretty soon, what with the time difference in Europe and all."

Alex patted his brother on the shoulder. "You know, Nic, Sam was right. You aren't as dumb as you look."

Give Us Your Tired,
Your Poor, Your Haunted
Masses Yearning to Be Free

The next night was one to give a person the willies. Pea soup fog inched outward, spreading across the pavement and winding its fingers around buildings and cars. The air was cold enough to penetrate the bones, unseasonably cold for October in New York. The ride across in the ferry had been bitterly uncomfortable, and fairly silent since Sam was pouting and Alex was canceling a date on his cell phone with some bimbo he had met. High in the dark heavens, the wind blew a thick cloud across the waxing moon, which would be full in a couple of days, Sam noted as she walked off the boat.

What was going to happen would happen tonight; she felt it in her bones just like the chill. Just what would happen she couldn't say, since there was neither rhyme nor reason to her gut instinct, just a feeling she couldn't shake. The conviction blanketed her mind like the cloud across the moon.

The others had scoffed at her insistence on the gorgon being infatuated with the Statue of Liberty. She could still hear Nic's parting shot as they'd split up to each go his merry way. Once again Sam had been tempted to tell him about the reference to the perverted sexual interest of Medusae, but some imp had kept her quiet. She and Alex had come her to kill the Meduse, and Nic could go hang. He and the others had split themselves between the various Goth clubs.

"Happy hunting," Nic had called to Sam and Alex's departing backs. Forest had shadowed him, standing too close for Sam's taste, but Nic was lapping up the Irish vampire's regard like Irish whiskey, she noted peevishly. Also it had been more than obvious that the pair thought she and Alex were on a fool's mission. Forest had been giggling as they'd left the hotel.

Well, let the woman laugh. Sam knew the old adage, *He who laughs last laughs best,* and she intended to be hysterical by the time she was in bed for the night.

Slamming her mind shut against any more thoughts of Nic and the vexatious vamp, Sam glanced up at the Statue of Liberty, taking in its proud majesty. A feeling of profound pride flooded her system, as it always did when she gazed upon the grand old lady. This dame was something else, with her hand held high, loftily lighting the way for new generations to find their American dream, just as she had done for millions before. The lady was a beauty, no doubt about it, and no self-respecting gorgon would be able to resist.

The poem inscribed at the base always affected Sam, that poem which had been changed slightly over the last eighty years to say, *"Give me your tired, your poor, your hungry haunted masses—your ghosts, your vampires, your werewolves and other supernatural predators yearning to be free."*

The poor saps, Sam thought. Americans just hadn't figured on the Meduse. No one would throw out the welcome mat for a creature like Nero.

Glancing over at Alex, who wore a light windbreaker, Sam wondered why the cold didn't bother him. She herself was dressed in a Columbo-like trench coat and fur-lined cap, and she was shivering, but he seemed oblivious to the cold ocean gusts all around.

Feeling Sam's eyes on him, he smiled. "She's something else," he remarked, his voice fraught with emotion as he glanced up at the grand old dame.

Sharing the moment, she smiled back. "She always gets to people, no matter their race, color or species—and no matter how many times you see her up close and personal." In the car on the way over, Sam had found out that this was Alex's second time to view the Statue. "America is quite a country."

"I guess," Alex agreed. "But I still miss Russia."

Sam smiled sympathetically. "At least your homeland is gorgon-free," she remarked.

"Yeah. Nic found out that there weren't any stonings there. Just in Italy, about a month ago. At least they think those two missing shapeshifters from Rome met with foul play, but with so many statues there, it's hard to tell."

"Well, there were no reported stonings on the West Coast, so I think we are best off assuming that the gorgon was hibernating around Rome somewhere. And for whatever reason, he decided to migrate here." Glancing back up at the Statue of Liberty, she added, "Maybe he couldn't resist the lure of this monument."

Alex shrugged. "In a crazy way, that makes perfect sense. Nero's a huge womanizer, so why wouldn't he carry a torch for the biggest woman in the world?" Observing the thin crowd outside the monument, he noted, "Nothing happening right now, though."

"Let's try indoors."

Inside, there was a small gathering of people.

"Not many here tonight," Alex commented.

"Too cold," Sam replied, scanning the crowd. Noting nothing, she nudged Alex's arm. "Let's go on up. Take the grand tour. I'm glad they're letting people do that again—I have something I want to confess."

Inside the crown, the crowd grew thin until it was only the two of them. There Sam confessed the odd reference to statuary rape. Alex gaped at her then grinned, giving her a very American thumbs-up for keeping her mouth shut about the bizarre reference. After a brief discussion about her omission, the two stared out into space. Below, the city of New York was a glittering, dazzling feast of lights, along with waves of drifting fog curling sluggishly around the rocks and foundations of buildings.

Finally Alex broke the silence. "Yes, I'm glad you didn't tell Nic about the sex thing. If we catch Nero then we'll be the heroes of the story. Still . . . poor Nic. You're barely talking to him. Are you ever going to forgive him for his deception?"

Sam turned to stare at him. "Is that any of your business?"

Alex grinned. "No, but why let that stop me?"

Sam couldn't help but smile. Alex was a cutup, and cute for a Strakhov. If she hadn't been hung up on Nic, she might have felt some physical attraction for him. Instead, Alex reminded her of her own brother, Bogart, with his sense of teasing misadventure and stupid practical jokes. She wondered how Bogart—or who Bogart—was doing. "You're a hopeless case, you know that?" she said wryly.

Alex nodded. "I wouldn't have it any other way. Now, speaking about my brother, remember that it's my fault he impersonated our cousin to get back at you. It was all a joke."

Sam gave him a quelling look. "Yes, Alex, I know. You're a riot, a laugh a minute."

"Now answer my question."

"Oh, didn't I?" Sam stared at him. "Perceptive of you to notice. Guess you have a head on your shoulders after all. Who would have thought, with those dirty stunts you pulled."

"Ow." Alex slapped a hand over his chest dramatically. "You wounded me."

Sam shook her head. "We're on duty here. Stop clowning around. I'd hate to see you stoned."

Alex snickered. "Nic feels the same way. Now I understand why Nic is so crazy for you. You're both too bossy."

Rolling her eyes, she laughed, but secretly she was jumping up and down. Did Nic really care so much? If he felt a fourth of what she felt for him, then maybe they had a chance.

Suddenly serious, Alex stared into Sam's eyes and willed her to believe. "It's true. I've never seen Nic like this with any other female. You're in his head and his heart."

In spite of herself, Sam's smile grew brighter.

Alex chortled. "See, you do care for Nic! I think you might just be as crazy about him as he is for you."

"Well, aren't you smart? Wipe that knowing smirk off your face, buster, and pay attention to our job. I'd hate to have to tell Nic that his little brother is a statue on top of a statue, target practice for pigeons."

"All right boss, you win. I'll behave."

And Alex was true to his words.

As the time passed, sometimes they talked, and sometimes they settled into a comfortable silence. The clock continued to tick. Two hours passed, and the fog thickened like a great gray blanket wrapping itself around the lower half of the city.

The call of a guard finally broke their thoughts, letting them know it was time to go. A reluctant Sam and a bored Alex slowly descended.

Boarding the ferry back to the city, both were lost in thought. She had failed tonight, and Sam didn't like that one little bit. Failure was not an option. The gorgon was out there, and she wasn't wrong about the Statue. For some reason, the Meduse had skipped his sexual hi-jinks tonight. But that didn't mean he would tomorrow or the night after that.

After the ferry landed, the crowd disappeared quickly into the gray fog, leaving Alex and Sam alone.

Life was a bitch at times like these, Sam thought ruefully. She felt like kicking somebody, hard. She had prepared herself for something to happen, and the gorgon hadn't shown. Ruefully, she shook her head as they headed for a street corner where they might hail a cab.

"I'll never live this down. And I hate like hell to admit it, but I guess Nic was right, at least about tonight. What rotten luck. And I just bet that Forest fires off some damn joke that's gonna make me want to kick her."

Alex slung his arm around her shoulder as they lurched forward into the white-gray darkness, their footsteps sounding a pitter-patter on the gritty, wet pavement.

"No, that book was most likely correct. I think your hunch is a good one. I like it. Just because the Meduse didn't show tonight doesn't mean he won't tomorrow."

Sam laughed half-heartedly, for he'd echoed her own thoughts. She chucked him on the chin. "Gee, thanks, kid."

Their banter was halted by a woman's scream, a woman who had been driven beyond terror. The shrillness of her cry was unforgettable. Again the unknown woman screamed, and Alex was off like a shot back towards the harbor and quickly swallowed up by the fog.

Sam followed, trying to get her bearings while surrounded by the chalky gray mist, feeling lost and alone in this dreamscape where nothing seemed real. Ahead of her she heard the sound of a body falling, a woman's horrified gasp, and the sound of clothing tearing; this was followed closely by growling.

Quickening her pace, she almost ran over a woman lying unconscious on the ground, but who was still very much flesh and blood, which was a good sign as far as Sam could tell. Touching fingers to the unconscious woman's neck, Sam quickly found a pulse. The woman was fine; she'd just fainted, probably due to the horrific sight she'd seen.

And it *was* horrific, Sam realized, gulping noisily and taking in the battle before her. There were two combatants: the Meduse and a huge black wolf.

"A wolf?" Sam questioned, blinking her eyes rapidly to see if she was hallucinating. It wasn't everyday a girl saw a gorgon doing battle with a really big wolf. But she wasn't hallucinating, and the gorgon charged.

Sam gasped. The gorgon was both awesome and awful, a sight to make sore eyes. He had a beautiful face but a forked tongue. Claws extended from his fingers; long wicked claws. They weren't as long as Freddy Krueger's, who Sam felt could use a really good manicure, but long enough, and razor sharp.

In repulsed fascination Sam stared at Nero's head, which was misshapen from a full mane of snake hair. The snakes were hissing, coiling and uncoiling, and so his coif was a real fright.

"Talk about a bad hair day," Sam muttered to herself, and she withdrew the golden sword she'd hidden in her trench coat. That hair was just awful—appalling really, the poor monster. "You could use a real makeover, fang-bangs."

Hearing her words, the Meduse turned to face Sam fully, to judge the threat. Then he rapidly snapped his attention back to the snarling wolf, who was crouched low, ready to spring, white fangs glistening in the nearby lamplight.

Snarling, the black wolf charged, rushing low, his fangs sinking into the gorgon's thigh. Then he lept back keeping far enough away from the snake heads to prevent being bitten.

The gorgon howled in pain, and blood spurted from his wound. Reacting in rage and pain, he clawed the wolf in the lower right flank, scoring the skin with three deep gashes. Just at that moment, the unconscious woman regained consciousness. Wild-eyed and shrieking, she ran off into the night.

Now that the woman was gone, Sam didn't have to worry about protecting her anymore; she charged into the thick of the battle. Swinging her sword in a wide arc . . . she managed to miss the gorgon's neck by a good four inches.

Luckily, the sword did bite into the gorgon's back, and he howled with pain and rage. Retaliating swiftly, the Meduse caught Sam across her shoulder with a tremendous swipe, and knocked her on her butt.

She landed hard, jarring her spine, shooting radiating twinges of pain throughout her body. Scrambling for her sword she got painfully back to her feet, waiting for another chance to attack as the wolf barely missed being bitten by their enemy's dreadful locks.

Raising her sword to attack again, Sam muttered, "Next time Prince V. gets me a weapon, it damn well better be twenty pounds lighter."

The wolf bit hard into the gorgon's other side just as Sam charged. Unfortunately, her sword slipped just as she managed to raise it high enough to swing. This time, she clipped the gorgon on the arm.

Nero's reprisal was again swift. His blow caught her hard on the back and sent her crashing to the ground; this time she hit her forehead against the gritty pavement. Yep, the mean streets of New York were living up to their reputation tonight, she mused dimly.

Shaking her head, Sam rolled over, sword in hand and prepared to be caught by a snake in the ass. Stunned, she watched the gorgon spin around and run off into the cold, thick fog, hissing as he went and holding his torn and bloody side.

My, What Big Teeth You Have

Her vision blurred, Sam slowly maneuvered herself into a half-sitting position; she had just gotten her butt kicked good. At the same time she became aware of the enormous black wolf standing over her. What rotten luck, she thought grimly. She had survived an attack of a gorgon and lived to tell the tale, only to be eaten by big, bad wolf.

Too dazed to do much more, she raised her hands to defend her neck and face. But instead of ripping out her throat, the wolf edged closer and licked the cut on her forehead, whimpering.

His tongue felt like scratchy sandpaper, but somehow managed to be comforting. After he licked her forehead, the wolf laid his head in her lap, and Sam ran her fingers through his thick fur.

At the petting, the wolf seemed to sigh, then stuck his head in her crotch. About the same time, a dazed Sam put two and two together—Alex's clothing shredded on the wet, glistening pavement, the wolf's black hair and massive size, and the deep soulful gray eyes—and got four.

She was nobody's fool. Quickly recognizing the werewolf for who he was, she bopped him on the head. "Alex, if you sniff my crotch for one more second I'll rip out all your fur with my bare hands!"

The wolf crawled backward, his head lowered in a submissive pose.

Standing slowly, her body aching, Sam griped, "Oh give me a break. Cut the innocent act, Alex. You're about as blameless as Ivan the Terrible. And as you need obedience lessons, I'll take it up with Nic."

Alex whined.

Ignoring him, Sam smacked her forehead, forgetting momentarily about the sore spot. Pointing a finger at the guilty wolf, she berated him.

"You're a Russian werewolf in New York—another secret Nic didn't tell me! You're masters of sleazy secrets. You and your lying, sneaking pack of brothers. Damn! Where are my silver bullets when I need them?"

Alex ducked his head under his forepaw, his tail ceasing to thump.

"Nuts! I could really bust your chops. You and that lying dog of a brother. Why didn't you guys tell me you were werewolves? Damn, but you shapeshifters are a closemouthed bunch, aren't you? First Ripley, and now you. I can't believe Nic didn't tell me he's not human!"

Sam was off on the rant, and Alex whimpered again, his pose staying totally submissive.

"Don't duck your head, you four-pawed Judas! I'm on to your game."

Sam began to pace, jabbing an accusatory finger at Alex as she walked.

"I should have seen this coming a mile away. Cousin to a vampire, and really, really knowledgeable about the supernatural. That wild, musky scent that's all Nic. The way he made love to me like a wild animal. But then, he's ruled by his nature, isn't he? Yeah, that's right. The man's a wolf! Boy, would Charles Darwin have a field day with you guys!"

Alex nudged her leg, looking up at her with big puppy dog eyes, imploring her to forgive the family deception.

"I've always been a sucker for dogs," Sam admitted. "All right, all right. I know you probably saved my life. Saved by a werewolf from a gorgon—who would have thought it?" She shook her head, nudging Alex away again. "But I helped save your skin too, buster, so don't forget it. We're lucky to get out of here with our skins intact!"

Glancing down at Alex, she ruefully shook her head. "Of course, you *didn't* get out of here with your skin intact, since you're all furred up. Still, we're alive and kicking—or howling, as the case may be," she muttered.

Sam started to pace, giving the werewolf a long hard glare. "Nic should have told me. I'm a Paranormalbuster. I can keep a secret. I wouldn't have ratted you guys out to anybody."

Alex whined, looking sweet, which got to Sam again. "I know, I know! A werewolf's gotta do what a werewolf's gotta do. Well, so does a woman. I'm going to kill Nic. Leader of the pack or not, I'll rip into him like nobody's business! He's a werewolf in creep's clothing."

With those words, Alex changed back. His fur dispersed, his bones popped and his jaws receded, and Sam was stunned by the transformation's beauty. Golden light formed a halo around him.

Alex rose to a standing position, wincing. Glancing down at the marks on his right buttock, he fingered them. They were only long red scratches now, with purple bruising, due to the healing characteristics of his metabolism.

"This is going to be sore for a couple of days," he said.

Her arms across her chest, her stance militant, Sam looked anything but sympathetic. "I don't know, I kind of think it's justice. You yourself have been one big pain in the butt."

"Nic's going to kill me. You seeing me naked and all."

Sam shrugged dismissively, although the naked Strakhov was a fine specimen of male. "Like I care? You haven't got anything I haven't seen before." Tugging off her trench coat, she handed it to Alex, her silence damning.

Alex assumed a hangdog expression. Looking guilty, he pulled the coat on, his arms four inches longer than the sleeves. It barely closed in front as he tied the belt.

"I suppose you're the real thing? Werewolves by birth, not by bite?" Sam asked.

"That's right. Actually, we're descended from a long line of werewolves. A royal line. Nic's a prince." Recalling Nic's face and hauteur, Sam could have kicked herself for not surmising so sooner. "How could I have forgotten? Russia used to be overrun with princes before the Revolution. So, why should I be surprised?" Glaring at Alex disgustedly, Sam gave up. This dog had fleas, even if he was the wrong dog.

"Come on, let's go. I've got a wolfman to see."

Alex hesitated. "What about the woman Nero attacked? What happened to her? I lost sight of her during the battle."

"She's okay. She ran off in the opposite direction."

"Just think," Alex remarked, his chest puffed out with pride. "I ran the gorgon off!"

"Get a grip. It wasn't just you; it was the odds. Two against one."

"Well, it certainly wasn't your swordplay," Alex riposted.

"I never claimed to be the Highlander."

"And I guess I can live without any pats on the head for saving that girl's life and yours," Alex groused.

"Be thankful I don't make Nic take you to obedience school. You deserve it, you know." She looked down and smoothed out her clothing.

"Touchy, touchy, aren't you? If you weren't that good at sword fighting, why didn't you practice before this?" Alex asked. He knew Sam was a professional and professionals usually didn't slip up like that.

"Who says I didn't?" Sam said.

Alex's eyes widened. "You practiced today?"

"Most of it. I just didn't get much better."

Eyeing her up and down, Alex exclaimed, "That's hard to believe. I thought you were good at everything you do."

"Not fencing." Sheepishly, she admitted, "I flunked it in college."

Alex snorted, amused.

"Twice."

He broke into laughter. "Wait until I tell my big brother!"

"Wait until I tell him that you were sniffing my crotch. He'll rip off your nose and lower parts best left unmentioned."

Alex actually shuddered. "You're just no fun, Sam. What ever does my hardheaded brother see in you?" Grabbing her arm, he hurried her off into the foggy night, their footsteps ringing on the pavement. Their voices became echoes.

"Bossy wench."

"Dog breath!"

The Laws of Attraction Between a Werewolf and a Woman

Sam sought Nic in his room at the Transylvania Hotel, leaving Alex to explain to Prince Varinski and the rest of the group what had transpired at the Statue of Liberty. Pounding on his door, she tapped her foot impatiently while waiting for Nic to answer, which he did in a pair of jeans and nothing else.

Shoving her way past, Sam searched the room. With relief she saw that Nic was totally alone.

"Where's that Irish potato biter?" Sam snapped, her back to Nic. She had plenty to say, but as she turned and saw his hard muscular chest, and the thin line of dark hair disappearing into his low-slung jeans, her mouth had a mind of its own. She wasn't made of stone. Although, if Nero had his way . . .

"Forest is down on six, with Petroff and the others in my cousin's room. Why? Did you think she'd be up here with me?"

"Where else? She's all over you like a fungus."

Nic laughed. He moved closer, and his laughter died as he saw her beat-up face and the blood in her hair. She looked like death warmed over, and by someone who didn't know how to cook.

He tenderly touched the cut on her forehead, where a purple knot was forming. "You're hurt."

"A lot you care," Sam retorted. She wasn't sure why she was acting so hostile.

"But I do. If you only knew. You're like some kind of disease I didn't want to catch, but I can't shake the bug now that I have it," he said. He smoothed a strand of lose hair behind her ear.

Sam batted his hand away. "Oh, great! I make you sick, is that what you're saying?"

"That's not what I mean and you know it. Now, what happened? How'd you get into trouble? If you didn't go to the Statue of Liberty—"

Stabbing a finger down at her muddy and ripped jeans, Sam interrupted, "I did. And, Mr. Know-It-All Nic, guess where Nero was tonight?" He had made light of her hunch, but her hunch had been right on the mark. He should have backed it.

Nic started cussing in Russian, German, and maybe Chinese—Sam wasn't sure, not being a scholar of Asian languages.

"I can't believe it. The one place I felt sure you'd be reasonably safe, and you got attacked!"

Glaring at him, hands on hips, she said caustically, "Poor you, being wrong. All things considered, I would have preferred being at American Gothic with you and Ms. Pining-for-You Forest. It's lots more fun standing around than being tossed on my head by some snake-haired man."

Nic felt a blast of terror. "What happened? Is Alex alright?"

Observing the worry in his eyes, Sam quickly explained what had occurred outside the Statue of Liberty; she didn't want him to fear for his brother. She could wait to blast him for his wolfish secret, since everything was relative.

Taking things from the beginning, she led Nic through the night's events, telling him all that had happened, with a few minor exceptions: She left out her seeing Alex naked and Alex's head in her crotch.

As Nic listened, his fists clenched and unclenched in anger, and the muscle in his jaw began to tick. The two of them might have been stoned tonight! He was furious; but then, so was Sam. And to be honest, Sam didn't seem nearly as angry about almost being made a rock woman and losing her quarry as she was about Alex turning into a werewolf. Suddenly a thought struck him, hard, smack-dab and dead center, and he was aware of just how mad Sam really was. And why. She knew he was a werewolf.

A little late, Nic tried to gather Sam into his arms. She backed away, shouting, "You secretive sneak! You four-footed beast! You impersonating impostor! You're a wolf in creep's clothing and you didn't bother to mention it!"

She'd called him worse, Nic realized. There was yet hope. He had a lot riding on what he said next, and he needed to proceed with caution to take the bite out of his words.

Hands on hips, eyes flashing, she snarled, "You . . . Marxist werewolf, you!"

Nic shook his head like a dog shakes off water. Of all the names she could have shouted, he wasn't expecting that. "I've been called names before, but never that. I'll have to give you an A for originality." He laughed.

"You cold-blooded Russian werewolf! You *royal* cold-blooded Russian werewolf! What other secrets are you keeping? Do you have a wife somewhere? Do you moonlight as a spook? Do you wear women's underwear? Were you alive during the Russian Revolution? Do you get dipped for fleas once a month?"

Nic addressed the second to last question; the others were not deserving of an answer. "I was a young boy during the Revolution, yes."

Sam's mouth opened to continue her rant—she was just getting started—but his words stopped her dead in her tracks. He'd been a boy in 1918, which made him really old. "You . . . look younger," she muttered finally. Was he too old for her?

Nic stared at her, as if reading her mind. "For an expert about these things, you really aren't using your head. You know we age slower than humans—about a year to your three."

Now it was Sam's turn to shake her head—like a dog, even though she wasn't related to any. Nic *was* too old for her; decades too old. He'd probably fought in World War II and knew Stalin personally. He'd actually had to live behind the iron curtain—not a pleasant situation for a werewolf, as they were allergic to iron. Yep, this man was *old*. If only he weren't also such a rugged, virile, magnificent male. "I hate your lying werewolf guts," she snapped.

She regretted the words the instant they left her mouth. *Well, wasn't that mature,* she thought. She should have just settled for a left hook to the groin.

She clasped her fist and raised it, then lowered it again.

"Why stop pulling punches now?" he growled.

Sam sniffed. "I believe in keeping something in reserve."

"Come on, Sam, don't be mad at me."

"Mad? Oh, I'm not mad. I'm howling furious. Or I would be howling if I were one of *your* kind. You should be horsewhipped," she stated emphatically, then hesitated a moment and corrected, "wolf-whipped, for all the secrets you've kept from me. And now you say you care? What a dog you are."

She was wound up and going strong. "How can I ever trust you? First you pretend to be Prince of the Playbats. Well, you really are a Prince, just not Prince Varinksi, who happens to be your cousin. Later I think you're a wolfish competitor, my arch business rival. Now I find out you're a *were*wolf, pretending to be human, who once pretended to be a vampire. Just what will I find out next?"

When Nic opened his mouth to defend himself, Sam sliced her hand through the air. "Don't answer. I know what you are—a first-rate jerk!"

Nic thought for a minute she might punch him, but she didn't. He didn't know why he found this ranting and raving fascinating, but he did. He didn't know why he liked these violent tendencies in her, but he did. Probably it was due to his werewolf DNA. "Come on, Sammy, you're making a mountain out of a mothball.""

"That's a molehill!" she shrieked. "Trust is not a molehill!"

"You know you can trust me, even with your life. I

only pretended to be something I'm not because of the business situation. But that won't happen anymore. You know all my secrets," he swore, his gray eyes smoldering with sincerity and concern. "Honestly, I'm telling you the truth and nothing but the truth now."

He looked so good, standing there half-naked. He smelled so good, too, with his woodsy, musky scent. She weakened. "I might trust you now and then."

Nic smiled.

Annoyed, Sam added one final thought. "But you'll just have to guess when. Maybe I'll trust you tomorrow, maybe next year. Maybe the year 2075. Of course, I'll be dead by then, but you might still be around—alive and licking."

Eyes darkening in anger, Nic cursed. Why was she not more forgiving? It seemed he would have to crawl, something a Strakhov just did not do. "I know what you want, Sam. You want me to crawl on my hands and knees and beg your forgiveness."

"In human form," she agreed. Somehow, a begging werewolf would use its puppy dog eyes and she'd cave in and rain kisses all over his handsome snout.

Pride always went before a fall. Nic fell. Dropping to his knees, his expression taut with disapproval at what he was doing, he said, "I'm truly sorry, Sam, for hurting you, for lying to you, and for not telling you about my heritage. And that is the whole truth."

"You wouldn't know the truth if it bit you on the behind," she grumped.

Controlling his anger, Nic explained, "I meant to tell you sooner about my heritage, but I wanted to wait until you had forgiven me for all the other stuff. Stuff you had every right to be angry about." He nuzzled her hand. "You've got me down on my knees, and you can have me eating out of your hand if you just whistle, Sam. I'm yours—beast and all."

Sam almost gave up, gave in; the man had too much animal appeal. But then, that was the nature of this beast. With willpower she didn't know she possessed, she backed away, maintaining her dignity. "Get up, Nic. I'll accept your apologies, but I won't forgive you."

Nic was on his feet in less than a second, accepting her challenge. He moved quickly, gracefully, and caught both her hands and forced them around behind her back. He hauled her resisting body against his own, took swift advantage. "Whistle for me, Sam—whistle because you're going to be mine."

Lowering his head, he kissed her long and hard, a ruthless kiss. It was a kiss of possession that devoured her, tasted and lastly cherished her. He had been too long without her, and the wolf in him had finally recognized its mate.

Sam didn't want to respond, but she couldn't help herself. He tasted of the richness of the earth and dark pleasure. His arms were strong and warm against her, holding her to him, pinning her. She could feel his desire, which increased her own. She was ready and able.

Unfortunately, she wasn't quite willing. Making a monumental effort, she pulled away from his questing lips. "It's too much, Nic. I need time to think. I . . . You hurt me bad."

Glancing down at the huge bulge straining the zipper of his jeans, he remarked, "I'm hurting myself. How do you expect me to get any sleep?"

She grinned impishly. "You could try counting sheep. If you don't eat them first." And then she walked out of his hotel room, trying to feel proud of her self-control.

Who's That Knocking at My Door?

Twenty minutes later, Sam had showered and was pacing her hotel room. Her hormones in overdrive, her overactive imagination had Nic buck naked and cavorting upon her hotel bed. It was an appealing image.

So, he had crawled and begged for forgiveness. Well, maybe not begged, Sam admitted, but he had asked for her to forgive him and had been on his knees. To have a werewolf prince on his knees—what more could a Paranormalbuster want?

Tapping her fingers on the headboard of the bed, she considered the situation. Could she understand why Nic had kept his heritage a secret? Sure, if she were totally honest with herself. She also believed he would have told her sooner or later. So why she was pacing in her room when she could be making love to the Russian werewolf of her dreams? Quickly she made her decision. Who was she going to call?

Nic stepped out of a long, cold shower, his body still aching with lust. The phone rang, and he grumpily picked it up. A long sharp whistle pierced his eardrums.

Sam!

After grabbing his jeans, he made it to her room in less than three seconds. Pounding hard, he found himself grinning like a fool. She had forgiven him! Hadn't she?

Behind the door, Sam wore a sneaky smile. She wasn't a dumb broad with spaghetti for brains; she knew exactly who was knocking on her door. The big bad wolf, of course, and he could come and be as bad as he wanted—provided he was bad with her. For his loving, she was a piggy, and she was ready to see him huff, puff, and get down to the blowing.

Sliding back the bolt and dropping her towel, she grinned. Werewolves sure could move fast when they needed to.

As the door flew open, Nic charged inside. His nostrils flared. He scented his prey and her spicy arousal, and his gray eyes shimmered with barely suppressed passion. He worshipped her body with those eyes.

Sam lost herself in those swirling gray depths. This man was a beast—wasn't she lucky? She could feel the tips of her nipples tingling, longed to have him bite and suckle them. The flesh puckered with white-hot heat, and she felt the area between her thighs grow damp. Parting her mouth in an open invitation, the tip of her tongue snaked out, wetting her lips.

Nic swept her into his arms, kicking the door shut and then dropping Sam onto the hotel's bed with a big bounce. The minute he had heard her whistle, he had gone into heat . . . werewolf mating mode, needing to possess Sam completely. He needed to mark her as his for all time. All others needed to know and beware.

Desire made Sam's eyes heavy as she stared up at her wolfman. He growled, looking like he was going to gobble her up—and now that she knew he was a werewolf, that was a distinct possibility. Thinking fast, she decided to keep still, to wait to see just what he decided to gobble.

Nic's desire crashed against him in waves, like an ocean gone mad. He didn't know how much longer he could wait; Sam was stretched out nude before him like a banquet. Growling again, he crouched between her knees, spreading her legs wider as he leaned down and took her in his mouth. Her spicy, wild scent drove him crazy. She tasted of warm honey and musk.

Nic gobbled, licked and sucked, and Sam realized she had landed smack-dab in the middle of paradise. Her nerves were screaming with pleasure. As wave after wave of ecstasy washed through her, moaning and writhing she called out his name over and over. Finally she erupted in a climax that had her crying.

Sliding up to kiss her, Nic said, "Remember, sweetheart?"

She nodded. "It's all coming back to me now. I'm a fool to have made us wait this long." She sighed.

He didn't agree or disagree; he simply parted her thighs and eased himself between them. His enormous length filled her in one thrust, and raw, primal sensations took over them both.

"Welcome home, peter," she whispered throatily.

"Oh, Sam, you feel so good, so hot, so sweet . . ." Nic gasped, his breaths short.

Kissing his neck, Sam urged him on. She was ready for the wild ride to come.

Sucking her nipple into his mouth, Nic laved it with his tongue, while he set up a hard-driving rhythm. His sex filled her over and over, reaching ever deeper into her wet and throbbing core.

He groaned.

She moaned.

His hand on her hips tightened as her fingers clutched his buttocks, digging in. Nic felt like he was king of the world, his emotions in wild flux. This female made him hunger like no other. She made him wild with need, and when he was inside her he was happier than he had ever been in his whole life and more fulfilled. He kept up the pace, losing himself in this paradise he had almost lost.

Sam cried out. The sound echoed in the room, and Nic saw her eyes flare. She bucked against him, soaring higher and higher into the heavens of pleasure. Her expression was like a ghost ascending who had finally found its way home after a long and empty time on earth.

"Oh, baby," she panted in violent pleasure. The world began to shimmer and fade. It was only she and Nic, together, soaring through the skies, their heartbeats matching, their movements in perfect accord.

Nic covered her mouth in a fierce kiss. His hard thrusts incited her into another long, heartrending climax, one of both emotional and physical impact. She came violently as Nic shouted her name, and his own release was so explosive that it went on and on and on.

He tenderly kissed her, rolling over, taking her with him. After a few moments of postcoital bliss, he remarked smugly, "I guess you've forgiven me."

"What gives you that impression?" she replied.

His eyes roamed her body. A smirk graced his handsome face, and he kissed her forehead. Sam loved every minute of it.

"So, I'm a sucker for a fast-running, sexy-biting, sweet-talking werewolf," she admitted.

"I take that as forgiveness."

"Smart man."

Wrinkling her nose, Sam lay her head on his chest and said, "I'm not a one-night stand, anymore—or even an hour-and-a-half lean."

"You never were, Sam." Staring into her gorgeous blues, he asked, "Do you believe me yet?"

"Yes." Nic was her wild thing. He made her heart sing, was a wild man in the bed, beside the bed, or under it. She loved him for his intensity as well as his kindness. This wolfman also got her jokes, and that was saying a lot.

Nic was the best man ever. He was one werewolf in a million, and she respected him for his business abilities, his humor and his intelligence, and she'd begun to understand his arrogance and chauvinism. She was crazy for his thick wavy black hair, the twinkle in his gray eyes and the way he looked at her like she was the most beautiful woman he had ever seen—even when she was having her worst hair day. And that meant something to a woman in a business where being too feminine got a girl killed.

"Forgiven and forgotten?" Nic questioned, running his fingers through the strands of her hair.

"Forgotten? Don't press your luck, buster."

Nic snorted. Sam was so wonderfully stubborn, he wanted to roar in approval since she was now his and his alone. "Don't press it? But I want to—again and again and again." He pushed his body against her.

She giggled. "Well, I might allow that. And I might consider forgetting all the bad stuff if you let me groom you when you're in wolf form."

Lifting his head, he studied the pinkish blush on her soft skin. "You're not bothered by my turning furry and clawed, are you?"

"Nope. We Paranormalbusters must take it all in stride. All in a night's work. Just another unnatural occurrence in another ordinary day."

Nic laughed and hugged her close. "What a lucky wolf I am. A human woman who doesn't mind my ancestry, and who only wants to groom me. Sure, Sam. Anytime."

"And you won't mind me putting a red bow in your hair?" she asked slyly.

Dropping his head back to the pillow, he gave her a whack on the butt. "Grooming, yes. Ribbons, no."

"Can't blame a girl for trying," she giggled.

Pulling her up so that they were turned face to face, he tenderly ran his fingers over her lips and nose. "You've bewitched me, Sam. All you have to do is laugh, breathe or wiggle your nose, and I want you." The feelings were fresh and new and frightening, but they were also exhilarating and erotic.

She kissed him. "And all *you* have to do is enter a room and I go all mushy inside." She was crazy about Nic, and he was crazy about her. Maybe they could merge their businesses and, even better, maybe they could merge their lives!

"You drive me crazy. I hunger for you so much that I doubt I'll ever get enough."

"Yeah, and you're better than a Hershey's bar," Sam admitted, half teasing, half not.

"The height of compliments. Now who's sweet-talking?"

Sam giggled.

"What's so funny?"

"When I opened the door tonight, I thought you were going to pounce on me."

"That's what wolves do when they're starving. And I was ravenous," Nic admitted. He nuzzled her ear.

"Well; I liked it. You know, Nicolas Petroff Strakhov, you can be a real jerk at times, but you're an irresistible jerk." Sam kissed his chest.

"And I think you've broken Pete. He's limp from all the hard work he just did," he teased. Glancing down at his flaccid flesh he made a face of mock sorrow.

Grinning evilly, Sam slid down his body. It was time to behead the Czar. Beginning a conversation with Pete, she praised and lavished him with kisses and sucking until he was Great again. It was indeed just what the weary, headstrong fellow had needed to rise to the occasion.

Sliding back up, she asked Nic pertly, "How's everyone down there now?"

"Perfect, just like you," Nic growled. And flipping

her over on her hands and knees, he put his head of state back in the Kremlin. He was home.

Transported again to paradise, Sam laughed. Who would have thought she'd love it doggie style?

Nic at Night and Nic in the Morning

Sam awoke and glanced out the window of the hotel. It was still night, though the sky was beginning to gray. She felt fantastic wrapped in Nic's arms, her back pressed against his hard body. The light from the bathroom revealed the bedsheet had slipped down to their hips, and as she glanced down at her breasts, she saw two prominent hickeys. She grinned. If she was going to lie down with werewolves, she was going to get bit.

Eight million stories in the Big Apple, and now hers was one of them. The Russian werewolf in New York with the American Parnormalbuster from Vermont; it would make a great movie of the week on the Ghost Network.

Snuggling closer to Nic's hot body, Sam knew that she should let sleeping werewolves lie; she was sore this morning from their all-night marathon. But as memories of their passion curled around her, she began to feel like she needed the hair of the dog that bit her. She wriggled herself against his crotch, smiling happily when she heard him growl.

Before the growl finished he'd grabbed her and turned her over for a passionate good morning kiss. Unfortunately it was interrupted by a knocking on the door. They drew apart and cursed.

"I'll get it," he snarled, yanking on his jeans and flipping on the bedroom light. "And I'll break the neck of whoever it is for interrupting us."

Sliding on her robe, Sam smiled ruefully as Nic opened the door.

Alex rushed in, fairly bursting at the seams. Seeing Nic and Sam half-dressed, a grin split his face from ear to ear.

"Nic wasn't in his room, so I took a guess and tried here," he said. He gleefully rubbed his hands together. "So, you two mule-headed people have finally gotten together." Taking in the destruction, the sheets and pillows on the floor, he added, "Looks like a hurricane hit here—Hurricane Strakhov."

"Alex!" Nic warned. There was an unspoken threat. He didn't want his practical-joking brother to embarrass Sam after the special night they had just shared, and he wasn't taking any chances. "This had better be good."

"Oh, it is," his baby brother confided, his eyes glittering with excitement. "We got a shapeshifter—a panther—who says he knows Nero from the clubs. He's been out of town hunting, and just got back in. He heard about the deaths in the supernatural community from Ripley. Four nights ago he was walking a girl he met in Club Dread to the subway station, and he saw Nero sneaking off into the tunnels. He thought it was odd that Nero was doing that, since it's more than obvious Nero's no homeless guy."

"I don't get it. Why would Nero be hiding out in the tunnels under the city? He has money, and New York is huge, a no-man's-land with plenty of places to hide." Nic chewed his lip thoughtfully, his brow furrowed in concentration.

Tapping her fingers on the headboard of the bed, Sam exclaimed, "I can't believe I forgot! Vanderbilt—of the railroad Vanderbilts—was said to have built a Greek pavilion to park his own personal railroad car. It's only rumor, and I've never found it on any map, but I do know that the Vanderbilts used to live near the St. James Church over on Hudson Street."

"So you think Nero is so homesick that he lives underground in an aging Greek pavilion?" Nic asked cautiously. He thought hard about the possibility. It seemed idiotic, but then so had the Statue of Liberty idea.

"I was right about the Statue," Sam pointed out. "I bet I'm dead-on about this. It makes sense. Nero has been hibernating for centuries in Italy, probably somewhere underground. He probably feels comfortable in a pavilion below the earth."

"I guess I can see that," Nic remarked, still a little skeptical.

"Yes," Sam said excitedly.

"All right, we buy the story. Now, which subway station did this panther see him at?" Nic asked, his heartbeat accelerating at the possibly of a good hunt.

"He couldn't remember exactly, since he doesn't live in this part of town and he'd drunk some Warlock's Blood at the club," Alex replied, knowing himself how potent the drink was, a beverage made from the blood of pigs and spiced and bespelled by a prince warlock. "He said they walked by Jeremy B.'s Cellar. You remember, the bar that used to be the old Falk biker vampire hangout. Now's it's run by biker wolfmen. It's the place on the corner of Eastwood and Hutton street."

Nic nodded.

"The panther guy said he turned right by St. James Church—the church where that Lansberry artist designed that eight-foot angel guarding the shepherd."

Sam put in her two cents: "The subway station is two to three blocks after the church, but before you get to Hell's Kitchen. Good thing, too. Hell's Kitchen is now a big devil hangout, and we've got enough troubles without adding one or two of them to the mix. Does Prince V. know?"

"Yeah, I alerted the whole gang. Our cousin is using his connections to get maps of the underground tunnels, since those shafts can stretch for miles. He's also getting us some equipment we'll need: miner's helmets with lights, flashlights and stuff. Petroff said he'd meet us downstairs in twenty minutes."

"So, what are we waiting for? Let's get going!" Sam's eyes were bright with anticipation. She wished that her baby brother could be along, knowing Bogie would be ready at the drop of a hat to rock and roll all over this gargon. She supposed it was safer if he wasn't here.

"How about getting dressed?" Alex teased, staring pointedly at her blue terry cloth robe.

Blushing, Sam admitted, "I forgot." Grabbing her jeans and a lumberjack shirt, she headed for the bathroom. Nic intercepted her.

"Where do you think you're going?" he asked.

"Where do you think?" What was wrong with him now? They had a strong lead, and she was chomping the bit to get at it.

"You stay here and coordinate the effort. Direct reinforcements if any are needed."

"Have you gone loco?"

"Look, Sam, there's no need for you to put your neck on the line when Alex and I are here."

She rolled her eyes. "Nic, get a grip. Get on board the train to the twenty-first century. Women everywhere are right now screaming 'chauvinist' at you."

Grabbing her shoulders, he pressed his fingers into the soft skin. "You could get *stoned*."

"I'm a big girl. I don't faint at the first sign of danger. This is my job. I'm a Paranormalbuster, for Pete's sake." Glancing down, she added, "Well, I don't mean *that* pete. And I'm going. It's a done deal—either I go with you guys, or I go it alone."

Seeing the grim resolution in Sam's eyes, Nic knew to give up the ghost. He might not like it; he might hate the possibility of losing Sam, but Sam she was. He knew good and well that this woman would carry out her threat. Why he was crazy about such a difficult female, he didn't understand. But he was. He had no choice.

Glancing at the bathroom door, which Sam had just shut, he shook his head. "I don't want her to go, so what do I do?" he asked himself.

"Roll over and play dead," Alex suggested cheerfully. "With a woman like Sam, you'll always either be in the doghouse or howling in delight."

Nic growled in agreement.

The Resident Evil
in the Tunnels of New York

An excited Alex, a taut Nic, a vibrating Ripley and a curious Sam all rode in one cab over to St. James Church; Boris, Natasha and Petroff rode in another. From the church they walked on, finding the subway station they sought only a few blocks farther. It was on the intersection of Pierce and Mirren Streets.

All were aware the clock was ticking on their search and destroy mission. Prince Varinksi could withstand several hours of daylight, but Natasha and Boris would fall into a deep sleep by midmorning. Nero must be vanquished long before high noon.

Once they were downstairs and in the subway tracks, the group split into three, each covering one of the tunnels that snaked off into the darkness of the underground perpetual night. Boris and Alex took the tunnel on the right, while Natasha and Prince Varinski took the one in the middle. This left Nic, Sam and Ripley the tunnel on the left. They had decided earlier that one of these tunnels was probably the one that held the Greek pavilion Vanderbilt built, and they were prepared to find the city below the earth where the disenfranchised and hopeless now lived.

Everyone donned their helmets, checked the battery lights and their water canteens, and began to walk into the eternal darkness. All of the others in the group were nocturnal except for Sam, which gave them a distinct advantage, but the pitch-blackness was so deep and dark that even preternatural predators needed help in seeing what lay ahead. Wishing each other well, the groups each headed off toward their date with destiny.

The shafts extended in straight lines through a world of utter blackness, a forgotten land of tunnels and cavernlike rooms beneath the earth, far from the harsh light of day or the soft glow of the moon. As Nic, Ripley and Sam followed their assigned tunnel, the air became musty with a strong odor of decay and moldy earth. Their lights cast gloomy shadows on the tunnel walls.

In less than a mile, the tunnel began to twist and turn, descending, and Nic slowed his step and said; "Sam, you stick close to me."

Noticing the tiny red eyes that watched her balefully from the shadows, and the sound of soft furry feet scrambling in the darkness, she remarked firmly, "You're kidding, right? I'm on you like feathers on a duck's back."

Nic snorted, amused.

"I really hate rats, you know," she said. "I'm glad you're not one anymore." Her skin crawled in apprehension.

In spite of the tension he was feeling, Nic laughed. He had to protect Sam at all costs, though he also wanted this gorgon's head on a platter.

Ripley just shook his head.

Sam felt a faint breeze of air stir. The rotten odor of decay faded, leaving a dusty smell of damp earth. In front of them, highlighted by their helmet lamps, steps led spiraling down into the greater unknown.

"This is creepy, Nic," she said. She was ecstatic that he was with her, for she felt clearly the taint of a cool evil presence seeping out from the great yawning depths. Her heart sped up with fear, and she forced herself to take each step.

Glancing back, Nic gave her a smile of encouragement.

"I had to trap a rogue hooker werefox once, in a mine in Mexico. It wasn't my cup of tea," Sam admitted.

"What happened?" Nic asked. He was curious to know everything about her, past and present and future.

"She'd been slashing up her male customers. Killed one of them. I remember Bogie running her to ground, and we finally trapped her in one of the shafts, trying to coax her out. She had beady brown eyes, and she acted like she couldn't hear us. She was plotting her next move. It was a Mexican stand-off for two days."

"How'd you get the little vixen out?"

"Psychology. I made Bogie dress up as a bunny."

Nic started laughing again, and this time Ripley joined in.

"I kid you not. Worked like a charm. She came out

and gave chase, and I trapped her with some iron netting." As she talked, Sam felt a little less afraid of the big, black unknown. "For months I teased Bogie about it. I said we'd always have a job for him come Easter."

Nic shook his head. His helmet light bobbed, making the shadows dance. "You, Sammy, are a pistol. Don't let anyone tell you different."

Their good humor was cut short as Ripley stumbled on something big and hard. Glancing down, he took a small leap backward. Sam and Nic both moved to stand beside him, their helmets illuminating the reclining figure of what had once been a man. The figure was now just a monument to the Meduse's destructive force, with the expression on his face preserving his terror for eternity.

"Nero's been here," Nic stated gravely. Bending over he inspected the man and the area around him, sniffing the air. "This coffee in this cup here behind him smells three, maybe four days old."

"We're on the right path then," Sam acknowledged grimly, both frightened and innervated by the thrill of the hunt. "Ripley, call Prince V. and the others and let them know we've got a dead one."

Ripley raised his state-of-the-art walkie-talkie to his mouth, but all he got was static. Apparently they were too deep in the ground.

"I guess we should go back and tell the others, since splitting up your forces is just plain stupid," Sam suggested.

But before the other two could agree or disagree, there came the sound of something coming at them from the end of the tunnel they had just traversed.

Both Nic and Ripley fell into a crouch. Sam's light beam ranged into the depths, but it reflected back only blackness.

Suddenly Boris appeared, flying through the air about three feet off the ground. He landed at once, and Nic asked harshly, "What's happened? What's going on?"

Breathing deeply, Boris explained, "We ran into Nero in our tunnel. Alex is hurt bad, Nic. Too bad to transform."

"Did the snakes bite him?" Sam asked, filled with concern.

"No. Nero's claws did the damage, but it's bad. I didn't want to move him without help. So here I am."

"You left him there with Nero around?" Nic growled, his eyes feral.

"Easy, Nic. Nero ran out the way we came in. I think he's going topside," Boris explained. Holding up his arms, he showed the claw marks and dark red stains decorating his own jacket. "I fought, too."

Nic was frantic to get to his brother, but he couldn't leave Sam, who couldn't move as fast as a paranormal. "Alright, let's hurry. Sam, jump on my back and I'll carry you."

She shook her head. "I'll slow you down, and every second counts for Alex. You and Boris go ahead, and Ripley and I will follow."

Nic didn't like the idea of leaving her with the other werewolf; but his brother could be dying. "Alright. Be careful, Sam. Ripley, guard her with your life." And with those words he kissed her on the lips and began to run, following Boris.

Their speed amazed Sam as she watched the lights

of their helmets fading rapidly into the blackness. "Come on, Ripley, let's hurry. I can run for a while." Sam felt distinctly uncomfortable when she saw the man's pupils had dilated and he looked half wolf, but Ripley simply said, "The ground here is too treacherous. We'll walk fast until we get back out into the tunnels. I'll lead."

They walked swiftly for a few minutes, their footsteps in the hard graveled dirt making the only sounds. Sam's mind was focused on Alex, concern for both him and Nic striking at her mind as she placed each foot in front of the other.

Her well-honed senses started screaming that something was wrong, and she felt the hairs on the back of her neck stand up. No, something wasn't right; she couldn't put her finger on what, but she felt it to the core of her being. Her tension mounted, almost suffocating her.

Cautiously, she reached inside her jacket pocket for her dagger. The ancient knife had been fashioned for protection against shapeshifters, since iron, like silver, had been revealed as dangerous to a werewolf; deadly if the metal penetrated either the eye or the heart. The blade had been a birthday gift from her Uncle Myles on her eighteenth birthday, and had cost an arm and leg—though luckily not the arm or the leg of anyone law-abiding.

Unfortunately, Sam didn't have long to wait for her premonition to come true. The enemy revealed himself. Ripley had turned, switching off his lamplight. From her own helmet's beam, Sam saw that the werewolf's eyes had dilated even further, and his claws were extending from the flesh of his hands, sharp and curved. His jaw had elongated, and he looked rather like the beast in the old black and white movie with Lon Chaney, *The Werewolf of London*.

Ripley scrambled to the side, shoving away what looked to be part of the tunnel wall. It was instead a cleverly camouflaged doorway to another tunnel, to another dark and scarier world.

As Ripley worked, Sam turned and began to run, which only incited the werewolf to violence. He leaped and brought her down hard to the ground, his breath harsh and stale on her cheek, his wicked teeth protruding from his half-human jaws.

Thrusting himself against her, he growled, "I can see why Nic has the hots for you. You're built."

Her arms were trapped, and she couldn't reach her dagger. She spit in his face. Ripley slapped her, knocking her head to the side. He leaped up and jerked her roughly to her feet.

"Come on, bitch! We're going in there," he snarled, and he practically threw her through the door.

"What the hell do you think you're doing?" Sam asked as they ascended into a new tunnel. Above and ahead, she could see some kind of light, like a beacon welcoming her into hell.

"What do you think, Miss Paranormalbuster? Use that expertise you're supposed to have."

Getting a damn good idea of what was going on, she tried to stop her shudder of revulsion and terror. "Ripley, I got news for you. Nobody rocks my world except Nic. That includes you and snake hair. I take it you're Nero's wolf, and you brought us here to lure us to our deaths."

"Bravely spoken, bitch—and you're right. You're soon to be stone-cold for eternity."

Unfortunately, Sam was afraid the wolfman was right. She had gotten in over her head, and the next few eons were going to be rocky ones.

Paper, Scissors, Meduse

The short tunnel ended, opening into a large cavernous room lit by lanterns, the kind used for camping. The roof of the cavern had been painted to imitate the night sky. Stars were marked on the ceiling in some kind of luminescent paint, as well as a large full moon. Sam could hear and see the trickle of water that ran down one cavern wall, draining into a small pool.

Below the fake sky was a small Greek pavilion made out of grimy white marble with round circular columns and steplike benches. A marble table was carved in the center, with cushioned chairs. The tabletop had a plate of grapes, grape leaves and what looked like cheese: typical Greek and Roman fare.

Plastered against the walls were various posters of the Statue of Liberty wearing a bikini. Sam took a double-take at the defacement. Jeez! It was worse than if someone had magic-markered a fake moustache on her.

Shaking of her disgust, Sam rapidly took in the rest of the pavilion.

Statues of women of various sizes and shapes were everywhere, all frozen in sexual poses. They were scattered throughout. In the corner of the pavilion, a drape made of some shiny material curtained off the front of a room.

Sam gasped. Here was where Nero presided over his court of stone women. She was receiving a stiff welcome.

Stepping out from the curtained area, Nero appeared. He stared at Sam from about twenty feet away. In human form, without his full head of snakes, he was a remarkably handsome man. At the moment he wore only boxer shorts.

Sam was struck by this as the height of absurdity: A classical Greek godlike figure in a pair of boxers. Who would have thought old Mr. Snakehead would be into Fruit of the Loom.

Ripley yanked on her arm, trying to drag her forward. Sam lost her sense of humor. She was going to be a stone sacrifice? Well, this was certainly not another day in paradise. What could she do? She was fighting against the odds when she had just found love. And she did love Nic, with all her heart and all her soul. She couldn't die now!

"So, you have brought the pretty Paranormal-buster to me," Nero said as Ripley threw her golden sword upon the bottom step of the pavilion. "I am impressed—both by your getting the sword and the girl. Will the others follow?"

"Her lover, the werewolf prince," Ripley answered, his voice even more harsh and guttural than it had been. His hand on her arm was elongating, and Sam knew that soon Ripley would complete his transformation. She knew she didn't want to be nearby when he did.

"Fine. Perhaps, little one, I will place you and your lover together for all eternity, my monument to the Goddess Aphrodite."

"You mean you've killed all these people to prove your devotion to gods who have been dead, buried and forgotten for thousands of years? What planet are you from? You're a dirty rotten rock-for-brains!" she ended up shouting.

"Silence, infidel! Aphrodite will approve. She is still on Mount Olympus awaiting my tribute. We shall rule together."

"Aphrodite is nothing but a myth," Sam snarled. "All this trouble because of your myth conceptions."

"Silence, human!" Nero commanded. "You know nothing! Bring her to me, werewolf, so I may begin her immortality in stone."

The monster ripped off his boxers, sporting a doric column so big that Sam thought she was seeing things. Now she understood the expression, "hung like an ox." And Nero wasn't even a Minotaur!

"Talk about cock of the walk," she muttered to herself. No way was that getting anywhere near her. Still, what was a girl to do? She despaired momentarily, caught between the moon, New York City, a werewolf and a giant gorgon penis.

Yet, she couldn't die here and be trapped for eternity with her butt left to the breeze. So she wouldn't, she thought with grim resolution; she was determined to beat the odious odds.

Fingering the knife in her pocket, Sam reacted so quickly that Ripley never saw it coming: She rammed her four-inch iron knife into his upper eyelid. Years of training and experience were her aid, and her aim was true. Howling in pain and anger, the werewolf clutched his paws to his face, and Sam ran like hell in the opposite direction.

Glancing back, she saw that her blow hadn't been lethal to Ripley, but it would slow Nero's wolf down and keep him from transforming. He couldn't pull the iron out himself without searing his paws, so Nero would have to help him.

She wanted to rush for her sword, but Nero was close to it, and she wasn't about to tempt fate. "Don't let that werewolf bite me on the ass," she prayed as she ran. "There's someone who likes it just the way it is."

Running as hard as she could the way she'd come in, she ducked back out the short tunnel and into the main one, glancing around to check on her pursuers. *Nuts!* her mind screamed. Obviously gorgons were fast monsters—maybe due to that third leg he wanted to stick into her. Nero was only a few feet behind, his snakeheads hissing and his red eyes glaring. In spite of her life being on the line, Sam couldn't help but think he'd look better in braids.

Breathing hard, her heart racing, she suddenly heard the sounds of running paws and growling. "Thank you, God," she gasped in relief. Her Russian man was rushing in just in the nick of time.

Two hundred pounds of enraged werewolf knocked the gorgon off its feet. The snakes were hissing, wolves were howling, and a vampire was suddenly flying through the air with a golden sword. The noise in the tunnel was almost deafening. Sam lent her own scream to the proceedings, then leaned against the cavern wall to catch her breath.

Nero spun, and a snake almost caught Nic on his flank. Nic dodged.

Sam screamed again. "Look out, Nic! He's trying to put the bite on you!" In werewolf form, Nic dodged another hissing snake.

As Prince Varinski landed, Nero leaped toward him, intending to deliver the headbutt of the century. But the Prince was ready. Swinging his sword with all his considerable vampiric strength, he hit the gorgon just below the shoulder and severed an arm. Blood gushed out and the Meduse howled in furious pain.

Snarling and crouching, Nic was about to leap when he saw Ripley start to charge his cousin. Sam picked up a rock and threw it. As the missile struck Ripley's forehead, causing him to lurch backward and howl in pain, Nic took advantage, surging forward and knocking Ripley over, his jaws clamping tight on the wolfman's throat. Pulling hard, he finished the kill.

In the meantime, Prince Varinski had swung again, this time sweeping Nero's head clean off his shoulders. The head flew in one direction, while the body fell in another.

"Teamwork—impressive!" Sam managed to gasp in relief. Nic and his cousin had saved the day, and her too. Looking over at the mess that was Ripley's throat, she whistled. "Talk about taking a bite out of crime."

As Nic transformed, Prince Petroff looked Sam over carefully. He said, "You're not hurt?"

Sam shook her head. "But I will say one thing, Prince V., your timing could use some work. Another minute and I would have been stone cold to your charm."

The Prince looked offended, but Nic, his transformation complete, threw back his head and laughed. "She's teasing you, Petroff!" he explained. Then he hurried to enfold Sam in his arms.

Naked as the day he was born and bloody from battle, Nic had never looked so beautiful. He was Sam's wild man, a magnificent warrior, saving his woman like they had in days of old. And despite her tough side, Sam was secretly thrilled. Her werewolf was really just an old-fashioned knight kind of guy. Jeez, how she loved him. Sam Spade, Mike Hammer, Rick Blaine and the rest didn't have a thing on him, and the real mystery was why it had taken them so long to get together.

Nic stared. Sam's face was smudged with dirt, her helmet gone and her hair a mess. Her shirt was ripped, and the knees of her jeans were black with grime. Well, nobody would call her princess right now—maybe not ever, since she was too spunky for that; too stubborn, and right now too dirty. But she was adorable to him and always would be. She'd make a good wife.

Squeezing her tightly, Nic held on to her. "You can cry you know," he said, his heart fraught with love.

"Nah. Crying is for wimps. Is Alex okay?"

"Yes. He's hurt a bit, but nothing that won't mend." Nic snuggled closer, loving the feel of her against him. "After we took care of Boris, who was working for Nero, we rushed over here."

Sam shoved away, looking up at him. "Boris? I never did trust those beady eyes of his. And Ripley was Nero's wolf!"

"We know. And they are truly among the dead now," Prince Varinski pronounced. "Natasha and Alex are waiting for us about two miles back, near the subway station entrance. I'll stay here for a bit and clean up, but you two should go back and get Alex a doctor." So saying, the Prince started back toward the short tunnel, carrying Nero's head by its now limp snake heads.

Nic thumbed Sam on the chin. "I think, my dear, that this is the beginning of a beautiful friendship."

Friendship? Sam gave him a haughty glare and trudged with grim determination back toward the world above.

Where's Paul Bunion's Axe When You Need It?

Almost a day had passed since the beheading of the Meduse. In true vampire fashion, Prince Varinski had ordered up a victory celebration, inviting several close friends who lived in New York, and many of the leaders of the supernatural community. Petroff had wanted to personally assure them that the threat to their community was over, besides flirting with several prominent female leaders.

Nic had stopped by and given Sam an update on his brother several hours after returning to the hotel; he had taken Alex to see a werewolf specialist about the vampire bites that had ripped huge hunks out of his shoulder and neck. His brother was in serious but guarded condition, so after kissing her on the cheek, Nic had gone back to watch over Alex, and Sam had fallen into a deep but troubled sleep.

Now she was entering the foyer of the grand ballroom located on the hotel's second floor. She didn't want to go to the Prince's victory party, but she felt it would be bad manners to not at least put in an appearance. She had booked a midnight flight to Denver, Colorado. Fortunately for her wounded heart, her brother was doing a little Bustin' job there, and she had decided he could use some help.

Sighing wearily, she knew that Nic was not going to be happy about going to bed alone tonight, but then, she wasn't either. What was wrong with that big Bustin' bozo that he didn't love her already? She might not be the loveliest lady on the block, or have legs that stretched to heaven and back, but she wasn't exactly bad-looking either. Besides, she had great hair.

She sighed again. Her excuse for leaving was that she needed to help Bogie; however, reality was a different matter. She truly needed some time away from the oversexed werewolf to come to terms with how she felt about him—and how he didn't feel about her. Nic had just professed feeling friendship for her, and she'd seen his hot, heavy lust, but she was crazy in love with him. She wanted to start planning a wedding and babies. She could just see their cute little cubs with their raven black hair and large gray eyes like their father's. Unfortunately, Nic only "cared" for her, and caring wasn't the same as loving. They wouldn't be trotting off into any sunset happily ever after.

Could she stay in a relationship where she loved so strongly and Nic felt less? Would he grow to love her, as she did him, or was she doomed to eventually watch him walk away? She didn't know if she was strong enough to put herself through that kind of misery, since she wanted guarantees of a happily-ever-after future and needed Nic to love her. If he didn't, then Sam was afraid that eventually she would grow to resent him. She couldn't help it; that was the way she was.

Shrugging her shoulders, Sam entered the room. She had dressed down tonight, due to her depression, in a plain black skirt and solid black sweater. Her hair was pulled up in a severe bun, and her makeup was spare.

Espying her, Prince Varinski strolled regally over, grasping both her hands in his. "Sam! Glad you're here. You did an outstanding job, not only by helping us rid New York of that deadly monster, but also in ridding my castle of its ghosts. I have a check for your latest efforts." And so saying, he handed one over, smiling pompously.

He has a right to be pompous, Sam thought wryly as she glanced at the check with so many little zeros. "Thanks, Prince V. My company can always use the dough and the business."

He touched a bruise on her cheek. "Any others?"

"A few, but it's the nature of the beast," she joked.

He chortled. "Nic is going to have his hands full with you."

"Yeah, well . . . ," Sam hedged; then she asked curiously, "How did Natasha take Boris's defection?"

"Not well. I'll admit to being surprised by it, too. Ripley I could believe, but Boris was a turncoat of a different color."

"Not to mention species."

Dark amusement sparkled in the Prince's gray eyes. "You *will* give my cousin a run for his money."

Shrugging her shoulders, Sam answered glumly, "I do my best—especially if it will keep him up at night."

The Prince chuckled. "Oh, by the way, I don't know if Nic had a chance to tell you, but he heard from the Hollywood agent he sent Rasputin to. The mad monk is going to be starring in a movie! *The Ghost and Miss More.*"

Tilting her head, Sam nodded, thinking about life's little ironies. "Miss More is that ex-stripper turned actress? The one with the 38-D's?"

Prince Varinski nodded. "The very same."

"Well, I guess the movie won't be a sleeper, since nobody could sleep through her assets—or Rasputin's." She wondered what genre the film would be. It was scary imagining Rasputin as a movie star.

Turning, she scanned the ballroom for Nic. He'd just entered, but before he got two feet, Forest appeared and was on him like a tick on a dog.

Forest, with her low-cut dress, which made Sam see as much red as that hair above the redhead's abundant cleavage. "What a dog," Sam muttered to herself.

Unfortunately, Nic was a female magnet. It was a fact she hated, which made her guts twist as threats filled her brain. If she kneed a werewolf in the groin near Forest, Sam wondered, would he make a sound? Or if a tree branch shaped like a very sharp stake fell on her, would anyone mind? "No way, I'd sell tickets."

Seeing her, Nic disentangled himself and came over to Sam.

"Who let you out of your cage?" she asked him peevishly.

Nic hid his grin. Sam was really terribly jealous of Forest. He found it cute—and foolish. Because all he wanted was her. "Be kind to me. I'm a vanishing species," he said.

"Ha!" Sam wrinkled her nose, which Nic leaned over and kissed.

"You look beautiful," he said, admiring the way her short skirt showcased her dynamite legs. He recalled the way her tight thigh muscles clutched him tightly when they were making love.

Sam moved a step back. "How's Alex?"

"His neck looks really bad. Boris almost got his jugular but, thank God, he didn't. He's upstairs asleep. Well, actually he's doped up pretty heavily. I need to go check on him in a little while. Why don't you come with me?"

"Sorry, but I can't. I just came to say good-bye. Bogie sprained his ankle and needs some help with a runaway dragon up in Colorado. I leave in a couple of hours."

Nic was anything but pleased. He had planned to celebrate in private with Sam tonight, off and on as he kept checking on his little brother. He also didn't like the thought of her chasing a fire-breathing dragon around the Rocky Mountains.

"If Bogie can wait a day, I'll go instead—or get my brother Gregor to go," Nic volunteered.

"Thanks but no thanks." Nic's concern cheered her, but then Nic was nothing if not loyal to friends and family. Sam didn't want to remain a friend; she wanted desperately to be his family.

"Sam, corralling dragons is dangerous business."

"Not when you know what you're doing," she retorted. "And I do."

"Let me guess. Dragon psychology?" Nic guessed,

his tone stiff with disapproval. Sam always lived on the edge, trying to chase and capture creatures who wanted to eat her for lunch as a crispy Paranormalbuster-and-jelly sandwich.

"You betcha. Along with riding lessons since I was eight"

"I should have guessed," he grumbled. "But what can you use on a dragon?"

"I'm surprised you don't know."

Nic sighed. Was she going to start taunting him again? "Dragons were outlawed for years in Russia," he said. "So, tell me, Sam, what scares a dragon?"

"Mice. Just like elephants are terrified of the tiny critters, so are dragons."

Nic snorted. "Come on, Sam—a mouse? A dragon could fry a mouse with one baby breath."

Sam shrugged. "You know that and I know that. Just don't tell it to the dragons."

He couldn't help himself; he threw back his head and howled with laughter. When he finished, he hugged her. "All right, Sam, but be careful anyway. I'd hate to see you go up in smoke."

Leaning over, he kissed her tenderly. Her response was lacking, and so he knew instinctively that something was wrong. His woman was distancing herself by going off to Colorado, physically and emotionally as well. "I'll go with you to the airport," he decided.

"No. You stay here in case Alex needs you."

"Well . . . call me from Colorado," Nic suggested forcefully, watching her eyes. "And be very, very careful."

She looked at the floor. "I'll try, but cell reception isn't great in the Rockies."

Before a protest could form on his lips, Forest sauntered up, placing a possessive hand on Nic's arm. Sam gave the vampiress a look that would have felled a redwood. Then, narrowing her eyes at Nic, she glanced back and forth between the two and remarked caustically, "Yeah, be careful yourself. You never know when there's a monster hanging around waiting to gobble you up."

Sam walked out of the room, her head held high, her eyes flashing, but left the field to Forest.

Who You Gonna Call?

Sam had just finished showering and dressing when her Uncle Myles arrived home from closing the bar. Her mind was on Nic, and on the odd flight from Colorado. Deciding she'd needed to think of something else—anything besides Nic, Nic and more Nic—she'd decided to watch the television monitor on the plane. They had been playing a cooking show, and guess who'd taken center stage? The galloping ghostly gourmet, Chef Jules—and he really was cookin' with his guest, some guy named Ramsey! At least he'd seemed happy. But that had made her wonder if all ghosts were so lucky. Were they luckier than she?

"Sweetheart," Myles said, his eyes glinting cheerfully. He hugged her. "You got back early."

Kissing his cheek, she managed a smile.

"Good to have you home, doll. How did the dragon hunt go?"

"He's back in his silo. Bogie's still in Colorado, finishing up the paperwork and instructions on how not to have a runaway dragon again. He should be back tomorrow night—if he doesn't get sidetracked by that pretty brunette dragon trainer."

Myles nodded. "I was surprised to hear of Bogie's sprained ankle. He didn't say anything to me about it," her uncle stated suspiciously.

"Hmm," Sam mumbled. Her pet goblin, Zeuss, came up and rubbed against her legs. She distractedly petted his soft striped fur.

"Sam, what gives, doll? Could it be that Strakhov fellow?"

"Could be," Sam replied, a slight smile on her face. She had been gone three and a half days, and in that time she had received over fourteen calls from Nic. A person might call to check on a friend four or five times in a period of less than four days, but fourteen meant more than friendship. It was her job to make sure Nic realized that.

"Nic came by yesterday," Myles remarked. "Said to tell you Alex is fine, but *he's* not." Her uncle was watching her shrewdly.

"I see." Sam could be the master of understatement when she chose to be.

"Said you hadn't answered any of his phone calls. I told him your cell phone must not be working up in the mountains."

"You know how cell reception is in the Rockies. Not good," she added, not really addressing her uncle's curiosity.

Sam had thought and thought, and now she knew she'd been a trifle hasty in leaving Nic without talking to him about their feelings for one another. A showdown was coming, and she wanted to pick an okay place to corral him.

"He and I had a long talk. I know he's a Russian werewolf prince," Myles went on.

Sam was surprised. "You don't mind me jumping species?" Zuess stretched out by the fireplace; his feet stuck straight up in the air.

"Nah, doll. Didn't I ever tell you about the time I fell in love with a beautiful little werelynx? She had the prettiest golden hair," her uncle reminisced. Sam grinned.

"I have to admit, Nic's a good Joe," Myles continued. "He's crazy about you. You could do a lot worse, sweetheart. Remember, doll, that life is easy—it's the living that's hard. And if you find love along the way, grab it with both hands."

Sam was overcome. "You know what? I love you, Uncle Myles."

"Of course you do. What's not to love?" he replied. He lit a cigarette. "Nicky boy also said to tell you that werewolves prefer blondes."

Sam's grin split her face from ear to ear. "Well, blondes—or at least this blonde—prefers black-haired wolves." She grabbed her coat and raced for the door. Chasing a fire-breathing monster through snow-capped mountains gave a girl time to think. Nic loved her and she loved him. This was as complex as she chose to make it. Therefore, she would make it simple.

"Where are you going?" Myles asked.

"To go play some piano at the bar," Sam replied. Opening the door, she headed out into the night.

"But Nic said to call him the minute you got in," her uncle warned. His eyes were twinkling. Young love was a sight to see, and he was glad to be around to watch Sam find her man, even if it was a wolfman. Species didn't mean jack.

"I'm counting on *you* to do just that," she replied. She shut the door, laughing.

Myles picked up the phone to call Nic, a big smile on his face. His niece was back in Dodge, but she was no longer dodging Nic. And maybe this town was big enough for the both of them.

All Through the Night

"Of all the gin joints in all the world, he had to walk into mine," Sam remarked smugly. She stopped playing "As Time Goes By," her fingers easing off the piano keys. In the emptiness of the bar, deserted as it was, she'd heard the door open and shut. With a loud click, the deadbolt slid into place.

Nic grinned as he appeared. He walked over to her, his step cocky. Sam was a sight for sore eyes, with her long blond hair hanging sleekly down her back, and her tight rear end encased in those faded jeans.

"I heard everybody comes to Rick's, sweetheart. Is that why you left the door open for me?"

"Maybe I'm just a sucker for a man who gets all wild and furry at the right times."

"Sounds promising. Does this mean you're speaking to me again?"

Instead of answering, she whistled.

Nic laughed. Bending over, he unlaced his boots. He now realized Sam loved him, and that he'd been a fool not to see it sooner. She was a one-man woman, and wolves mated for life. Sam was his,

319

would always be his, and he couldn't think of anything better than to go to bed and wake each morning beside her. They had decades to make love with
their whole hearts, bodies and souls. They would
share the moonlight, shadows and laughter, and
spend many nights chasing ghosts together. He
would always delight in this tough-talking, hard-
driven woman, with her heart of pure gold and a
passion to match his own insatiable hunger.

"I'm looking for a certain dame who drives me
crazy. She's been on the lam, but I got her cornered
in the Casablanca Bar."

Sam arched a brow. He sounded just like Uncle
Myles. "Jeez, Nic—either you've been watching a
Bogart movie marathon, or the Hammett craziness
is infectious. But then, you did compare me to a disease once."

"One I've caught for life."

Plopping a statue of a black bird down beside her
on the piano bench, he grinned. Forcing his lust to
take a backseat, he tried not to breathe in the scent
of her, since he wanted to go slow. It wasn't everyday
a werewolf got to propose to his true love. She deserved flowers and candy; she was getting a black
bird for her uncle—and of course a naked werewolf
to love her for eternity.

He drew in a deep breath, trying to gain control
of his raging hormones. The deep breath made it
worse as the scent of her drove him wild.

"For your Uncle Myles," he said, his voice raspy.
Before he jumped her bones he was going to make
his marriage proposal, his declaration of love. He

would hear Sam's own avowal that she was his for forever and a day.

Cocking her head, Sam studied the black bird. "He looks like a crow rather than a Maltese Falcon. But a gift's a gift, and my uncle's never one to look a gift in the mouth, or a wolf, either."

"Smart man. Too bad his niece isn't as smart," Nic replied.

Staring up at him from her piano bench, Sam devoured Nic with her eyes, "How do you mean?" He was dressed in jeans and a green flannel shirt. His eyes were glowing gray, and his expression was smug.

"Because she didn't answer my calls, and she's been gone three days, sixteen hours and twenty-two minutes. And I missed her like hell," he replied. He began to unbutton his shirt, slipping out of his unlaced boots at the same time. Sam watched with interest as his muscular chest came into view.

"Three days, sixteen hours and thirty-three minutes buster," she said at last, her blue eyes alight with love and humor. "I'm counting too."

He slung his shirt over the back of a bar chair. "I'm glad. Maybe you aren't just another pretty broad."

As he unsnapped his Levi's, he stepped closer, taking her breath. "At first I didn't gct why you pulled away in New York, then I finally got it through my thick skull that I hadn't said the thing that women love to hear. A certain phrase that I have never said to any female besides my immediate family."

"Oh, and what's that?" Sam already knew, but she'd been waiting for weeks to hear these words.

She would play her cards close to her chest for a few minutes longer, then she'd kiss silly the half-naked man standing before her.

"I love you, Sam Hammett," he said. He delivered the statement without fireworks, without a marching band or Ravel's Bolero. He stated it as if it were a simple fact of life, and she loved him for that absolute certainty.

"I want you to be my mate for life. I want you to bear my children—our cubs."

"Far be it from me to spoil your breeding plans, but is this a marriage proposal?" Sam asked.

"Only if you love me back." Nic dropped his jeans next to his discarded shirt, standing clad only in his underwear.

Sam tried to keep her drooling to a minimum. "Yes, I love you—warts, fangs, fur and all. I love you with everything I am and everything I can be." She'd got a taste of the brass ring, won her American dream and her Russian werewolf. They now had a lifetime together, and the feeling was so remarkable that her eyes began to water with unbound bliss. A single tear slid down her check.

Noting it, Nic was deeply touched. "I thought you said crying was for wimps?" he teased her gently.

Sam shrugged. "What can I say? I'm a sucker for a romantic ending."

Throwing his boxer shorts aside, Nic leapt onto the piano, settling his bare butt against the smooth grain, his legs on either side of Sam's shoulders. "Pete's missed you something fierce," he said.

"I can see that," she managed to say, her mouth dry as her eyes widened in stunned fascination. Passion rushed through her in crashing waves as she sat eye to eye with her good friend Pete, who was up and rearing to go. He looked more than a little happy to see her, flush as he was with pleasure.

"My, my, Mr. Strakhov, I never thought to see you sitting naked as a jaybird on a piano top. I thought that would be beneath your dignity, the dignity of Monsters-R-Us." Sam tore her eyes away from Nic's powerful erection and finished her sentence staring into his beautiful gray eyes, which were filled with love, lust and amusement.

"The only thing beneath me is you," he said, giving her a wicked grin. "Got it, my competitor, my love?"

Sam didn't need any help to get Nic's thrust, which was generally in the direction of her heart— or soon would be. But she was happy to help him drive the point home.

"Oh yeah," she said, her mouth going dry, her thighs humming with anticipation. Her heart ached with a love that was gloriously, finally returned. "This chess match is over." She leaned over and took him in her mouth.

"Then let's play it again, Sam," Nic rasped. "Forever."

The Remarkable Miss Frankenstein
Minda Webber

The problem, Clair realizes, is that she's a Frankenstein. Everyone in the family is a success, while all she's managed is a humiliating misadventure with pigs. But her spirits are rising. The Journal of Scientific Discovery promises to publish a paper on the Discovery of the Decade, and she has a doozy. She simply has to prove Baron Huntsley—man of distinction—is a vampire. With his midnight-black hair, soul-piercing eyes and shiny white teeth, what else could he be? Oh yes, the Baron wants a bite of her or she's no scientist. Pretty soon she'll expose him, and on everybody's lips will be…*The Remarkable Miss Frankenstein.*

The Reluctant Miss Van Helsing

Minda Webber

Having lived long amongst London's *ton*, Ethel Jane Van Helsing is an astute female who well knows her faults. She has a face unremarkable in its plainness. And yet...at a masquerade ball, anything can happen. There, even an ugly duckling can become a swan.

But tonight is not for fowl play. You see, plain or not, Jane comes from distinguished stock: Van Helsings. And Van Helsings are slayers. Her father, the Major, showed her very early on how to use the sharp end of a stick. Tonight, everything is at stake. Something is going to get driven very deep into a heart, or she isn't...

The Reluctant Miss Van Helsing

Just One Sip
Katie MacAlister
Jennifer Ashley
Minda Webber

A sunbathing vamp in Vegas? Meredith Black is absolutely positive the tanned god with the gorgeous smile couldn't have possibly made her his for eternity with just one glance. But he'll sure have fun proving it.

‡ ‡ ‡

Battling a demon lord is all in a day's work for the Dark One named Sebastian. But now he must take on a horde of unhappy zombies and an obnoxious teen vampire if he wants to win the hand of the one woman who can make him whole.

‡ ‡ ‡

Talk show host Lucy Campbell has made a career of interviewing Druid witches, trolls, and an occasional goblin. But now she wants more. Only she wasn't expecting to get involved with a vampire detective who has a slight incubus problem.

The Invasion of Falgannon Isle

DEBORAH MACGILLIVRAY

There is something about Falgannon, something that keeps most of its male inhabitants unwed. Every male of the Isle has happiness dependent upon that of its Lady. So things have been since Pictish times, and so they will be long after the present day.

Despite her machinations, to this point B. A. Montgomerie has been unable to make her men happy. Now, a new son of Eire has arrived and is making the natives restless. Yes, everyone can sense Desmond Mershan's desire for B.A. And while the men of Falgannon will never let anything happen that she doesn't want, this Irishman has come to pillage, and nothing is going to stop him. B.A. can taste the battle to come.
